Sabine Baring-Gould

Jacquetta and Other Stories

Sabine Baring-Gould

Jacquetta and Other Stories

ISBN/EAN: 9783744747851

Printed in Europe, USA, Canada, Australia, Japan

Cover: Foto ©Andreas Hilbeck / pixelio.de

More available books at **www.hansebooks.com**

JACQUETTA

AND OTHER STORIES

BY

S. BARING GOULD.

AUTHOR OF
'MEHALAH,' 'OLD COUNTRY LIFE,' ETC.

LONDON

METHUEN & CO., 18 BURY STREET, W.C.

1890

CONTENTS

By permission of Messrs MACMILLAN & CO., *and* Messrs SMITH, ELDER & CO.

THE STORY OF JAEL

CHAPTER I

GULL-FLEET

The river Colne, once upon a time, was seized with the desire of being a second Nile. We are speaking of course of that præhistoric age in which imagination runs riot, and sets down all its fancies as facts. The Nile brings down mud which it deposits over the surface of Egypt, and fertilizes it. Mud! thought the Colne, I can do a neat thing in mud. I can beat the Nile in the amount of slimy material I can bring on my waters and cast down where my waters reach. But it was not in mud that the Nile was to be equalled and excelled. A delta! thought the Colne. I can delticulate—a præhistoric verb and passable —into any number of mouths. Then the Colne proceeded near its embouchure to ramify in various directions, like a fan. But the attempt proved a failure, and in the end the Colne was forced to find her way to the sea through a single channel out of the many abortive ones she had run, leaving these latter some longer, some shorter, all smothering them-

A

selves in mud, and annually contracting. The Colne in the world of rivers is an instance of the great pretence and poor execution, and has its counterpart in the world of men.

Crafty millers have cast their eyes on these channels, and have run dams across their extremities with sluices in them, and when the tide flows into the creeks and flushes them full, it pours up through the sluice gate and brims the basin beyond; but when the water tries to return with the ebb, No, no, says the miller, you come as you will, you go as I choose! The trap is shut, and the water is caught and allowed to run away as the miller orders, and is made to turn a wheel and grind corn before it goes.

That water, as it trickles down the empty channel blushing brown with humiliation, finds that channel which erewhile was an arm of green and glittering water, deteriorated into a gulf of ill-savoured ooze, alive with gulls chattering, leaping, fluttering, arguing, gobbling.

At the mouth of the Colne, and yet not on it, nor on the sea, but lost and entangled among the creeks that end in mud-smother, lies the port of Brightlingsea. The name it takes from its first settler, Brit-helm, the Dane with the bright helmet by which he was known, who ran his boat across an arm of the sea, and squatted on what was then an island. It was Brithelm's Isle; but now it is no more an island. One long creek runs past it for several miles eastward to St Osyth's Priory, and almost reaches the ocean, perhaps at one day it may have done so. Another, in an opposite direction, cuts across the land to the Maldon river, and actually reaches the great bay of the Blackwater, so that in its mid channel the tides meet, and strike each other in their wavelets angrily.   And again, another above Brightlingsea runs behind the little port and tries to reach the sea, and did reach it in historic times, but is now stopped by a causeway and a miller's dam.   That road marks the spot where Brithelm's boat crossed in ancient days.   In later times a causeway was carried over on piles driven into the ooze, and then the sea began to choke itself at the extremity, and to deposit banks of mud behind the causeway, which finally became dry land, and so Brithelm's Isle ceased to be an Isle.

Nowadays, it is along this road that the Brightlingsea people have to go when they drive or walk to the market town of Colchester, and a very long *détour* it obliges them to make.   When a railway was run by a private company up the river, it was carried across the mouth of this creek three miles down over a timber bridge, but as boats were accustomed to enter the channel and run up to the quay by the mill, the bridge was fashioned so as to open and allow a small craft to pass through.   Then, to make sure that the bridge was complete for the train to pass across it, a guard or pointsman was stationed in a wooden hut near the end of the bridge, whose duty it was to let the boats through, and also to close the bridge again for the passage of the train.

Conceive of an express rushing along the bridge whilst a schooner was in the act of passing, and consider to which would the encounter be the most unpleasant.   The object in life set before the pilot of the bridge over Gull-Fleet was to prevent such encounters.

That railway from Brightlingsea up the Colne went no further than the next village, Wyvenhoe, where it touched the G.E.R., but was there ever, among coy railways such a coquette as this little affair? It sidled up to the burly, stately G.E.R. and said, 'Take me on,' and 'Let us love one another,' and then, when the G.E.R. grunted, and puffed, and said, 'I don't particularly like you, I don't—to be plain—see much good in you,' then this little pouting Mignon went into sulks, and turned her back on the G.E.R. and said, 'You nasty, ugly monster, I hate you! I can have my own puff-puffs! I will have my own dear little cosy station, and my own servants—officials in my own livery.' So the little coquette set up her private establishment, and got to spending money lavishly, and, it was whispered, but the whisper may have been wicked scandal—got dipped. So then she set up a little scream from the whistles of one of her little engines, and drew a long puff, and cast two piteous little lines of rail towards the G.E.R., and said, not in words, but by gestures, 'I have been naughty, take me on, on your own terms.' Then the G.E.R. grandly put out his hand to her and took her. Now, at the time when our story moves its course, this little absurd, coy little railway was not married to G.E.R., but was only coughing to draw attention to her, and making signals that meant, if they meant anything, 'Come to my help, dear duck of a G.E.R.' But G.E.R. was looking another way, to Walton, and had shut his ears and would not hear the appeals. And the little B. and W.R. was unhappy, and a little careless about the times it kept, and the charges it made, and did capricious things which old and well-conducted railways would never think of doing. But B. and W.R. was in a sulky mood, and didn't care what it did, didn't care what folks said, didn't care to do its duty, and seemed to have lost all moral discrimination between right and wrong.

But there was one point on which the B. and W.R. did not fail, and that was in the maintenance of the pilot at Gull-Fleet Bridge. It let the paint come off its wood-work, and the waiting-rooms be without fire, and diminished its staff to a sort of maid-of-all-work, who sold tickets, station-mastered, stoked and poked, and acted as guard—but it never gave notice to quit to the pilot, Shamgar Tapp.

On the marsh in the sun on a blazing summer day, lay the daughter of the said Shamgar Tapp, a tall handsome girl—tall when standing up, handsome always—playing with a tame gull.

The marsh was now dry and hard. It is a tract of turf with veins and arteries ramifying through it, that flush with water at high tide, the refluence of the Colne river rolled back by the invading sea. But the turf itself is not overflowed except at neap tides. Now it was baked to the consistency of brick, and the thrift that grew over it was in flower, from white to pink in satiny shades that flickered and shifted with every breath of air over the water. The girl's name was Jael, and she came by it in this way: When Mrs Tapp presented her husband with a daughter, 'The finest and biggest she-baby as ever was or ought to be,' said her intimate friend, Mrs Bagg, who nursed her. Mrs Tapp thought she had done enough for Shamgar and the world, and shrank from the rearing of the finest and biggest she-baby into a big and masculine girl, so she gave her husband and baby and nurse the slip, and left them to make the best of life without her.

'And now,' said Shamgar, 'what the dooce am I to do

with this wopping baby? I wish it had pleased the Lord to leave Clementina' (that was his wife) 'and take the baby.' He looked at the creature then smacking its lips. 'What in the world shall I do with it? If it were oyster-spat I'd know what to do with it. I'd put it on a light gravelly bottom, and see it didn't get choked with mud, and may be, now and again, feed it with barley-meal. But a real live rampaging and roaring female baby, and so big too! What ever shall I do? And as to naming it. It don't look a Clementina, there is black hair on its thing of a head; and my Clementina had fair hair, a sort of a parsnip, and pale eyes, and this thing has eyes that look about to be as dark as mine. It don't seem to me to have any elements of a name ending in *ina* about it. I know what I'll do. I'll go to Scripture. I'll see in the book of Judges whether Shamgar the son of Anath, the which slew of the Philistines six hundred men with an ox-goad. What was I saying? oh!—whether my Scriptural ancestor, or whatever he was, had a daughter, and if he had, what was her name?'

Then he pulled down his Bible, not a book much read, as might be seem by the cleanness of the edges and the dustiness of the cover.

'I can't see that he had,' mused Shamgar, studying the book, with his dark, bushy brows contracted. 'In the days of Shamgar, the son of Anath, in the days of Jael, the highways were unoccupied. What was the relation in which they stood to one another is not particularised; but as Jael became the wife of Heber, and struck a tent-peg through the temples of Sisera long after Shamgar was gone to glory, I guess she was his daughter. Therefore, and so because—you darned blustering, howling babe—Jael shall you be. Amen.'

Seventeen years had passed, and Jael, from being a big babe, had grown into a big girl—strong, finely built, who strode about the marshes, leaped the tidal runs, shouted to the gulls and skuas and the kittiwakes that flew about the flats, and had a face a nutty brown, and black, thick hair, cut short like a boy's, and lips red as 'butter-haves' Do you know what butter-haves are? They are the rose hips in the hedges. That is their Essex name.

An idle girl was Jael, brought up to no particular work. She did, indeed, in a fashion, manage her father's house, but that house was very small, and his demands not great. The major portion of her day was spent racing over the marshes, playing with the gull, sometimes bathing in the 'fleet,' where there was a 'hard' or gravelly bed, sometimes rowing, and when at home sometimes quarrelling with her father.

He was a headstrong man, and she was a headstrong girl. He a man full of passion and will; and she—one could see it in the swelling dark veins, in the sharp-cut, contracting nostrils, in the flashing eyes—a very little was needed, a few years, maybe only a few months, a hard opposition to her will, a great wrong, and the girl would flare and rage as her father flared and raged.

If one could have stood over her now, like the sun, and looked down into her face, one would not have been surprised at the sun looking so long and ardently at it. The brow was broad and low, but the curling, glossy dark hair over it made it look lower than it really was. The dark eyebrows were arched and the lashes long. Under them were splendid, eager, brown eyes, set within these long lashes. The lower part of the face was oval. Those red, merry lips were, when smiling, accompanied by deep, satellite dimples in the gold-brown cheeks.

As she lay on the marsh turf, with her knees up, she held her hands above her face, not to screen the sun from it, but to serve as a perch for the gull, and a protection to her eyes from his beak.

'Again,' she said, 'come, Jack, again! You missed last time,' and she put a piece of bread between her lips and threw the bird into the air.

It fluttered about her, using its wings without confidence, for a couple of pin-feathers had been clipped in one, and yet not enough to prevent it from rising and taking a short flight. The white bird hovered, lurched, wheeled over her, casting shadows across her face, and then made a sudden drop and drive at her lips. Instantly, she struck and sent the bird back into the air, and, as the gull screamed with mortification, she laughed joyously. As she laughed the bit of bread fell out of her mouth.

'Here!' she called, 'Jack, here is another. Come, boy, don't be beaten. Try again. What! Skulking? No, no, Jack! Once more. Ha-hah, old fellow! Supposing some other, and bigger Jacks, some day make a dash at my lips! Sha'n't I only beat them away? Ay, old bird, with a much rougher stroke than I give you. Psha! I've hit away some of your breast feathers, and they are falling about me like snow! Ah—' she made a stroke with both hands now, and started up—'you mean, cowardly creature! That was a peck at my eyes! Jack, you might have blinded me! Jack, that was not fair! You do not understand fun.

You lose your temper. I had not put the bread between my lips, and was unprepared for you, and down you dive at my eyes. Spite, old bird! Wicked bird! Spite, that! You shall not do that again.'

She sprang to her feet.

'Now—you rascal, you!' she exclaimed, threatening the gull, which had settled at her feet on the ground. 'I shall not forget and forgive that. I hate meanness. I hate cowardice, and it was cowardly of you to strike at my eyes when I was not expecting you. Come, Jack, hop on my hand, and now, fair play. I will put the bread in my lips, and you shall peck and try to take it—without flying, and I without striking. I will hold my other hand behind my back. No! Tired of playing? Very well. I bear no malice; let us kiss and be chums.' She had put her right hand behind her, and had raised the left, on the wrist of which sat the gull, expanding and closing its wings, balancing itself as she changed her position. All at once Jael's right hand was caught, a hand was thrust under her chin, her face was turned up, and a kiss pressed on her lips.

Then a laugh and she was let go. 'Pecked and got my ripe fruit, and made friends,' was shouted in her ear. She turned, flaming with anger and shame to the roots of her hair, and saw before her a young man in a blue jersey, and dark blue breeches, and a straw hat on his head.

CHAPTER II

THAT was the beginning of their acquaintance, or friendship, or love affair. I say *or*, not *and*, because it was not acquaintanceship and friendship and love in one, or in rapid development from one to the other. The tie between them was elastic, sometimes very close, sometimes very loose; sometimes it was real love, and sometimes only cold, nodding acquaintance. The reason for this variation of relation was to be sought in Jael, not in Jeremiah Mustard.

Jael was impulsive, hot and capricious. Sometimes she quarrelled with Jeremiah, as—it must be confessed—she quarrelled with her father, and as—but that was allowable—she quarrelled with her gull.

It is a curious fact that man—and woman also—is never contented with what he has, but always wishes for what he has not; grumbles at what is, and desires what is not; and pants with unutterable longing for what cannot be. The artist who paints exquisitely sulks over his pictures and craves to be a musician, and curses his folly when he was a

boy in not practising his fingers on the piano; and the
sailor wants to be a soldier, and the soldier longs for a deck
and the blue sea; and the girl's ideal of happiness is to be
a wife, and the wife sighs to be an unencumbered maiden
again; and the first fiddle in the great orchestra of life
envies the cornopean, and the cornopean longs for the
double bass, and the man who saws on that elephantine
instrument is conscious how absurd he looks poking his
head from behind the great stem, and sighs 'I want to be
a fluter!' and the conductor is disgusted at swaying the
bâton, and would like to sit in the audience; and in the
audience those in the reserved seats say that the only
situation for hearing the music properly is back in the
shilling or sixpenny places, and those in the rear growl
because they are where the draught creeps round their feet
and ears, and their benches are uncushioned, and—because
they are not in the *fauteuils* reserved for the wealthy.

So was it with Shamgar Tapp. He was condemned by
his profession as pilot over Gull-Fleet to be always at his
post—to have indeed a very light task, but a monotonous
and trying one—and his soul was full of ambition to see
the world, to visit Asia, Africa, and America. Why
should every young cub at Brightlingsea be able to follow
his desires and go in a sailing craft somewhere, and see
something beyond the flat coast of Essex, and sea, purer,
bluer than the estuary of the Colne?

'I've heard tell,' said Mr Shamgar Tapp, 'that there be
black people—niggers. Why am I never to set my eyes
on a nigger? Why has Providence so ordained that I can
never go sailing to Africa, and see niggers?—Or—if that
be too much—why doesn't niggers come here and show

theirselves off to me? There was a parcel of 'em came to Colchester and performed on the banjo and knuckle-bones there, but I couldn't go. I must stay here, and mind the bridge—always so. Everything in this world goes contrary. The parson, he came here t'other day, and said we couldn't expect to have everything in this world. No, I dare say not—but shall I see niggers in the world to come? I doubt but such as go there will have left their black skins behind them, and there'll be a pretty state of things for me—never seen a nigger in all my life, and never a chance of seeing any for all eternity. It isn't,' argued Shamgar, 'the nigger himself I care for so much; it is that I want to satisfy my mind about him. From all I can see, the sun burns us brown, just the same as roasting coffee or doing a chop; it don't make smut of us. Well, I believe —and till I see and satisfy myself with my own eyes, I will believe—that the real nigger is a sort of a deep red brown—a very dark chestnut; but as for being black— real black—get along!'

Tapp was working the crank turning the bridge, which had been opened to allow of a boat laden with straw to pass out with the falling tide.

'What are reason and the faculty of observation given to a man for, if they are to lead him to knock his nose against stone walls, or lose his way in a marsh? Doesn't reason, and the light of nature, and daily observation show that the sun browns the skin, and doesn't blacken? The sun black a man's skin as a shoe-boy blacks a boot!—get along!'

The bridge was closed, the lines united.

'Life is made up of contrarinesses,' said Tapp; 'else why

should I have been left a widower with that rollicking she-baby—that Jael to bring up. Lord! what a bother I had with her, and spoon-feeding and teething, and now—she'll be running after all the boys. That's the way with gals. Then there's her money, that is, her mother's money; it was thirty-eight pounds, but I've made it up to forty; the which is potted and put away. I'll go and see it is all right.'

He took his spade and went into the marsh; at one spot known only to himself he removed the turf. 'Right it is,' said Tapp. 'Forty pounds all in gold. I'm not a fool to trust that to banks and speculators, and sink in railways, and put into funds that goes up and down, up and down, like a ship's deck, and may go down, down some day altogether. Not I. There is the pot—an old preserved ginger pot, and forty sovereigns in it—Jael's own money. I'll give it her when she marries, and I've seen the back of her.'

'Look there!' said Jael, touching the arm of Jeremiah —they were together, sitting under a thorn-tree on the land above the marsh. 'Father's looking at my treasure. I never told you of that. My mother had some money, and father keeps it for me.'

'How much?'

'Oh I do not know—forty or fifty pounds.'

'That's a great lot.'

'Is it? I have no use for it now; but I may some day, if we get married. Father hides the pot about in different places, so that no one may discover where it is; but I always know. He's not afraid of telling me. But if he didn't tell me, I should know. I could watch him.'

'Fifty pounds! Why you might buy a boat with that.,

'I dare say I might, but father won't let me havo tho money till I marry ; then I shall have it, and then you may do what you like with it.'

'Fifty pounds!' again repeated Jeremiah, 'Why, if I had that I could buy a share in the *Cordelia* along with Tom May. He was saying yesterday in the 'Anchor' he wanted a mate. We'd go after chalk to Kent—there's a lot required for the new sea wall, and we'd catch sprats when we couldn't go after oysters. I'd make a pint of money in no time. That's the worst of it ; if you want to reap money, you must sow money. There's the trouble with me. I've nothing, and so I never can get anything. I see lots of chances before me, but I can't take hold of them, because, like the man without arms, I can't grip. It's all money does it. You'd soon see ; if I had a little to start with, what a lot I'd make. I've brains. I can see through a milestone, but I can't make a start without some-thing to start on. Fifty pounds would just do it. Pot your money! What an idea! Invest it. Lend it to me, and I will turn it over and over, and every time it turns it will grow. Go and ask your father to lend me the money.'

'It is of no use. He is suspicious of all speculations.'

'Then take it.'

'What—my money ?'

'Yes, your money.'

'But father would not let me.'

'It is your money, not his.'

Jael shook her head. 'Father will not part with the money till I marry ; so he who wants the money must take me along with it.'

'How old are you, Jael?'

'I'm just on eighteen.'

'And I am twenty-one; just of age, and come into my property.'

'What is your property, Jerry?'

'Nothing—nothing at all. There is the aggravation. I have brains. I was the best boy in the school; always head of the class; but I can do nothing, begin nothing, gain nothing, because I've nothing to begin with. If you were a mathematician, Jael, you'd know that you may try to multiply naught till you're black in the face, and naught is the product. You must have a cipher of some value, and tack naughts to that before you can make tens, and hundreds, and thousands, and millions. But without a cipher to begin with, with naught but a naught, all the adding of naughts makes naught but naught. That's my situation. I could do wonders if I had something to begin upon.'

'There's nothing for it, then,' said Jael, with her face grave, 'but for you to go to father and ask him to give us to you.'

'Us? What do you mean?'

'Me, and the pot, and the sovereigns, and the gull.'

'I'll risk it,' said Jeremiah; 'but I don't want the gull no more than I do the pot.'

'Who takes me takes the gull, and he who takes the money must have the ginger pot also to hold it in.'

'What do you say, Jael? Shall I risk it?'

'Yes,' she said. 'Why not? We are both as strong as ever we are likely to be, and able to keep house together.'

Afar off stood Shamgar. He had caught sight of the two.'

'Ah,' said he, 'there they are—that pair of chattering

good-for-nothing, mischievous jays—Jael and Jerry—J. and
J.   Looking on, were they, whilst I was digging up the pot.
I shouldn't be surprised if Jael were to tell that fellow all
about it.   I must hide it elsewhere.   I don't trust him or
any one knowing where the girl's money is hid.   It would
be as bad as putting it in a bank, or speculating with it.
I wonder what they're a-talking about?   A pair of darned
chattering, good-for-nothing, pecking, mischievous jays.   Up
to wickedness of some sort, I'll be bound.   Whatever did
my wife, Clementina, mean by leaving of me with that girl
to bring up.   I wish she'd come back from the world of
spirits, just for a moment—I wish she would—and, by
Gorr! I'd pull her nose.'

CHAPTER III

JAEL went on the railway bridge, climbed to the rail and sat on it, swinging her feet, and looking round at her father's cottage. Jerry had risked it—he had gone in to see old Tapp, and ask for the ginger pot, and Jael, and the gull, and the sovereigns. The tide was rushing away below, through the tarred posts of the bridge, swirling and sweeping along with it strands of sea-tangle.

'Hah!' exclaimed Jael, 'there goes a shepherd's purse?' as she saw a black seaweed pouch drive by. 'If Jerry gets the money we shall want purses into which to put it.'

In the broad estuary of the Colne was the little vessel that had recently passed through the swing bridge; its sail was spread, and it was speeding out with the rapidly ebbing tide. Down Mersea Fleet, the channel opposite, another boat was coming, also with wings spread, also straw laden; both were on their way to town with their loads, to supply some of the many mews of the metropolis.

'See!' exclaimed Jael, 'there's yonder boat coming this

B

way, and the boat that has gone through the bridge is going from just the opposite direction, and they will both sail out together with the tide and wind into the blue deep sea, and take their course together—just like Jerry and me. Why!' she suddenly exclaimed, 'what is the meaning of that? Here comes Jerry, jumping and running as if father had touched him with the red-hot poker. Jerry! what is it? Stay!—where are you going? What has father said?'

The young man, looking hot, angry, and agitated, came up. 'It is no use,' he swore. 'Confound it! What an ass I was to go, and what a fool you were to advise me. I shall enlist; it is of no use staying here. Good-bye, Jael— when I'm gone, you will think of me.'

Not another word of farewell—he was off, over the bridge, running, and, having reached the further side, leaped the light rail that divided the line from the marsh, and went across it, in the direction of his own home. Jael had descended from the rail on which she had been sitting; she stood with her hands behind her, holding it, looking after young Mustard, her feet planted together on one of the sleepers of the line.

The colour rose and dyed her brown cheek a rich apricot, and then went. What was the meaning of Jerry running away?

Then she heard her father calling her, but was too pre-occupied by her thoughts to attend and answer. She was roused by his hand roughly grasping her shoulder.

'Come! come in, you girl; come in at once,' and he dragged her by sheer force to his cottage. When there, he shut the door.

'It has come to this,' said he; 'you send lovers to me with the impertinence to ask for you—and such lovers too.'

Jael folded her arms.

'Only one, father.'

'And isn't that one enough? A boy of twenty, or one-and-twenty, without a trade, a good-for-naught! And pray how long has this been going on?'

'What, father?'

'What! What? This love-making, without axing of my leave, and just picking up the worst fish in the whole net.'

'Jerry and I have been friends many months. I love him, and am going to marry him, and then we're going shares with Tom May in the *Cordelia*.'

'Oh, indeed! All is settled, is it?'

'Yes, father.'

'It takes three to settle such a matter as that. Do you suppose I'm going to give you to that whipper-snapper?— a lad who never did enough honest work to earn his bread, a lad without a father—'

'Well, and I am without a mother.'

'That's a different matter altogether. He's a good-for-nothing chap, and I won't have it.'

'Every one is against him,' said Jael; 'every one has something hard, and unkind, and unjust to say of him; but you know he was head boy in the school.'

'Oh, yes, and that spoiled him for hard work. Look at his hands, they are soft as a girl's. I tell you he don't like work. He likes to be in the 'Anchor,' smoking and drinking, and—' with concentrated wrath—'it's the likes of he as can go all round the globe and see niggers, and rub them and see if it be burnt cork or not, and I am forced to stay at home. Talk of slaves, do you?—get along.'

'I thought, father,' said Jael, 'that if I married Jeremiah he'd be useful to you. He might attend to the bridge, and pilot the trains over, and allow you sometimes to get away.'

'Indeed! bring him into my little cabin, would you? Let him take some of my work! I'd see him hanged first, for I never could trust that chap. He'd let engine and train run into the Fleet. If that happened, on whom would the blame lie but on me? I won't hear of it. That's flat, flat as turbot.'

'But, father, I love him, and I care for no one else, and I want him.   Besides, we have arranged about the *Cordelia*. If he is not to have me, I think I should let him have some of the money out of the pot, to start him in life, to make up to him for the disappointment.'

'Do you!' roared old Tapp.   'Lord! what did Clementina mean with leaving me saddled with such an incumbrance. Hold your tongue, you make me mad. I shall strike you if you say more. Jeremiah!—all Brightlingsea knows he is an idle fellow, with no good in him, never sticks regularly to one trade. He's drove an engine; he's been at sea——what do you mean, trying to interrupt me. I know what I'll do—I'll go to Fingrinhoe after Mrs Bagg. She shall be a mother to you; she shall comb your hair; she shall put you in traces and set blinkers over your eyes, that you look straight afore you at the road where your best interests lie, and don't be peering all about you at the boys. I'll pull on my best coat—let's see, there won't be a train till 5.35—and I'll go to Fingrinhoe and propose to Mrs Bagg, and come and be a mother to you.'

'Father, you do not mean it !' Jael's veins swelled.

'Ay, I do; I'll go at once. Get your room ready, she shall share it with you, and see how she likes the situation, and the whipping and the driving of such a colt as you. I'll have you broken in, I will.'

'Father, if you do that I shall run away.'

'Will you? Where will you run to? See here, Jael. Did you ever know boys play at dobb-nuts; Two does it; each has a chestnut with a string through it, and one strikes at the other nut, and if he splits it he conquers. I take it your head and mine are set against each other, and we'll see which cracks first, which proves hardest. Dobb-nuts it is! I pity your skull, I do, for my head is hard, uncommon hard.'

Mr Shamgar Tapp put on his best coat, and went down to the water's edge, where he got into a boat; and at once took off his coat again and laid it in the bows. Then he began to row.

'Drat the girl!' he said. 'What do I know of the management of girls, that Providence should have given me one, and left me to manage her? Providence might just as well have dropped an elephant down my chimney, and told me to rear that, and given me no instructions what victuals to give it, or what diseases it was troubled with, and when and how it might become dangerous. But there—I won't think of that Jael any more. I'll change the subject. When I think of her taking up with that loafer, Jeremiah Mustard, it makes my blood boil. Talking of boiling too,' he pulled long strokes, 'talking of boiling, don't I know by experience that a black kettle takes half the time to bring to the boil as does a polished tin one? Don't it, so to speak, suck in the heat? Very well. What is the human reason and experience given to a man for if he ain't to apply his experience and exercise his reason. Don't tell me that African niggers are by nature black. Why, bless me! if a nigger were by nature black, and was to sit down on the burning desert he'd begin to boil at once, and the steam come out of his nose. He'd take in the heat and suffer from it twice as fast as if he were white. It's with niggers as with kettles. I don't believe, I won't believe, that there is one law of nature for kettles, and another for human beings—get along.'

Presently his boat touched the land, and he drew it up the slope from the shore to Fingrinhoe, where was the cottage now occupied by the widow Bagg. Mr Tapp came in.

'Do, Mrs Bagg, do?' He took a seat. 'How do you feel yourself?'

Mrs Bagg was a fine woman of about forty-five, fresh for her age, with an aquiline nose, fine dark eyes, her hair, parted on one side, was drawn over to the other; a tidy woman, who kept her cottage scrupulously clean, and her person scrupulously neat. Folks said she had a temper, but tidy women, and good housewives generally have tempers, there is energy, go, in them; they have no patience with slovenly people, and work half done.

'Mrs Bagg,' said Tapp, 'I've come to call you to task. Why didn't you smother it?'

'Smother what!'

'The baby—my Jael. It is nigh on eighteen years ago

you were in my house, and was almost a mother to that creature. You never considered my wishes, you never had a spark of human feeling and neighbourly consideration for me. You might as well have gone and sown tares in my field, or thrown a firebrand in at my window, or let loose a hyæna in my kitchen. It was your duty to have smothered it.'

'But, Master Tapp, I did not think—'

'No. In course you did not think. Women never do think. If you'd have thought you'd have known how inconvenient it would have been to me with a she-baby yowling for its meat, and I called away to open the bridge, or to leave it alone, after it could toddle, with the lamp on the table burning, and the fire in the grate blazing, and me off closing the bridge over the Fleet. No, you never thought, not you.'

'But, master Tapp, surely—'

'You never asked me my opinion. You treated me as if I were a cipher in the house, as if that baby was everything, and I must have no will of my own, no wishes concerning it, no chance for myself. I did not think you was that unfeeling and ungenerous—but so you acted, and it has left me as tangled as twine.'

'I couldn't do it, you know, Master Tapp.'

'In course you couldn't,' he said sarcastically ; 'just you come over and see the consequence. There's that girl grown up, and tearing over the marshes after the young men. What am I to do? What can I do? She is that daring and audacious, that she defies me. You should have smothered her when she was born. You'd have done it if you'd had any Christian and womanly feelings in your bosom, Mrs Bagg.'

That lady was so disconcerted at the sudden and unexpected attack that she was incapable of defending herself. She looked about her, and for lack of something else to say, asked, 'Will you have a cup of tea, Master Tapp?'

'I don't mind if I do,' he replied. 'It'll soothe the inflammation I feel within me. Ah! Mistress Bagg, did you ever reckon on changing your name?'

'Well, master,' answered the widow, 'I can't say I have never thought on it, because the men press it so on me. The offers I've had since my dear man died would dress a potato field; but I put them from me—I waited for better offers.'

'Now, see this,' said Shamgar, 'I change my shirt once a week, so there's washing to do. And I wear a hole in the foot of my worsted socks once a week, so there's darning to do. And I like my victuals hot and reg'lar, so there's cooking to do—a chop or a steak on Sundays, and a bit of pudding and gravy on Tuesday. Then with these sewing-machines come in all one's coats and trousers and waistcoats go to pieces at the seams.'

'I know they do,' said Mrs Bagg.

'How do you know?' asked Shamgar. 'Have you been overhauling my chest of drawers?'

'I was speaking promiscuous,' explained the widow, 'of work done by sewing machines. You see they don't knot the ends of the thread.'

'I don't know nor care how it comes about, but I know my garments are ever giving way at the seams and letting in air—and it's a windy place is Gull-Fleet Bridge. So there's tailoring to be done. And then, and above all, there's that Jael, that girl, to be kept under, and held in tight, and taught her duties, and made to stay at home, and held from the boys, and so,' said Mr Tapp, 'there's also Jaeloring to be done.'

'There must be,' agreed Mrs Bagg.

'Now, if she goes off, I'll want someone to manage for me, and if she don't go off, still I want someone. So if you please, you can come and try it, and I'll see what you're like, and there's no saying—more wonderful things have happened—but you may come in the end to changing your name. That depends, you see, mistress, on how you get on with the washing, and the mending, and the cooking, and the tailoring, and the Jaeloring.'

'I don't mind, I'm no ways particular,' said Mrs Bagg. 'I'll come and try it.'

'Very well,' said Mr Tapp. 'Then I'll wait here whilst you put your few things together, and I'll row you back. That girl wants looking after continually and regularly as Gull-Fleet Bridge.'

CHAPTER IV

THAT night Jael was expected by her father to share her room and bed with the woman who was to be her second mother. Jael's heart was full, her bosom heaved, at one moment the tears rushed into her eyes, and then, in pride and anger, she restrained them. Her dark brows met loweringly above her eyes, and she looked at Mrs Bagg with a scowl. At one moment her lip quivered, and then she bit it, and in biting it gave a hard look to her mouth, with hard lines on either side.

She would hardly speak to Mrs Bagg. At supper she laid the table in her rough, untidy way, and was reprimanded by the widow.

'Do look here! The ends of the cloth are not even,' said Mrs Bagg. 'It looks as if it were chucked on anyhow.'

'It is chucked on anyhow,' answered Jael, surlily. 'If you can't eat off the cloth you can leave alone eating till you get home.'

'Jael,' said her father, 'I will not allow you to speak in that impertinent fashion to Mrs Bagg, as has been, and is to be a mother to you. Get down your catechism, and see what that says about respect due to them as is set over you.'

Jael thereupon refused to speak at all.

'Show the lady up to your room,' said her father, after supper. 'We keep early hours here, for with me times is irreg'lar—according to tide. My rest is broken with vessels as wants to come up and go down through the bridge.'

For this reason Mr Shamgar Tapp occupied a little room on the ground floor. His duties took him out at night occasionally, and he was able, by having his room below to leave the house and return to it without disturbing his daughter.

When Mrs Bagg came into the room devoted to Jael, she looked around her. Jael's clothes were scattered about in untidy fashion. She shook her head.

'Sack o' dew!'* exclaimed Mrs Bagg. 'We shall have to make a power of changes here. There's a place for everything, and let everything be in its proper place.'

'Right,' said Jael; 'act on it, and take yourself back to Fingrinhoe.'

Mrs Bagg pretended not to hear her, and proceeded to divest herself of her garments. Such an eminently tidy woman was she that she folded up her clothes and laid them on the chair as if she laid them there for their long last rest; her shoes she set with toes in line under the chair,

---

* An Essex exclamation, corrupted from the *Sacre Dieu* of the Huguenot settlers at the revocation of the Edict of Nantes.

and having suspended her gown to a crook on the door, she proceeded to stroke it down, to get the plaits in lines, with as much care and pains as if she were curry-combing a horse.

'And now,' said Mrs Bagg, 'where's the cap-stand?'

'I don't wear caps,' answered Jael.

'If there was a swing-glass here,' mused the widow, 'I'd manage to put the cap on that, but there bain't, mussy on me if I know what to do. I can't have that crumpled. Deary life! I know what shall be done. Run, Jael, down stairs, and fetch a broom up here, and I'll plant the broom up between the backs of two chairs set ag'in one another, and the cap a-top. It'll do. Necessity is the mother of invention.'

'Sack o' dew!' exclaimed Mrs Bagg, when she had provided herself with a besom and placed it in the required position, and adjusted her cap on the top, and brought down the ribbons on each side evenly, and had walked round it admiringly, holding the candle. 'Sack o' dew!' she said, 'it's almost human, it's so lovely.'

That was more than could be said for the lady herself at that moment, attired in a very short crimson skirt—a cut down gown that served as petticoat, and had been cut and cut till it reached but little below her knees. She wore black stockings, and had very stout calves. There was a bald patch on the top of her head, on account of which she divided her hair on the left side and rolled it over the bald place, and made a curl on the right side, like a breaking seventh wave. She had removed her gown and wore her stays.

'That I should have lived to see this!' said Mrs Bagg.

'What creatures men—I mean human beings—be. How they rises to emergencies, and when put to their mettles how their talents appear.' 'That besom does beautifully, doesn't it, Jael?'

Jael remained in a corner ; she crouched, with her elbows on her knees, looking sullenly at the floor in front of her. No appeal of Mrs Bagg could induce her to look up and admire the cap on the extemporised stand. The widow, however, was content to talk without eliciting answers ; and when she had completely undressed herself she got into bed, without taking the least heed of Jael, and blew out the candle.

In a very few minutes she was asleep.

The cool manner in which the woman appropriated Jael's room and bed, her indifference to Jael's comfort and feelings, heightened the girl's dislike and stirred up bitter and angry passions in her heart.

Mrs Bagg was snoring, snoring already—snoring vociferously, triumphantly, with defiant snorts, like those of the warhorse ready for the battle.

Jael's nerves were not finely strung, but, such as they were, and at that time they were in a condition of irritation, the trumpetings from Mrs Bagg's nose jarred them and tortured them to exasperation. If Mrs Bagg had snored evenly and in moderate tones, it might have been supportable, but she had a Baggonian snore of her own. She inhaled the air through her nose, which vibrated at each inhalation as if filled with concertina metallic tongues, and then blew it forth between her lips in a blunted whistle. Jael could not, had she wished it, sleep with a woman so noisy at night, who shook the bed as though she was worked by a screw propeller.

Just as she was resolved to put a towel over the lady's mouth, so as to force her to do all breathing through her nostrils, Jael heard a scratching sound at the window, and looking towards it, saw a stick with some holly leaves at the end being rubbed against the glass.

She stole across the room to the window, and cautiously opened the casement. The night was so full of twilight that she could see and distinguish Jerry standing below.

'I say, Jael,' he whispered, 'come down, I want to tell you something.'

'What is it?' she asked also in a loud whisper.

'Come down, it's a long story, and a bad one. You only can help me. I'm all but undone.'

'What is it, Jerry?'

'Come down, I say, I can't halloo my secrets for the scamews to know them.'

She slipped off her shoes, and descended the stairs so lightly, that even had not Mrs Bagg's trumpet drowned all inferior sounds, she would not have been heard. The door was never locked; she opened it and went out. 'Come on to the bridge, Jerry,' she said; 'I won't go far from the house, nor stay out many minutes, so you must be quick in telling me what you want.' She was in a defiant mood, indifferent to what her father might say if he found her going out at night, and yet she had sufficient self-regard to curtail the interview, and not to leave the line of rails near the cottage.

When she reached the bridge she leaned against it, as customary, with her hands behind her, and her feet together on one of the sleepers. The night was still, the gulls were awake and chattering, calling to one another, and chuckling over their catches in the empty channel. What was mud by daylight was silver now, reflecting the clear illumined sky. The gulls' white wings caught the light from above, and as they fluttered down they seemed like great falling snowflakes. To the north-east a clump of fine trees about an old manor-house stood out against the luminous sky as blots of ink, and the noble tower of Brightlingsea church rose against it distinctly visible in the night—more distinct than it was often by day, when the haze obscured it. 'What do you think, Jerry?' she said, her bosom heaving, 'what do you think? Father has brought home Mistress Bagg to be a mother to me, and she has turned me out of my bed.'

'You're in trouble then,' said Mustard. 'By George! so am I. What do you suppose I have done? I have made an ass of myself—I have enlisted. I have taken the Queen's money, and whatever is to be the end of it, I do not know.'

'Enlisted, Jerry!'

'Yes, I have; and I was a fool. I know very well that I shall be sent out to India or to Africa, and have to fight, and be killed, or die of cholera, or rattlesnakes, or ticdolor-eux.'

'Oh, Jerry!'

'Do you believe in presentment? I do. But I won't go out. I'll desert, and if I'm caught, I shall be shot, and that will be the end of me.'

'But—why did you enlist?'

Jael took her hands from behind her and folded them over her beating heart, then unlaced them, and put one hand on the bridge rail and drew it forward and backward ; she had forgotten her own distress for the moment at these unexpected tidings.

'Why did I enlist!' repeated Jeremiah. 'There's a cold-blooded question for a girl to ask! Why did I enlist?' in a tender tone, 'Because your father insulted me that grossly that I couldn't bear it, but felt I must drown myself or become a soldier.'

'How many years will you have, Jerry?' Her voice shook, she was pained to think she would lose him, and yet—a little proud to think of him as a gallant soldier in scarlet.

'Not a year, not half a year, not two months. Are you deaf? Did you not hear me? I said I should desert.'

'But you cannot desert, Jerry.'

'I can and I will, unless I am bought out. You must do that. It costs only ten pounds under three months, and fifteen over that. Ten pounds—what is ten pounds when my life and happiness is concerned? You would not have me whiten the desert with my bones, and saturate the soil of the Indies with my gore, would you?'

'Have you got ten pounds, Jerry?'

'No I haven't, but you have.'

'I—Jerry!'

'Yes—you have; you've a pot full of sovereigns. You are flush with gold; what's ten pounds to you? You told me yourself you had fifty.'

'But, Jerry, my father has that, it is not mine yet. If it were mine I would gladly let you have the money—but—'

'Oh, yes, I understand ifs and buts.

'"If all the loaves were made of But
And all the seas of If,
There'd be no paupers in the land
For all would have enough.'

'You must pronounce the last word *eniff*, or the rhyme don't come right,' explained Jerry.

'But, Jerry, my father would never consent—'

'Do you take me for a jackass? I, that was first boy in the school, and gained a Bible and Prayer-book out of Lord Thistlethwaite's charity by learning a score of the Psalms of David by heart? I never thought of asking your father. The money is yours, not his.'

'But he has the charge of it.'

'I'll tell you what it is,' said Jeremiah Mustard, sententiously; 'you told me yourself he was going to give you a second mother. He'll have heaps on heaps of children by her, and you'll be put out in the cold and your nose be turned out of joint; and they'll make use of you as a nurse to the squallers; and—what was I saying? Why—that woman will twist your father round her finger, and wheedle out of him all your money, and gild herself with it from top to toe—or—if she don't herself, she will her brats of children. I know what stepmothers are. I've read about them in print, and what's in print must be true. Why, she has driven you out of your bed already, she'll turn you out of the house next, because it is too small for you and her, aud her swarm of babies——. As for your father, he'll love you no more, he'll be so wrapped up in the new babies, and he'll be led about by that woman, tied to her apron strings. It always is so. I believe there's something about it somewhere in Scripture, only I cannot name the chapter and verse, I'm so excited and angry.'

'But—Jerry.'

'Let me say my say,' he went on; 'I see clear as daylight that you have no one to stand by you but myself, and what you must do is to throw in your lot with mine. I've hit it, Jael! We'll go to America together. You dig up that pot of gold, and we will start at once for London, and see the agent for Canada, and get a free passage, as for man and wife. They'll perfectly scream for joy out there to have such a settler as me, able-bodied, young, and clever having been first boy in the school, and able to say a lot of Psalms by heart, among others the one hundred and nineteenth. We'll get a free passage, and then, with your fifty pounds, we'll buy a farm. Why, Jael, they sell the land there for half-a-crown an acre, and that will make four hundred acres. Farmer Marriage hasn't got one so big as that, and he's churchwarden and guardian, and he *rents* his from the squire; we shall *own* ours. By George! we shall be grand folks! That will be happiness. No soldiering for me, and no·mother-in-lawing—no, I mean step-mothering for you.'

Jael put up her hand to her brow, then over her lips which were trembling, but the hand trembled also; she stayed it by resting her elbow in the hollow of the other hand crossed before her. A tear came out of her eye and hung on her long dark lash, but Jeremiah could not see it, though the light from the north was on her face. He could not see the tear, but he saw how handsome she was, and her face was pale and cold in that mysterious light from the hidden sun, shining far away within the arctic circle. 'That will be happiness,' he continued; 'you and I will have a nice little house together, with a green door and windows, and white curtains, and an umbrella stand in the hall.'

He took her hand from her mouth, and held it between his. His hand was hot, she felt his pulses beating, she tried to withdraw her fingers, but he would not allow her.

'No, no, Jael,' he said, 'hand in hand we shall go through life together. You have no one else to look after you and care for you and love you. Now that your father has taken up with that old tabby, and is patting of her, and scratching her under the chin, and she a purring, he has no thoughts for you, not a bit of love left in his heart fit to set on a threepenny piece, not as much as makes a dose of quinine for the ague.'

'If I thought my father did not love me——' began Jael, and then broke down. She had not been an accommodating daughter, had followed her own will, but she loved her rough father, and she believed that in his rude, unshapen heart, he loved her.

'He don't love you. I ask any one who hears me,' said Jeremiah, 'is it possible that he can love you when he goes over to Fingrinhoe and fetches you a mother from there, and that woman, Mrs Bagg? It is impossible. Every scrap of love is gone out of him—if he ever had any.'

Then for a few minutes they stood silent, hand in hand, Jael looking dreamily across the silver of the empty channel—dull silver, with one thread in it of liquid, quivering mercury. The tide was rising and flowing in, up the channel, gurgling round the beams that supported the bridge.

'The tide has begun to flow,' said Jeremiah. 'The day after to-morrow at four o'clock in the morning the *Cordelia* is going to sail for London. She's got a load of peas and beans, and is coming back with drain tiles. I'll tell Tom May to expect you, and about half-past three you come aboard and slip into the fo'castle crib, and no one will say a-word, and lie hid there till we're off. When we get to town we'll go and see the Agent for the Dominion of Canada, somewhere in Victoria Street, I think he is, and we'll get our passages out. You bring your fifty pounds along with you——'

'But, Jerry, how about your enlisting?'

'I'll chance that. I told you I should desert, and if there be a fuss and I be caught, why we must shell out ten pound to clear me. But we'll try to get off without that. It would be a shame and a sin to throw away ten pound, that is eighty acres, when we can keep them. So, I say, we will chance it. Then we shall go to Liverpool together and cross the great Atlantic, and, as the story books say, be happy ever after on our estate of four hundred acres, and umbrella stand in the hall.'

'No, Jerry, I cannot take the money.'

'You must, Jael. We shall want it. We cannot do without it. You will see what a figure I shall cut, what a fortune I shall make when I've something to start from. That has always stood against me—having nothing. You can't begin from nothing, any more than you can stand upon nothing. They call money in hand capital, but I don't, I call it pedestal. It is not that which crowns but that which supports. What would this bridge be, if it were not for these sustaining posts? Well, your fifty pounds will be the supporting beams on which the line of our life will be carried.'

'I cannot take it, Jerry, without my father's consent.'

'You will leave your mother's money to this second woman to use, I suppose. Jael! I thought you'd more good feeling and respect for the memory of her that's gone than to think of such a thing. What will be your poor dear mother's feelings, in heaven when she sees Mrs Bagg buy a crinolette, and a chignon for herself, and a perambulator for the baby—bought out of her savings, out of her money which she intended for you, which she always desired you to have?'

Jeremiah felt Jael's hand twitch in his own.

'Oh, Jael!' he said, 'if you love me, consider my feelings, and do what I ask.' He put his arms round her.

Then they heard—was it a sea-bird screaming? No, it was Mrs Bagg at the window calling, 'Jael! Jael! Oh, you wicked, oh you audacious girl! That ever! What will your poor dear father say? Come in this instant.'

The girl withdrew from Jeremiah's embrace, her brows contracted, all the softness and tremulousness that had come over her went away; she was hard and firm now.

'Jeremiah,' she said, 'I must go in. Perhaps she has not seen you. But it does not matter. Good-bye, Jerry!'

'Good-bye, dear Jael, till to-morrow twenty-four hours at four in the morning, when we go off together with the tide—and don't forget the preserved ginger, I'm partial to that.'

CHAPTER V

NEXT morning, when Jael entered the kitchen, she found that Mrs Bagg had prepared breakfast and was at table with her father. Jael had spread a mattress in the corner of her room and cast herself on it, holding her hands to her ears to shut out the scolding of the widow, and had fallen asleep without taking off her clothes. She had slept heavily and long, and did not awake till Mrs Bagg had risen and been down for an hour and a half. As she entered the kitchen she heard her say to her father, 'Now mind, Master Tapp, to whatever I say, mind you say "Amen."'

Jael was a little ashamed of herself for having overslept herself and neglected her duties so that Mrs Bagg had been enabled to step into her place without a struggle or protest. Mrs Bagg had lighted the fire, boiled the kettle, spread the table, put the bread and butter on the table, and done the rasher of bacon. Not only so, but Mrs Bagg had done all better than she—Jael—had been accustomed to do things.

The table had a cloth on it—Jael had never considered it worth while putting one on for breakfast—and the four corners of the cloth hung evenly about the table.

'There,' said Mrs Bagg, 'take your place, child; we have kept a rasher for you.'

Jael's anger swelled up in her heart again. This woman was exercising authority over her, as mistress of the house, and mother by right divine.

She looked at her father, but he bowed his head over his plate and did not raise his eyes to meet hers.

'I don't want anything,' said Jael, roughly; 'if I am hungry presently, I shall take what I want.'

'Sit down, anyhow, in your place,' said her father, still without looking at her.

She obeyed. Her face was like a landscape across which shadows and flashes of light sweep alternately, when a gale is blowing aloft and driving clouds athwart the sun. At one moment it lowered, dark with sullen wrath, and then there came a gleam of fire into her eyes and cheeks, as her anger mounted and threatened an outbreak.

'Is it only barnacles as grows on to the bridge?' asked Mrs Bagg, looking from Mr Tapp to his daughter.

'And tangles,' responded Shamgar.

'Tangles it is,' said Mrs Bagg, and pretty tangles they be. The sea-tangles have bubbles in 'em filled with a jelly, and the tangles I've noticed on the bridge hasn't got no more than jelly in the bubble it calls its head. Tangles, indeed!' She poured herself out another cup of tea. 'Pretty tangles they be, with a pair of legs and two arms, and a tongue, a reg'lar intangling tangle it is.'

Shamgar looked up at the woman, then at his daughter.

'I've heard,' said Mrs Bagg, 'of living tangles, a sort of fish with two great eyes and a lot of long arms, and its head and stomach all in one. And I've heard,' she continued, looking hard at Jael, 'that when that same creature gets its arms about a human being, then it's a bad look-out for that same. And I know that there be human octopuses too, that likes to throw their arms round girl's necks, and then I pity the girl, that's all. And from what I saw and judged last night, I suppose that there has been a human octopus and a human tangle about this house, and has been a longing and a trying to devour a certain person not a hundred miles off, nay—with only a table and a rasher of bacon between us.'

Jael stood up, and flushed a dark red. She knew to what the widow alluded.

'I'm not surprised,' said Mrs Bagg, 'that this poor dear man here'—she waved her spoon towards Mr Tapp—'has been vexed and worried out of his life, by having to deal with idiots as can't keep out of the way of octopuses. Any one with a grain of sense would steer clear of them brutes, but some run into their arms and offer themselves to be swallowed. Jonah didn't go and chuck himself into the whale's belly, he was chucked in by heathens and papists, as were in the boat with him. I'm not surprised that Master Tapp has asked me to come and circumvent and supervise his house, when there are such goings on, and such creatures in it to be brought into order and obedience. Am I wrong, Master Tapp?'

'No, Mistress Bagg, not at all.'

'Now don't you go and turn your back on me whilst I'm talking,' pursued the widow, 'especially when your hair is hanging down behind, all in a rummage, not properly pinned up, and when there's an end of your staylace poking out through the joints of your gown where it isn't fastened, nor can be because of the bursting of an eye, or the coming away of a hook. I'm not surprised at your father calling me over the coals for not a-smothering you when you were born.'

Jael turned sharply round, and looked at Mr Tapp, whose eyes fell.

Mrs Bagg felt she had gained an advantage, so she pursued the subject. 'The poor dear man came up to me at Fingrinhoe, wringing of his hands, and saying, "Oh, why, my dear, dear Jemima"—which is my Christian name——'

'I did not call you Jemima,' corrected Shamgar.

'Was it Bagg, you said?' asked the widow. 'Bagg it shall be ; it was the expression of your face as you said it, and the tenderness in your voice, and the general affection that pervaded you made me think it was Jemima you said, but it was Bagg, maybe, so softened and honeyed, and spiced, that it sounded like Jemima.'

'Did my father wish I had been smothered?' asked Jael.

'He did. He was that cross with me for not having put the pillow over your mouth and made an end of you when you were born, that I'd the greatest difficulty to pacify him ; and to make amends for not having done so, I said I'd come here and see what I could do with you now. Of course now, Jael, smothering is out of the question, but—'

'Father,' said Jael, 'is this true?'

'Ay!' he said loudly and angrily, to cover his confusion. 'Of course it is. Have not you been a plague and a vexation to me ever since you were born? Ain't you now a

harassing of me, as if you were going over me with a garden
rake? I do—I do say, that Mrs Bagg was very much to
blame that she didn't consider my feelings and smother
you right off on end when you were born.'

'I suppose you'd just as soon I were smothered now,' said
Jael in a tone of mingled bitterness and distress.

'If the law would allow of it, I would,' answered Tapp
in a loud tone to disguise his real uneasiness, and under the
impression that he must back up Mrs Bagg, and carry out
the arrangement made with her. 'It would be an end of
worry to me, and I could mind the bridge with nothing else
in my thoughts to vex me.'

'I am sorry for it—that I am such a trouble to you. I
will vex you no more,' said Jael, hardly controlling herself,
and she went out of the door.

Mr Tapp thought he had gone too far, spoken too
strongly, and he half rose from his seat.

'You let her alone,' said Mrs Bagg.

'Hard words break no bones. You've given her a pill
that will set her to rights. I understand female nature.
Haven't I got it myself? If a person has it and has had
it these forty—I mean thirty-five years, experiencing of it
and experimentalising on it day and night, winter and
summer, one must be a fool not to understand it. It will
do her good. Trust me. I know what does for such
constitutions as hers. Why, when I was a girl, myself,
'tother day, I was as skittish as she—not that I ever
runned into the arms of octopuses. I let the octopuses run
after me, and I kicked and struggled before I let them
throw their arms about me.'

'How you must have changed since then,' said Shamgar

grimly. He was uneasy in his mind. 'Now you've come across the mouth of the Colne, left your own cottage for the chance of getting me. It is a chance. Mind you, unless you manage that girl properly, I'll have nothing to say to you more. Bagg you was, and Bagg you shall be, and Bagg shall stand on your tombstone. Yes,' he said testily, 'the Bagg shall find her mate, I'll give her the sack.'

Jael did not appear throughout the day. Mr Tapp was not greatly concerned at this, Mrs Bagg not at all.

'It is wonderful how it tames wild creatures to be without their victuals,' said the father.

Evening arrived, and still she had not returned.

In fact, Jael was rambling about the country, on the marsh, in the copse-woods. She kept out of sight of her father's house; there was a fire in her veins which made her restless, but in the afternoon she fell asleep in a nut-wood.

When she awoke the evening had closed in. She was hungry, but she would not go home. The sun had set, and there was summer-lightning flashing in the sky, fitful, as the pulses in her own heart. She could not remain in the nut-wood. There is an Essex saying that if you go nutting on a certain day, and the sun sets ere you leave, you will meet the Evil One, also nutting, but the nut he will want is your soul. He will put his hand to you, just as you put yours to a hazel tree, and grope, and all at once lay hold of your heart, and give it a twist, exactly as you twist the nut off the bough, and in a moment it will be in his hand. Then he will put your heart to his teeth, and crack—in a moment he will have gulped your soul down, just as you eat the kernel of your nut.

Jael remembered this superstition, though she could not recall in what night it was that the Evil One went nutting, or whether he did not go every night, always seeking for those nuts. The idea of meeting him frightened her, and she emerged from the wood, and in the dusk stole nearer home. She had vainly sought nuts in the copse, nuts that is with formed kernels. All were empty, the time for the swelled and pleasant fruit was not come. She broke the shells and found they contained nothing edible, nothing but a sort of white cottony fibre

The horizon was flushing, and it was hard to say where the lightning really was, for the original flashes repeated themselves over the whole sky with such vividness that the reflections seemed to be themselves electric discharges. No thunder could be heard. The storm that raged elsewhere was raging at a distance, but a haze of black vapour began to spread over the southern arc of sky, and thence, if the storm came, it would come to the Colne estuary.

Jael sat on a bank watching the sky for long; she could see the light in her father's cottage kindled, and the red signal lamps on the line. To the south the darkness was spreading, and the pulsation of light in it became more frequent, and once or twice she thought that she could hear a distant rumble.

The night would not be as clear as the last, even now a bank of vapour was forming over the north, like a repeated shadow there, as the lightning reflected itself there in flashes.

Presently Jael felt a drop on her hand, a warm large drop,

like a tear fallen out of heaven—a tear of pity for her, hungry, forlorn, exposed to peril, homeless.

Then she went cautiously down to the railway bridge, looking about her, so as not to allow herself to be observed, and took refuge on the turf under the bridge where it made its first stride from the mainland. There she could stand, and if the rain came down would find shelter, so long as it was not driven by wind; and of wind, as yet, there was little, and what there was came in sighs at intervals.

She seated herself on a patch of thrift, and leaned her back against one of the huge balks of creosoted timber that held up the bridge. There were many of them. By night, looking away to the flashing horizon, through the crossing spars, she seemed like a fly caught in a great black spider-web.

She could hear now the patter of the rain in the mud of the Fleet, and its rustle on the coarse turf. Then far off she heard a mutter from the sea, and in another moment a puff of wind rushed through the bridge girders and supports, sighing, moaning, whistling, and aloft, above the roadway, playing on the telegraph wires as on an Æolian harp. Sometimes the distant lightning was white, sometimes reddish-yellow; it became more intense, and the night became darker.

Peering forth at the sky she could see no stars, no entangled light from the north, only black, driving vapour, flashing and fading.

'There!' she exclaimed, as she saw a flash over the estuary as though the heavens were torn open, and in the white vista she perceived as it were a zigzag rent from top to bottom; and under that blaze the water was visible, as white as if run out of moonlight, and in its brilliancy she could trace the shape of a ship black as ink, and lines of breaking waves, vivid above the light of day on their crests, dark as deepest night in their laps.

'There!' she said again, as she heard the roar of thunder, still distant, but withal loud.

She was not conscious now of hunger, but of lassitude and faintness. She felt a sense of pleasure stir in her at the sight of the lightning and the sound of the approaching storm.

'There!' she exclaimed again, and drew in her feet, and contracted herself against the timber, as she saw a yellow speck of light travel along the sea-wall, and then approach where she was. As it approached, it widened and brightened.

'It is father's lantern,' she said to herself in a whisper. She did not think of going to him. She considered only how she might conceal herself from him.

He drew nearer, and by the lightning and his lantern light she could make him out, could see the red tie about his throat. He was carrying a spade in one hand, and something under the other arm.

He came near to where she was, but he did not see her. The flashing of the lightning dazzled the eyes. He saw only what was within the radius of the light from his lantern. He stood still. There were three great balks rose out of the marsh to the roadway, serving as piers for the single line of rail, and these were braced and girded with other beams a very little way above the ground.

'One—two,' said Mr Shamgar Tapp.

Jael heard his words. The wind set inwards. She was hidden behind the third balk.

Then her father set down the lantern and turned up the turf with his spade.

Now Jael saw what he had been carrying under his arm. It was the preserved-ginger pot that contained the sovereigns that belonged to her mother, and were left to her.

Now, also, Jael knew what he was about. He was aware that the place where the pot had been hidden was known to her. He was afraid lest she should go to it, and take the money, so he was removing it and hiding it in a place where she would not find it.

Jael laughed bitterly, laughed loudly, but Shamgar did not hear, the wind carried her laugh away from him up the Fleet.

'And now,' said Mr Tapp, as he replaced the turf over the pot which he had buried, 'now she can't lay hand on it without my consent.'

Then he went away, swinging his lantern, with the spade over his shoulder, and a sudden, dazzling, blinding explosion of lightning showed him to her, mounting the sea-wall, with his back to her, going home.

Then again she laughed, and her laugh was like the cry of a gull—but it was blotted out by the boom and bolt and rattle of thunder that shook the bridge, and made the very ground on which she sat, and the balk against which she leaned, quiver as though the dissolution of all things was at hand.

CHAPTER VI

ON THE 'CORDELIA'

In the raw morning light, cold, wet, haggard, Jael crept down the beach at Brightlingsea. The tide had flowed and reached its full height, now it was on the turn, and the *Cordelia* would go out with it.

The rain had ceased, the thunderstorm had passed away and left a wet, chill world behind it. The wind was cold, or seemed so to the girl who had been exposed to it all night, crouched under the railway bridge. She had eaten nothing for many hours.

'Hold hard, there you are,' said Jeremiah. 'I knew you would come. Get into the boat and I will row you aboard.'

A few men stood about, they looked at Jael.

'What, Jael, you going a sea-faring?' asked one.

'Ay! Going to see the sights of London,' answered Jeremiah, 'under my protection. Here, Jael, be alive; put your foot there, and sit in the bows.'

In another moment they were afloat, launched—to go whither?

On reaching the *Cordelia* she was helped up the side.

'There, Jael,' said Jeremiah. 'Slip into the fo'castle crib and lie quiet till we're off.'

The forecastle did not form a cabin, but a covered space so low that though one might sit up in it, to stand up in it was not possible. It was a convenient place to stow goods away, as it was sheltered from the wind and from the wash of the waves. Jerry threw in a couple of sacks and bade the girl lie on them.

'Oh, Jerry!' she pleaded. 'Give me something to eat. I have had nothing for a day and a half.'

Then he brought her some bread and cheese.

'We shall be off,' he said, 'in half a jiffy, and then you have said Good-bye to your old life and How-do-you-do to the new one.'

It was as he said. The anchor was raised, the little vessel swung over on her side, Jael heard the pleasant swash of the water parted by the bows, and through the opening of the forecastle saw the grey, dull landscape change. The Martello towers passed before the opening, and the shingly beach with the breakers on it, then the vessel strained and went over steeply, and Jael saw nothing but sky, morning clouds kindled pink and amber and gold from the rising sun.

She lay quietly on her sacks, resting her cheek in her hand, looking out, but only imperfectly seeing the changing view, for her mind was otherwise occupied. A feeling of alarm crept over her. She had taken a step impossible to retrace. She was leaving her home and her father, and her girlhood, and was seeking a new home, and new associations, and—she knew not what lay before her. Hitherto she had been sustained by sense of wrong done her, wrath against the odious woman who had supplanted her, resentment against her father for his indifference to her happiness; but now a reaction set in, and her breast was full of quiverings, fear and incipient remorse and painful suspense.

Tom May, a coarse sailor, who did not bear a good character, came and looked in, and cut a rude joke, that brought the colour to her brow, and then the tears into her eyes. She did not answer him but turned and looked away from the opening to the planks. Then May went off. She knew he was gone, for more light filled the low cabin when he did not stop the hatch with his body, and she reverted to her former position, and again, with dreamy eyes looked out. Swash! The water rushed up the bows and fell over the deck, raining down before the cabin entrance. Some of the water ran in, some of the drops were carried on to her lips, and were salt, but there were other drops as salt on her cheeks that fell from her lashes, and came from another sea, a deep sea within, that tossed and foamed, and threw up brine, and filled her heart with bitterness.

Then Jeremiah Mustard came to the entrance and crept in a little way, kneeling on one knee, stooping, and holding the sides of the hatch.

'How are you, Jael? You do not mind the sea?'

'No, Jerry.'

'Glad to be away from Mrs Bagg, eh? Glad to have turned your back on wretchedness and set your face towards prosperity, eh?'

'I don't know that I am glad,' she said simply, then raised her face from her hand, and laid her hands folded on the planks. Her right cheek was crimson as a carnation, through the pressure of her hand, but the other was very pale. 'I am not glad, I am not happy at all. I do not feel as if I were sailing out of shadow into sun, but as if my boat were dipping and would never come up on another wave.'

'That is because you haven't had your proper victuals,' explained Jeremiah. 'It is always so, when the meals ain't regular.'

She made no answer to this, neither consenting to the interpretation, not disputing it, but she drew her hand across her cheek.

'Has the sea water been in?' asked Jerry.

'Yes—there's been a good deal of salt water here,' she meant in her eyes, but he did not understand her; 'and,' she went on sadly, 'I think I shall be better when there has been more.' Then suddenly she drew herself up from her posture of lying on the sacks in the low cabin, to her knees and so faced him. The light was behind him, brilliant, for the sun was rising, and the clouds were dazzling as they had been when heaven opened in the lightning flash last night. He was between her and the sky, cloud and light and sun, and she could not see his face distinctly for the brightness behind him. His arms were extended clasping the sides of the door, and he was on one knee, the other foot was within the little cabin.

She knelt before him, she clasped her hands and laid them on her bosom.

'Jerry,' she said, 'you mean fairly, truly, honestly by me?'

'My dear Jael,' he replied, 'of course I do. You must trust me.'

'Trust you,' she said ; 'I have no one else to trust. I loved my father, and he has turned against me ; he does not love me. He wishes I had been smothered as a babe by Mrs Bagg. He told me so. He was angry with her because she had not killed me, when my dear mother died, and I was left helpless.' Her voice quivered with emotion, her notes were deep, almost masculine, in their hoarseness, the hoarseness of intense emotion.

She recovered herself a little, and, still kneeling to him, looking at him with great eyes full of entreaty, and with the mark of her hand crimson on her right cheek, so that every finger was printed as with blood, she said, 'Jerry, my mother died, my father hates me. I have no home, I have no one to look to, no one to trust, no one to love, no one to hold by—but you.'

'Well,' said he, 'that's right.'

'What! Right that I should be all alone? No, Jerry, I am driven from home because of you. I pray you be just, be true to me. I have but you.' Then she fell forward, with her hands outstretched on the planks before him, and her fingers touched his foot, her head sank between her arms, on the floor, and she burst into a storm of tears.

'It's want of victuals,' said Jerry. 'I'll see if there's a bit of cold pie.' Then he got up, and went away, and left her lying thus, with face and arms on the deck. 'For,' said he, 'I can't bear women's tears.' Then a great wave rushed up and spouted over the bows, and swept the forecastle and swirled in at the lurch and washed over her prostrate head and extended arms and hands.

Presently Jeremiah returned.

'There you are,' said he. 'Here's veal pie and a cold

potato, and in this bottle you'll find rum and water ready mixed and not too strong of water. You creep further in, and shut the trap, and amuse yourself with what I've brought. Take my word for it, Jael, after you've got the better of that pie and come to an understanding with the bottle, by that time the world will look a different colour to you than it does at this minute; and what is more, by and by we'll be out of this nasty sea, and under the lea of the Kent coast and be running into the Thames. If you'd prefer to be below in the cabin, come along, but the chaps are free-tongued, and you mightn't like it.'

'I will stay here,' said Jael, in a tone of indifference, and then, with sudden vehemence, 'Jerry! you mean me fair. You will not be false with me.' She paused. 'Oh, Jerry! if after I have trusted you, and come away from my home with you, were you to be untrue, I would—I would—' she gasped for breath.

'What would you do?'

Then her momentary energy gave way, she sank forward, with her clenched hands on the boards, and said, 'I do not know—I do not know.'

'There,' said Jeremiah, 'let me close the hatch; you go further back, and the water will not come in; you can go to sleep and pass the time in pleasant dreams.' Then he drew the hatch together and shut her in.

'I thought her a beauty once,' he said, 'but she looks as if all the beauty had been washed out of her this morning.'

CHAPTER VII

IN AN EATING-HOUSE

'So—this is London,' said Jael, looking round at the masts and warehouses. She was not cheerful in tone or in appearance. The vessel had taken a long time creeping up the Thames. She had not been able to remain in her forecastle berth, but had come out, leaned over the bulwarks and watched the coast, and the ships, the pretty wooded hills of Kent, the white chalk pits, the cement works smoking, the steamers shooting past, the long flax of Essex marsh, the chemical works, that made the air poisonous that wafted from them.

Jael had asked no questions; she was not greatly interested in what she saw, for she was occupied with her own troubles.

There were four men on the *Cordelia*, Tom May, Jerry Mustard, and two others; one of these latter was, however, hardly to be designated a man, he was a gawky boy. The man she did not know was a swarthy fellow with rings in his ears, and spoke broken English. He and May addressed her occasionally with offensive familiarity, and May put his arm round her waist as she leaned against the side looking at the coast.

'Let me go,' said Jael angrily.

'You're so light,' answered May, 'I'm afraid of your being blown away.'

His tone, his look, his freedom offended her, and she complained to Jerry, who shrugged his shoulders, and said they would soon be in London, and then be quit of May and the rest of them.

At length they entered dock, and Jael looking about her, in a tone of discouragement and disappointment said, 'So —this is London.'

'Ay,' answered Jeremiah. 'It is down Surrey side, Rotherhithe. You don't suppose, do you, that we can sail up to Westminster Abbey, or Madame Tussaud's, or Buckingham Palace to deliver over our cargo of beans? Come along ashore with me, you have no baggage, and we'll go to an eating-shop and have something good to dine on.'

She followed him with some reluctance, and yet with the consciouness that she had committed herself to his charge, and that she had gone too far to draw back. But she could not shake off her uneasiness and growing regret at having acted with such lack of consideration. She argued with herself that no other course was open to her, that she had no other friend, and yet was unable to convince herself that she had done right. The conflict in her mind had worn her, and her face had lost its freshness, and her eye its fire. Moreover, her clothes, exposed to rain and sea-water, had become draggled and discoloured.

She looked about the wharfs, at the men and bales, and

the warehouses.   Rotherhithe seemed to her a very dingy place, not at all equal to her anticipation of what London should be.

Jerry led her to an eating-house, and ordered dinner.   As they sat alone together in a compartment, with a table between them, and a dirty cloth over it, stained with ale and gravy, she was silent for a while, and then abruptly asked :

'Jerry ! Why did Captain May say I was light and might be blown overboard ?'

'How am I to understand his words ?' asked the young man in reply.

'He chuckled and looked at that foreign fellow with the earrings, and then at the boy and laughed, and the boy laughed aloud.   What did he mean ?'

'He was a fool to say it.   He showed his ignorance,' answered Jeremiah Mustard.

'But what did he mean ?'   She looked across the table at him, and leaned her chin in her hands, and her elbows on the dirty table, and with her great dark eyes fixed on his, insisted on an explanation.

The young man played with the steel-pronged fork set in a black handle, tapping it on the table, and laughed.   He was a handsome fellow, remarkably handsome, with curly chestnut hair, and fine eyes, dark as those of Jael, but without their fire and expressiveness.   His nose was well-shaped, and the mouth would have been beautiful had it been furnished with lips less thick.

'Well, Jael,' he said reluctantly, 'I suppose he thought you light to fly away with me ; but he was wrong, you know.   He knew nothing of how you were weighted.'

'Now,' said the girl, slowly, 'I do not understand you.'

Neither spoke for a while. Presently Jeremiah began to complain that the dinner was not served, they were kept waiting an unreasonable time, and then explained that the hour was not that at which customers were expected at the eating-house, so that nothing was ready. Jael did not pay attention to his complaints and explanations.

'We'll have something to drink first,' he said.

'Jerry,' said the girl, 'when are we to be married? It must be at once.'

'How can it be at once?' he asked roughly. 'Our banns have not been called, and if we get a licence it will cost us at least a guinea. You don't suppose it worth a guinea — why that would be eight acres in the Dominion of Canada. And for banns we should have to spend three weeks waiting. We must get to Liverpool and on to the sea before that. We can be married in America, or, if there's a parson on the ship that takes us over, we will get spliced then. Don't bother yourself about that.'

'But I do, Jerry. We must be married at once if it does cost a guinea.'

'Here!' called Jerry to the shabby woman who attended on the tables as waitress, 'you bring a pint of bitter, and be sharp.'

This was produced more quickly than the required meat and vegetables. Jeremiah took a long draught, and then passed the pewter across to Jael, who shook her head.

'Well, if you won't, others will,' said Mustard, and again applied his lips to the tankard. When he had set it down, he said, 'You don't guess what a chance I have given up for you, Jael. Do you know Argent Soames?'

'Only by name.'

He has got a mighty fine daughter—Julia.'

Jael looked at him hastily.

'Argent Soames has sometimes to do with the B. & W. Railway, and I might have had a post on it, if I had liked, that would have suited me beautifully.'

'But you could not take it.   You had enlisted.'

'Oh, gammon about that!'

'What do you mean, Jerry?'

'You are not so soft as that, are you?'

She looked intently at him with perplexity in her great eyes.   She was still resting her chin in her hands.

'That was all fudge,' explained Jeremiah.   'You don't mean to tell me that you believed I had enlisted?'

'You told me that you had.'

'Oh yes, I did say so, but that is no reason why you should have believed it.'

'You said it, so of course I believed it.   Did you not enlist, Jerry?'

He raised the pewter again to drink, partly to cover his confusion, for her true eyes searchingly fixed on him made him feel uncomfortable.

'By George!' he said, 'I wish you would not stare a fellow out of countenance.   It isn't womanly, it isn't respectful.'

'I want to know if you did not enlist, Jerry.'

'No, I did not.'

'Then why did you say you had?'

'Because—I didn't think I'd persuade you otherwise to come away with me.'

'It was a lie,' she said, and worked her elbows impatiently, angrily, on the table.

'Now, don't put yourself out,' said Mustard, 'you're irritable for want of victuals. It is always so when the meals aren't regular. Have some bitter, it is cool, and rare stuff.' He thrust the tankard towards her again. Again she shook her head, this time angrily. And now her eyes began to flash.

'It was a lie, then,' she said.

'Well,' he apologised, 'I wouldn't call it that. I had more than half a mind to enlist, and I swear to you, I would have done so, had not Argent Soames offered to take me on to the line. I would have liked that. I've tried it afore, and I can drive an engine as well as any one. Besides, it's not hard to run one between Wyvenhoe and Brightlingsea, and back again from Brightlingsea to Wyvenhoe—a chap can't go wrong so long as the bridge be right. You see the B. and W. has got across with the G.E.R. again, and she's going to set up her own station, and work her own engines, and not allow a G.E.R. man on her premises. By gorr! She's right. Why should the G.E.R. suck her blood? derive all the profits? The profits must be great, such a lot of oysters travel now-a-days from Brightlingsea. Shut those confounded eyes of yours, or look elsewhere. There's an advertisement of Guinness's Stout may interest you. Stare at that, if you please, and not at me.'

'If you did not enlist, you did not desert?'

He attempted to put her down with bluster. 'You are a fool to ask such a question. How could I desert if I did not enlist? As well expect a man to take off his coat when

he has not drawn one on. I wish I'd a paper here. You—'
(to the waitress) 'bring me the *Daily Telegraph.*'

He was given the newspaper; he opened it and held it up before him as a screen between himself and Jael. She put up her hand and beat it down, tearing it in two as she did so.

'Now, then,' said he, 'see what you have done. You'll have to pay a penny for that. Look at that woman if you want an engaging object of study, not at me.'

'Why did you tell me you had deserted?' asked Jael with persistency. She was a girl with strong will and much passion, and both were being roused by the falsehood and treachery of the man she had loved.

'Why did I tell you?' he repeated, and laughed mockingly, and held up his hand between himself and her to shut off the level steady glance of her eyes. 'Why? If you want to be satisfied, I won't balk you of your pleasure. Because I thought you wouldn't take the money unless you had to buy me out.'

'I am glad,' she said, with constraint in her voice, 'I am glad for one thing that you are not a deserter.'

'And what is that one reason?'

He looked at her, but could not bear her eyes, and put up his open hand again. Her eyes pierced him, shone like the sun into the vile chamber of his heart, and showed even to himself how full of foulness it was.

'I am glad,' she said, 'because only for that ten pounds was I tempted to take the money.'

'But as I do not want it for Her Majesty, we will spend it in acres—eighty of them.'

'I have not got the money. I did not take it.'

'What?' He started to his feet with an oath.

'No, Jeremiah! I was tempted—for the sake of the ten pounds to buy you out—but I did not touch it.'

'You have not the fifty sovereigns?'

'No, Jeremiah, I could not touch them. I tried to reason with myself that I might take—not all, that I never could have taken—but a part, just ten pounds; but—'

'But what?' He had clenched his fists; he stood opposite her, at the table, she with her chin in her hands, and her elbows on the table, looking up at him. His blood mounted to his face, flushed his cheeks, kindled his eyes.

'But,' she continued, 'I could not touch any of the money. It seemed to me that it would be like robbing my father. I knew that the money was mine—and yet I could not believe I had a right to it against his will. So—I let it lie where it was.'

'You fool!' he shouted, with a curse, and struck her in the face with his clenched fist. 'You fool! Do you think I cared a snap of the fingers for *you!* There are other and handsomer girls in the world than you. And now—I have lost the place Argent Soames offered me all through you.'

He would have struck her again, but she stood up. The blow had dazed her for a moment and made sparks shoot before her eyes, but she speedily recovered herself. She stood up, drew herself to her full height, and tried to speak. Not a word would come. Her bosom was heaving as the sea in a storm. Flashes came and went in her eyes as the summer lightning had come and gone in the sky that night as she watched it from under the railway bridge that spanned Gull-Fleet. Her hands were clenched at her side. Between her eyes, on her brow, was a red mark, where his hand had struck her.

At that moment the waitress appeared with plates.

'Irish stew, by all that is glorious! It is want of victuals has upset me, and I did express myself too strongly. There, Jael, sit down to the stew.'

She did not speak; with her hands still clenched, with her teeth set, her brows contracted, without a word she left the eating-house.

'Well,' said Jeremiah, 'I must eat both portions. What a mercy it is I do dote on Irish stew!'

CHAPTER VIII

Jael left the eating-house, left the neighbourhood of the Rotherhithe Docks, found her way from the Surrey side of the Thames into London proper, and thence, as quickly as she could, disentangled herself from the endless, monotonous, and hideous streets of the outskirts of the great city that sprawled to the east and north-east. She had plenty of intelligence, and though she had lost her power of speech under provocation, found it when she had occasion to ask her way. She was not without money, though she had not taken any of the contents of the preserved ginger pot. Her father had been wont to entrust some of his weekly earnings to her, and she had this with her, tied up in a pocket-hand-kerchief. It was not much, but it was sufficient for her modest requirements—enough to enable her to take a ticket on the Great Eastern Railway back to Colchester, but it did not occur to her to take it. Indeed, she had asked solely for the road to Colchester ; she could not think out what was best to be done under the circumstances. She acted on the impulse of the moment, and when she had discovered how unworthy Jeremiah Mustard was of the trust she had reposed in him, she felt the necessity for her immediate return to her father—and the nearest town, the market town, the point of gravitation for all the neighbourhood to which she belonged, was Colchester. Accordingly, she asked the road to Colchester. Of Bishopsgate Street Station she knew nothing. That it was possible for her to get across by a ticket from Rotherhithe, by Wapping and Whitechapel, to Shoreditch, could not occur to her, profoundly ignorant of London topography, and the routes and ramifications of the lines.

She was content to cross to Limehouse, and through Poplar, to reach the road by Barking to Chelmsford.

But Jael did not get far along this road at once. The exposure to rain, to sea-water and cold, the distress of her mind, her disappointment, and her wrath at the insult offered her by the man to whom she had clung, combined to break down her robust health. She knew that she was going to be ill, she felt that fever had hold of her, and she fought against it. She walked on, determined not to yield.

There were tramps on the road. There had been a gaol delivery that morning, and some of those who had come forth were starting on the eastern circuit. She was caught up by men in ragged clothes, with short hair, and repulsive faces, large jaws, and retreating brows, who sought to get into conversation with her, who joked, and attempted familiarities. They mistook her for one of themselves, or at least for a tramp, in her draggled garments, battered straw hat, with her uncombed hair, and because unencumbered with luggage. She halted, to let them pass. She affected to be lame, that she might not detain them, but time was not precious to persons of this sort. They would lounge along, by choice, slowly ; a brisk walk was what they did not affect. Then, when Jael discovered this, she put forth her utmost strength, and these fellows, out of wickedness suspecting her intention, strode out at her side.

Tears of mortification and anger came into her eyes. This was all part of the shame and humiliation brought on her by Jerry. She hated him, she clenched her teeth, when she thought of him. How much she owed him which she could never repay ! Oh ! if only the chance should come to her, when she could settle her account with him. To escape the odious persecutions of her companions she turned down a side road, and along this they were indisposed to follow her. She would not travel by the main highway, she would ramble along the coast. If she followed the coast she must, in time reach Bradwell Point, with its ancient chapel, a point she could see from Brightlingsea. Then she would manage to get put by boat across the mouth of the Blackwater, and walk to Fingringhoe, and thence take the ferry to Wyvenhoe, and so along the well-known line, home to the little wooden hut by the bridge. Now she found herself more entangled than she had been in the suburbs of London. There she was able to give a clear direction when she asked her way, now, she could not. When she inquired, she was told to return to the high-road.

After wandering ineffectually for some time she returned to the great artery of traffic.

A man with a cart was going along as she entered it, and in the cart were coals. She was very tired, the hedges danced before her eyes, and her knees gave way under her.

She went to the driver and asked if he were going far on the road.

'A matter of three or four miles,' he replied.

Would he give her a lift? She would pay him. Yes, she might step up on the shaft, and sit in front, and if she wanted something for her back, there was a sack of coals not clean, to be sure, but, as he judged, her gown was past taking much hurt from coals.

He helped her up, and she took her place.

'From town?' he asked, looking scrutinisingly at her. She nodded.

'But you ain't a cockney, I can see.'

'No, I am not.'

'No; gals from London ain't got your complexion. Been in London long?'

'No—a very little while.'

He whipped the horse, and the cart went on. The position was not a comfortable one that Jael occupied. She held the front of the cart on which she sat with both hands firmly to keep herself in place. She did not like to lean back against the filthy coal sacks.

Her feet swung very near the tail of the horse, and now and then the horse switched his tail and drew the long hairs over her soiled boots. The horse was a chestnut, with very light mane and tail, the colour of tan. Jael looked down, in a dream, and watched the muscles in the back of the horse as he went heavily on. She was thinking of Jeremiah; anger simmered in her heart. Had she ever loved him? She did not know. She had liked him, had believed in him; but she had never felt hot and dominant love for him. Now she felt nothing but hatred against him, and a consuming desire to revenge herself on him. Why had she not snatched up the knife on the table, when he struck her, and driven it into his heart? It had not occurred to her at the moment to do so. Dazzled by the blow, she had not seen the knife. Had she seen it then, undoubtedly she would have killed him with it. She would have been sent to prison and been hanged, had she killed him. She laughed. That was nothing to her. She would gladly die to be able to revenge herself on him.

What did he mean by that hint about Argent Soames' daughter Julia? Jael knew that Julia Soames was reputed to be a good-looking girl, but not a beauty.

What was Jeremiah going to do now that his fine scheme of going to America had fallen through? He wanted to start in Canada on her—Jael's—money. If he had got that money into his possession, he would have retained it for himself and given her—Jael—the go-by. He was capable of any meanness.

She had not thought it possible that a man could be so base.

She was startled from her reverie by the voice of the carter.

'Where do you come from?'

'Essex.'

'We're in Essex now. S and X are two letters, but there's a lot of space between them.'

'Near Colchester.'

'You have not been long in town?'

'No—I said not.'

'I know you've not, or you would have lost the sun's kisses off your cheeks. Have you relations there?'

'No.'

'Have you been in a situation ?'

'No.'

'Nor friends there ?'

'No.'

'What then took you there ?'

Jael was silent.   She could not answer him.

'Any brothers and sisters, eh ?'

'No.'

'Mother and father alive ?'

'Father.'

'Did you go alone to town ?'

Again she was silent.

Then he laughed, and said, 'Had enough of town, eh ?'

She did not answer him.

Then with the end of his whip he nudged her ribs and under her arm, and said giggling, 'I see it all. The old story.   Went with a sweetheart, eh ?'

She was silent.   Her brows were drawn together and over her eyes, and her fingers clenched the rail of the cart as if they would drive their way into the hard wood. 'And he's deserted you.   The old tale, the old tale !'

He put up his whip end again to jog her in the side, but she flared up in rage, wrenched it from his hand, and lashed with it—this way, that way—at him, at the horse, crying out, blind and bewildered with anger, and fever, and delirium, thinking that she was striking at Jeremiah, that the carter was he, and he was jeering her, and making merry at her misery.

Then the chestnut horse dashed forward, and the whip fell from her hand, and she remembered no more, only that the tawny tail of the horse was not a tail at all, but a wave of the sea that rushed over her; and that the rattle of the cart was not the rattle of the cart at all, but the rumble and roar of the thunder, that followed the summer lightning. But why there was thunder and no lightning, and why the wave washed over her without chilling her—that she could not understand. The chestnut horse was too old, unaccustomed to run, too used to the whip, and too heavily taxed with the coals to run far and run fast. The carter was after him, shouting, and the chestnut was speedily brought to a standstill. Then with curses the fellow scrambled up on the shaft and saw that Jael had fallen back among the coal sacks and was unconscious.

'Here's a go,' said the man. 'Dang me if I know what is to be done. Whether she's a crazy thing or whether she's sick. How am I to know? However, she can lie as she is.' He whipped on the horse. 'We ain't far from Romford, and the relieving officer lives just outside. I can knock him up, and chuck her in at his door.'

The sun had set, and the soft summer twilight had descended as a veil over the landscape. Lights were kindled in the windows of Romford, and the glow over London in the rear began to take the place of the haze of smoke that marked the site of the metropolis during the day—even a summer's day.

The carter drew up at a house in the outskirts of the town of Romford, and knocked at the door.

'I say,' he remarked to the florid man who came out, 'here's a pretty kick-up. 'Tain't a corpse, it's a poor lost creature I've got in my cart tumbled in somewhere among the coals. There'd be no peace for me if I were to take such as she home; the missus would sweep her out with one end of the besom, and give my back and head a taste of the other.'

'She must go to the workhouse,' said the relieving officer. 'Take her there at once.'

'Oh, yes,' retorted the carter. 'But I've my coals. I'm not going out of the way with her. What be you called a relieving officer for, but because you're paid by the rates to relieve us of the nuisance of caring for the sick and the poor and the old?'

'Get out, hussy!' shouted the functionary of mercy, going to the side of the cart and hammering with his fist on the shaft. 'Now then! No shamming. I know your ways—you're all alike,' then he turned to the carter and with raised eyebrows inquired, 'Drunk?'

'Don't know,' answered the fellow. 'Can't be sure; didn't smell any spirits. But she's gone on in a wonderfully comical style. Nigh on upset the cart, she did.'

'Drunk,' said the relieving officer. 'We'll see to her! We'll make her dance! We'll bring her to her senses! Come along, you! Ain't you ashamed of yourself wallowing in the coals that fashion? Ugh! You old Jezebel.'

'She's quite young—not above nineteen, and un-common pretty,' said the carter.

'Is she so?' asked the officer; then in a soft and winning tone to Jael, 'Come, my pretty. Hop up, my duck! I'll see to your comforts and take you to the workhouse, and there you shall have a nice supper and a bed, and—and—and after them coals you'll want it—a good wash.'

CHAPTER IX

VAN PASSENGERS

Six weeks had passed since Jael ran away from home, and she had not returned. She had been taken to the workhouse and thence to the hospital, as she was ill, in a fever and unconscious. She pulled through because she had a splendid constitution, but she did not recover rapidly. Her mind was ever working. She could not rest and recruit. The overstrained body needs relaxation that it may recover its vigour. The mind also, when it has been disturbed by harrowing cares, should also lie down, stretch itself, thaw in the sun, close its spiritual eyes, think of nothing, ask no questions of the present, and especially of the future, roll up the past and put it out of sight, and exist. It should be as the still basking butterfly on the wall in autumn, enjoy the soft air and the warm sun, and put out of consideration the storms and frosts of winter that are coming. When the mind can do this, it rapidly recovers fibre and elasticity, but if it goes on working, tossing, grasping, beating itself, then it takes a long time for renewal. The body may gain its losses, but the mind does not keep pace with it, and the result is a feeble flight like that of the bird with lopped wing.

Jael did not at all know how her father would receive her. She reproached herself for having run away. She had been angry with Mrs Bagg, but had not her father a right to bring the widow into the house? She, Jael, had not made him as comfortable as might be. She had brought herself up without system, with no one to direct her, to show her how household duties should be performed. She had preferred to play on the marsh, to tease her gull, to row on the water, to loiter along the sea wall watching the ships. She had preferred idleness to work, and the result had been that her father had become impatient at his discomforts, and had resolved to make for himself a better home than she could give him. Was he to blame? Did he · take Mrs Bagg because he had forgotten Jael's mother? He took Mrs Bagg to manage for him because Mrs Bagg cooked beef instead of converting it into leather, and baked bread without forgetting the salt and making it insipid, and put on the table-cloth evenly, and made the beds without leaving a strip of blanket at the bottom exposed, and swept up the hearth, and polished the brass candlesticks, and sewed up the splits in Mr Tapp's garments.

What would be her own reception when she returned? Jael asked, and trembled at the answer she gave herself. What would be thought of her? How could she vindicate her character? Was not that irretrievably smirched? Would all her assurances serve to wash it clean? Now she saw how foolish she had been to trust to the word of

Jeremiah, to put the least weight on his advice. All might have been well had he proved true. They might have been married and on their way to America. From Liverpool she would have written to her father and told him how sorry she was to have run away, but that she could not bear to live in the same house with Mrs Bagg, whether as housekeeper or wife to her father. She had been forced to throw herself on the protection of the man who loved her and promised to make a home for her in the New World. As for the money her mother had left, he must do with that as he deemed best. If by her running away, she had forfeited it, let him keep it and do with it what he willed, she would not reproach him, but if he forgave her, and thought she still had a claim on the money, then—but there! as Jael's mind ran on in this fashion, and she was in imagination writing her letter to the deserted, offended parent, the chilling remembrance came on her that it was in vain; Jeremiah had proved false, and she was returning to her father, as to the only one who could shelter her. Whether he would receive her after what had taken place— that was the question and with this question she proceeded to torture herself.

Even if he did receive her, he could not maintain her for long in idleness. For what was she fit? No respectable man would wish to marry her after her elopement to London, no decent housewife would desire to have her as servant. Besides, she was not fit for domestic service. She did all things badly. She sewed barbarously, she cooked atrociously, she was not tidy in housework. The only thing she could do was row. Yes, she could mind a bridge—a swing bridge—but what railway would entrust a swing bridge to her? Besides, swing bridges were not plentiful.

Jerry—Jerry was the cause of all this doubt and wretchedness. He it was who had lured her from home, and cast a blight over her life and made the future blank to her. Where now was he? What was he doing? Then she tossed in body as in mind, and moaned, and bit her bedclothes and tore holes in them, and when rebuked, bit her fingers and tore them till they bled and stained the pillow and sheets, and was scolded again.

At length, in spite of the fevered mind that would not sleep and smile and become cool, she was pronounced sufficiently recovered to leave the hospital. Then a kind lady who had seen her in the ward gave her an old gown of her own, and a dark bonnet, for her straw hat was battered and torn, and her cotton dress was stained with the sea-water and coal grime past use; she gave her also a shawl for her shoulders, and spoiled her kindness, not intentionally, by giving Jael much moral advice and earnest adjuration, believing her to be what she was not. This angered Jael, and she refused the garments, but then considered that the hospital visitor was not to blame in misreading her story. Jael could not tell her the truth, she was too proud. But she humbled herself somewhat, and half penitently, half sulkily, accepted the gown and bonnet and shawl, and the packet of tracts that was thrust into her hands, and trudged away, with bitterness in her heart, and shame and anger staining her cheek.

She threw the tracts over the hedge into a pond when she got outside Romford. She had looked at the titles of some, and they made her more angry.

In her pocket was still a little money. She went to the station and took a third-class ticket for Colchester. When she had taken this she had but a sixpence left.

'That will serve,' she muttered. 'I will go by carrier to Wyvenhoe, and walk thence along the railway embankment. It is not allowed, but that doesn't matter. I belong to the B. and W. R.'

The good lady who had supplied her with the tracts had thought also of bodily nourishment, and Jael found a packet of sandwiches in the pocket of the gown. 'The sixpence will just do,' she said. 'To-day is market day at Colchester, the carrier's van will be at the "Plough." I can get into it, sit behind, draw my shawl over my face, and eat the sandwiches, and wait till the horse be put to. No one will interfere with me. No one will know me.'

Jael did not leave Romford till after noon, and it was evening when she reached Colchester. She at once went to the inn where the Wyvenhoe carrier put up, and entered his van. This was a long covered waggon, with side and back of black tarpaulin stretched on a frame. It was open only in front; it had seats down the sides and at the end. Jael ensconced herself at the extremity, in the darkest corner, and drew her shawl about her, so as to partly screen her face.

'Now then,' said the carrier, climbing in. 'Oh! how doy' do, ma'am—or miss is it ? A passenger to Wyvenhoe ?'

'Yes.'

'We don't start for twenty minutes. I've to pack in all my commissions. You'll excuse me if I incommode you, miss. Let me see ! There's the camellia from Mr Cant, the nurseryman, for the vicar; and there's the writing stand-up desk from the National Society De-pot for the schoolmaster; and the laundry stove, and the flat irons, and the elbow and chimney, and the painted iron wire, from Messrs Catchpool, for the Laundry Company, Limited; and there's four pairs of stays to choose from for Mrs Pudney from Ager's; and there's four and twenty copies of the *Police News* to distribute, and one *Ancient and Modern*, and a baby's bottle.' He checked off his commissions on his fingers. 'Then there's the drench for Master Pullen's cow, and the boots to choose from sent by Mr Pocock; and the cold-drawn castor oil, and a packet of butterscotch from Sheldrake; and to mind and tell Malonie, the chimney-sweep, that if he don't come sharp and clean the chimleys at the old Hall, they'll shoot guns up 'em and do without chimney-sweeps' brushes. Now then, miss, would you mind? Come—will you sit for'ard and enjoy the air and the scenery, or will you sit back and let me pack the commissions in afront of you? Back is it? Very well, miss. Here's the schoolmaster's desk, takes up a lot of room, but I'll stow the camellia under it, and so too the ironing stove. Perhaps you won't mind putting of your foot between them, lest in the jolting of the van the stove should crack the pot. I might shove in straw, but then in going up hill the heavy articles will work back'ards, and in going down they'll be for'ard in their movements, and the straw might get displaced; so, miss, if you don't mind, I'd prefer your foot. If you could conveniently get the foot across so as to hold the stove with the heel, and the camellia pot with the toe, it would be more springy, and safer for both. Lor' bless me! I'd almost forgotten the rolls of wall-paper, at eightpence, for Mrs Baker. Perhaps miss, you'd find it no inconvenience to take the cow-drench, and the feeding-bottle, and the cold-drawn castor oil on your lap. It would be safer for them, and greatly oblige me. I've shoved the bag of boots under the seat, and you can sit upon the pairs of stays.' Then the carrier surveyed his arrangements. 'Lord love you! I'm sorry you're so stuffed in behind, but it was your own wish not to be forward. I don't think we shall have many passengers back. Coming with me, sir?' (addressing a young man who approached the van.)

'Yes—room for two to Wyvenhoe?'

'Room for a score, sir—you and Miss Soames, certainly.'

A spasm shot through Jael's heart; the voice was that of Jeremiah, and he was with Julia, the daughter of Argent Soames.

She drew her shawl over her bonnet, so as to completely hide her face, but she saw the young man help up his companion on the box.

'How long before you start, Fincham?'

'Directly, sir. I shall harness the horse at once.'

'Time for me to go to the tap and have a drink,' said Jeremiah, and disappeared into the bar.

In ten minutes the grey horse was between the shafts, and Jeremiah Mustard appeared, wiping his mouth, and sprang on the shaft, and without looking into the depths of the van, said to the carrier, 'Fincham! you've a good load.'

'Middling, Mr Mustard. Not much in the way of passengers—I mean in quantity: quality is everything I could wish.

'Going to have a dirty night,' said Jeremiah.

'Middling, sir,' answered the carrier. 'I don't think

there'll be wind; but it's the fog is driving in from the sea, we'll have it thick as smoke.' Then he cracked his whip, and the grey horse, understanding the signal, shambled on.

Either Jerry and his companion did not notice that there was a third passenger in the van, or they were indifferent to the presence of one, for they talked to each other unconcernedly, and Jerry put his arm round Julia's waist to hold her, lest the shaking of the van should dislodge her from her seat. At first, as the wheels went over the pavement of the street, Jael could not hear what was said, perhaps they did not speak much, owing to the rattle, but when once out of the town, on the sandy road, they talked with great freedom and unconcern.

'What time have you to be back at Brightlingsea?' asked Julia.

'I've got to run the engine with a score of empty trucks at ten, not before, and we shall go together then. Well, now, what will your father say when we spring the news on him?'

'I don't know,' said Julia, with a falter in her voice. 'It doesn't seem to me quite right, going and getting married at the Registrar's without his knowing anything about it—and when it's done, telling him.'

'My dear, it is all right. Trust me. What is the good of loving a man if you don't trust him? I like runaway matches on principle. It does put the father into such a corner; he must come round; he can't help himself. He has no other way out than coming round.'

'But he will be angry.'

'Oh, yes, at first because he has not been asked; but he must come round. I put it to you frankly. Can he do anything else? He can't stick in the corner all the rest of his natural life with his face to the wall. Look here, Julia?'

He unfolded a great sheet of paper, coloured red.

'There's going to be a grand concert of African Serenaders to-night at the Town Hall in Colchester. Sixteen of them—black as coffins. If we hadn't been married to-day, and weren't expected back at Brightlingsea by my mother, I'd have gone and heard them sing.'

'We are expected?'

'Yes. I told my mother to make all ready for us. You shall come with me on the engine when I run the empty trucks. I told mother to have supper ready—Irish stew. I do love Irish stew above everything.'

'But—my father——'

'We'll announce it to him when we get to Wyvenhoe —knock old Argent Soames into a heap; and we shall be off whether he comes round to-night or not. Take my word for it, he'll come round more rapid than an engine on a turn-table. No man likes a corner.'

Julia was silent.

'I say,' observed Jeremiah, 'was it a hundred you said your mother left you in the funds?'

'Yes, Jerry.'

'And no one can meddle with it—I mean your father can't keep you out of it, even if he remains in his corner rubbing his nose against the wall?'

'I think not.'

'By George! Julia, we'll buy the *Cordelia*; Tom May will have to sell her; and we'll build a beautiful house with green doors and windows and white curtains, and an umbrella stand in the hall.'

Again a silence ensued. Julia began to fidget.

'Jerry,' she said in a low voice, but with some sharpness in it, although so low—like a very small pocket-knife blade, 'Jerry, I never properly understood about you and that—that girl Jael. What was that story?'

'I'm glad you've mentioned it,' said Jeremiah, clearing his throat. 'Drat it! how the fog fills one's lungs. I'm glad you've mentioned it, because I can explain the whole matter so easy. Poor thing! poor thing! I and Tom May were going in the *Cordelia* to London with a cargo of beans and peas, and when we'd got to sea I chanced to go for'ard and look into the fo'castle, 'twixt decks, and what should I see but a young woman curled up there "Hullo!" shouted I, "how came you there? And who are you?" Then she came out looking awful frightened, and said as how her father was going to marry again, and she didn't like it, and wanted to go to London and see a bit of life there, and so she'd come and hid in the *Cordelia* unbeknown to me and May.'

'What happened to her?'

'Well, we couldn't pitch her overboard. We took her on to Rotherhithe, and there we lost her. She went her way, we went ours. But I do confess,' said Jeremiah, 'I did deal handsome by the poor creature. I took her to an eating-house, and I ordered a pint of bitter, and the *Daily News*, and Irish stew. What more could she have?'

'Then you lost sight of her?'

'Yes; I didn't want to see more of her. I was sighing for my Julia. I came back and took the situation I had been offered, owing to the quarrel between the G.E.R. and the B. and W. R., and the strike of the engine-drivers. You see, I've been on the line a while before, and know the working of an engine just as I know that of a ship. But if you love me, Julia, and wish to make home a paradise, and fill it with sunshine and smiles, have Irish stew on Tuesdays—once a week, anyhow. By George! here we are at Wyvenhoe. Get out, Julia. You must do it—break the news to your father. I'll go into the public-house close by, and when it's done you come by the window, warbling "I dreamt that I dwelt in marble halls," and I'll come out and go to your father with you—that is, behind you—and throw myself on my knees before him, and he'll tell me about that hundred pounds.'

CHAPTER X

THE SWING BRIDGE

WHEN the author was a child his nurse was wont to tell him stories. They began well, they proceeded well, but presently—as his little heart palpitated with wonder, sympathy, interest—a chill came over it, as he perceived that all the *dramatis personæ* of the tale were converging, by various paths, towards one point, and that point was a bridge, and he knew that inevitably the end of the stories would be

'The bridge bended
And so my story ended.'

However well they began, however skilfully they were worked to a climax, the miserable conclusion in all was the same, with pitiful detested uniformity—

'The bridge bended
And so my story ended.'

How he would writhe on his nurse's knee, and hold up his hands entreatingly, and plead with earnest eyes, and try to stay the words on her lips, or divert her thoughts into another channel, that there might be some variety in the conclusions, that Jack and Jill, and Tom and Poll, and Launcelot and Guinever, might not all put their feet on that unstable bridge,'and so their story go down in a tragic, yet impotent conclusion. 'It is of no use, my dear boy,' said nurse, 'it can't be otherwise. It is impossible for me to change the *dénouement.*'—no! she did not use that word, I forget the word she employed. There is but one end permissible, but one conceivable—

> 'The bridge bended
> And so my story ended.'

When the author of this tale had written the heading to this final chapter, a qualm came over him; he knew that to some of his readers reminiscences would arise of nursery tales, and with a scream they would start from the perusal, run away with their hands over their eyes, and shriek, 'We know it—

> ' "The bridge bended
> And so the story ended." '

But, dear readers, have patience. The writer is not your nurse. He is emancipated from the thraldom of those rules once believed inexorable; he is not bound to end his story by the pattern prescribed in the nursery.

When Clovis came to his baptism, St Remigius thus addressed the haughty king: 'Bend thy head, Sigambrian! Adore what thou hast burned! burn what thou hast adored!'

Alas! Are we not all doing this—going clean contrary to our ancient belief, defying to-day the rules to which we bowed yesterday, adoring what we scorned, and scorning what we adored?

Well, let the reader be content. The author has gone through his baptism—his literary baptism—and he does not conclude all his tales by the inexorable rule of the nursery.

Jael walked along the railway bank towards her home; the fog was thick, it drove up the river like steam, but it was cold and it smelt ill, for it bore with it the exhalation of decaying weed and shell-fish in the ooze.

Jael did not, however, feel the cold any more than the engine which rushes along the rails, for, like the locomotive, she had a fire within her. She had not by word or sign allowed Jeremiah and Julia to discover who had been their disregarded companion in the van. She had heard all, and her heart was in flames, and the smoke of the fire within and the heat and sparks mounted to her brain, and set that on fire also.

If she had hated Jeremiah before, she hated him with a tenfold—nay, a hundredfold hatred now. She hated Julia also, but in a less degree; she despised her too deeply to hate her with strength; but for Jeremiah she entertained no other feeling than intense, implacable hate, a rage at her weakness in being unable to punish him as he deserved.

As she walked on her feet went fast, because her pulses galloped, and she would have run, keeping time with her feet to the throb of her heart, had she been on other ground than the iron path of the engine. She thought of nothing but Jeremiah. She forgot about her father, Mrs Bagg, her own self. Oh, if but the means were in her hands to revenge herself on Jeremiah. Oh! that when he struck her she had stabbed him! She would have danced up the scaffold steps, and clapped her hands and sung as the fatal noose was adjusted.

All at once she stood still and knelt down, and through the cold fog raised her eyes and hands to heaven, and prayed as she had never prayed before, that she might be given the opportunity and the strength to mete out to Jeremiah the measure he deserved.

As she prayed she saw flames flickering in a field by the side of the railway, a little way up the land side. She knew what occasioned them. There was a seed farm there, and the old flowers, sticks, and stems and leaves were being consumed.

She rose from her knees and walked on, with the same throbbing pulse, the same fire in her heart, and came to the cottage of her father, and saw a light shining through the window, dully, because a curtain was drawn down between the glass and the lamp. She put her hand on the door and tried it. It was locked. Then she knocked.

A voice from within asked who was there?

Jael did not answer. Now she began to tremble.

She stood on the doorstep, with a hand on each shoulder, clasping her shawl, pressing her arms over her bosom, restraining it, lest it should burst with emotion.

'Who is there? Can't you answer?' asked the voice again.

Then the lock was turned, and the door was cautiously unclosed. Jael put forth her right hand and thrust it back, but took no step forward.

'Mrs Bagg!' she exclaimed.

'Ah! It is you, is it?' asked the widow. 'Bagging me, indeed?—when I am Mrs Tapp, lawfully banned and wedded at Brightlingsea Church. Did you mean to insult me by it? It is you, is it? What has brought you here?'

'Where is my father?'

'Mr Tapp?   Now don't you take a step in here——'

'I am not doing so.   Where is my father?'

'Mr Tapp has gone into Colchester.   There is an exhibition or a concert of live niggers, and he grew that desperate, there was no constraining him.   He have took with him a bit of a sponge, and he'll make his way out of the hindermost seats for'ards, up to the platform, and try his wet sponge on those niggers.   He will—he'd never be quiet till he knew the rights about them; "for," said he, "we must know whether reason is given to man to be his guide, or the contrary."   As for the bridge,' continued the new Mrs Tapp, 'with this sea-fog there'll be no ships wanting to come up the creek; and even if they wanted, they must wait.   Shamgar might never have such another chance to sponge a nigger.   Now, you stay where you are.   I'm mistress of the house, not you—and afore ever I let you in——'

'I will not come in,' said Jael peremptorily.   'I will not pass through the door till I have seen my father.'

'Then,' said Mrs Tapp, 'you may wait outside till he comes home from sponging them niggers.'

She slammed the door upon her and locked it.

Jael turned away.   Every particle of gentleness and love in her was gone; in her heart boiled only rage and bitterness. She was shut out from her home and was cast adrift, with nowhere to go.   When her father came home, would he be more pitiful than the woman who now ruled in his house? Would he be able to withstand her will, alter her decision?

Then Jael laughed and said, 'I am to be homeless.   I will go and see the home Jeremiah has prepared for his Julia;' and she walked across the bridge.   She walked slowly now, with her head down, and her arms folded on her breast. Her dark eyes, hard as polished stones, looked before her at the rails, and marked each sleeper through the fog, as she came to it, on which she was to plant her foot. She heard the tide rushing in through the channel below, swirling about the posts. It was cold in the fog— colder below in the water, she thought. Then she turned and looked back, and saw still the flicker of the flower-stalk bonfire, magnified in the mist to an immense conflagration. She walked on, and no longer turned or halted till she came to the outskirts of Brightlingsea, then crossed a field, and stood before the house. There was a bright light within, a lamp on the table, a fire burning in the grate ; the window was uncurtained, the house door was ajar. No one was within. Mrs Mustard, Jeremiah's mother, had gone into the town to buy some groceries necessary for the supper and the reception of her daughter-in-law. Jael stood at the door looking in. How cosy the house was ! How pleasant would be Julia's reception.

Jael thrust the door a little further open, and as she stood hesitating at it, looked back along the line to the glare of the fire of flower-stalks. How that fire throbbed and swelled and then contracted. Then her heart leaped and swelled, and then grew tight and still. How if she were to set fire to that little wooden house, and so— Jeremiah would bring his wife, the woman who had sup- planted her, to glowing, smoking embers ! She snapped her teeth at the thought, and went in.

There were muslin curtains to the window. There was a table-cloth laid ready for supper. She tore down the curtains and plucked off the cloth, and looked about for other things that might burn.

Then she saw a cat by the fire with its kittens, little things—there were three of them—that were old enough to see, and were playing over their mother's back, and the cat patted them and threw them down, and they leaped on her back again, and she purred and rolled over, and pawed at them.

'If I burn the house,' said Jael, 'I will not burn them,' and she went to the little family to remove it.

But instantly the kittens started from her, and ran and hid themselves beneath an oak chest against the wall, and the mother ran after them and dived also beneath it. In vain did Jael try to allure them forth, then to drive them out. The kittens would not allow themselves to be cajoled or scared away. As soon as Jael left the box she saw their comical little heads and bright eyes peering out at her from beneath it. Then she stamped angrily and turned away.

' I cannot,' she said, 'I cannot burn the cat and her kittens.' And she left the house.

She walked hastily back, angry with the kittens, angry with herself, till she came to the bridge, and then stood and listened to the gurgling water sweeping in. The night had become much darker. The fire of stalks had gone down as suddenly as it had flashed up. The fog rolled about her cold and deathly.

Then she heard the Brightlingsea church clock strike ten.

Ten! At ten o'clock Jeremiah would start with the train of empty trucks, he driving the engine, with Julia at his side.

She stepped on, putting forth her hand and touched the crank that opened the bridge. Then instantly all the sky, all the earth, the rushing tide, were alight about her, in a blaze such as that she had seen on the night when she stood under the bridge, but this light was red—red as blood. There was no lightning in the sky that thus illumined all things; the lightning was within; it was caused by the rush of blood to her brain; and that rush was occasioned by the thought that now—now at last, her opportunity was come. God had answered the prayer she had made kneeling on the rails.

Instantly she threw herself on the crank and worked it, and felt that the bridge was opening. She worked with all her strength, with feverish haste. Hark! A snap! It mattered not; a cog had given way. A little more, a few more turns, and now she let go. The bridge was in half and the train that came on would leap headlong into the cold, inrushing tide below, and sink into the deep ooze beneath it.

Then she leaned back against the bridge rail, in her old attitude, with her hands behind her back, and her feet planted on a sleeper, and waited. She would see the end. She would see her revenge accomplished, her prayer fulfilled to its Amen. She snorted with excitement. The bonnet compressed her head, and her head was swelling. She put up her hand and tore it off; she had become heated by her exertions at the crank; the fog, the sea air that puffed it inland, was grateful to her hot face, was pleasant to inhale into lungs that were on fire.

Ha, ha! that should be the home to which the happy pair would go—that cold, slimy bottom of Gull-Fleet. Here it was that Jeremiah had spoken to her, and persuaded her to go away with him, and here she would send him before the Judge who would condemn him for his treachery.

Hark! She heard a whistle, muffled by the fog, but audible from the direction of Wyvenhoe. It was the whistle of the train of empty trucks. Jeremiah had started, and every moment brought him nearer destruction. The whistle continued.

'I know why that is,' she said. 'Because of the fog, and to give warning about the bridge.'

She listened, and the whistle shrilled louder, in fits, palpitations, screams, and it shook her nerves.

All at once—how she knew not—the horror of what she was meditating came over her—of the *crime*. It was the whistle—the shrieking, appealing whistle—that caused the revulsion, but the revulsion was instantaneous. The passion for revenge went out, as had that fire of dry turf and stalks, and in its place surged up a sea of terror, self-reproach, agony, and pity. She threw herself on the crank, and strove to bring the bridge back into its place, but failed. A cog had been broken, and the crank would no longer work.

She beat her head. What could she do? Still that piercing scream, waxing louder. Not a moment was to be lost. She ran towards the cottage, and struck at the door. 'Open!' she shrieked, 'for God's sake! The red light! the red lamp!'

But Mrs Tapp, her stepmother, did not understand what she said. She knew the voice, and muttered, 'She'll bust in with violence, will she? She's going to be mistress in this house, is she? We'll see which is strongest. And if

the bolts and hinges give way, over my body must she go.'
Then she took her chair, and set it against the door, and
planted herself therein with her back to the door, and her
arms folded, and a pleasant smile on her face, murmuring,
'Will she! Let her try it on. We'll see which is mistress
here!'

And Jael, almost flat against the door, beat and cried,
'The red light! the red lamp!' and looked up the line.

She saw the red light through the fog. It was coming
on. Not the red lamp she asked for, but that set in front
of the engine. It was coming on quickly, in a very little
span it would be extinguished, and two other lights—the
lights of life—would go out with it. Then Jael left the
door at which she had vainly battered and cried, and leaped
on to the line, and ran forward towards the coming eye of
ruby fire, towards that screaming monster—by no other
means could it be arrested, by no other means those lives
be saved.

*　　　*　　　*　　　*

'Jerry,' said Julia, standing beside her husband on the
engine, 'I suppose it is all right with the bridge?'

'Of course it is,' answered he. 'How could it be otherwise? No mortal ship would venture up in such a fog as
this, and without a ship is passing, the bridge is never opened.
In a few minutes we shall be home—Then—Halloo! we've
run over something. Drat it! I must reverse the engine.
I do hope the Irish stew won't be overdone.'

*　　　*　　　*　　　*

An hour later Mr Tapp came home on foot. He was heated and excited.

As he entered his cottage, 'There!' shouted he to his wife, 'I said as much. Look at the sponge. I made up to 'em, and quite unexpected wiped the face of him with the banjo. And it came off. I have it here on the sponge. I brought it away with me. Burnt cork, or lamp smut. The human reason is given to be his guide—'

'Hush!' said Mrs Tapp. She was white and trembling.

'What are you a-hushing of me for? You forget I ain't a baby.'

'Hush!' said Mrs Tapp. She held the table; she was nearly fainting. 'Up-stairs. In her room. Run over by the engine.'

'What—who?'

'Jael.'

THE END

JACQUETTA

CHAPTER I

A BRILLIANT day in early summer, the sea blue as the alpine
gentian, the deep large dark flower; and the overarching
sky blue as the paler but yet intensely azure gentianella.
Not a white horse on the sea, only twinkles where the
water-surface wreathed in laughter to the sun's smile.   The
little steamer, *Sir Francis Drake*, was paddling her way
very leisurely from Guernsey to St. Malo, and her wake lay
behind her as far as the eye could trace.   She had left
Plymouth the preceding evening, and at early morning
arrived off the harbour of St. Pierre, Guernsey, where she
picked up a couple of passengers, two gentlemen, both
young, who sat on deck, smoked, and talked together in
French.

Presently, from the first cabin emerged two ladies, one
old, the other young, who also took up their place on deck,
and talked together, not in French, but in English.   These
ladies had come from England and had accordingly slept on

board.   Neither presented that dishevelled, haggard, and battered appearance so conspicuous in travellers who have crossed the Channel.   Neither had that look of utter break down of self-esteem that may be seen daily on the Dover or Calais pier, but both were fresh, hearty, and neat.   There was not much in the elder lady to attract attention—at least, the attention of young men—but it was other with the second lady.   She was a girl of eighteen, very pretty, bright, happy, and with the clearest complexion, and with the purest colour in her sweet cheeks.   She had honest eyes, of brown, and rather dark-brown hair.   Self-consciousness is the bane of most girls' faces, especially if they have any pretence to beauty, or are well dressed.   There was nothing of this in the girl on deck.   The gentlemen were struck with the tenderness and consideration she showed for her mother.   That same mother wore what was at one time known as an 'ugly'; it was a sort of hood of blue silk stretched on wires or whalebones, that folded up or drew down in front of her bonnet, like the hood of a carriage. Nothing more disfiguring can be conceived ; only an English-woman would venture to assume it.   A Frenchwoman would die at the stake rather than appear in an 'ugly.'

By that 'ugly' the date of this story can be fixed.   Let our lady readers, if they are old enough, throw back their thoughts to the time when ladies did not blush to wear uglies.   At that time the steamers did not run from South-ampton or Weymouth to the French port of St. Malo, touching on the way at Guernsey and Jersey.   At that time the Channel Islanders did not dream of sending early vegetables to Covent Garden Market.   At that time there was no railway from St. Malo to Nantes and Bordeaux.

'I think, my dear Jacket, we will breakfast on deck,' said the elder lady. 'It would upset me going down the ladder again. The insides do smell of paint—I mean the cabin.' Then to the gentlemen, or rather, indiscriminately to one of them, 'Can you tell me, sir, when we reach our destination?'

'*Ca dépend, madame,*' answered one, and added in English with a foreign accent, 'If madame is going to Jersey—or to St. Malo?'

'Oh, we're for France, sir,' explained the lady. 'My poor Aunt Betsy has been taken bad there, and we're sent for—that is, I am, as her nearest relative, and I've taken my daughter, Jacket, along with me. Bless my heart! I can't speak a word of *Parlez-vous*, but Jacket has had the best advantages money could procure, and has been at a boarding-school, and can talk French like a fish.'

'Mamma,' said the young lady, with a smile, and the slightest deepening of colour in her cheek, 'thinks because I have read *Télémaque* that I am fluent in French, but I have had no experience. We are going to St. Malo.'

Then the gentlemen ordered breakfast on deck as well. The ice was broken, and the two little separate parties coalesced and became almost one for the rest of the voyage. Mrs Fairbrother, the old lady, indeed, to use one of the gentlemen's expressions, ran alongside of them and threw out grappling-irons. She had never been out of England before, she was profoundly ignorant of foreign ways, she was mightily afraid of imaginary dangers and difficulties; and she clung to these strangers as likely to assist her to surmount the first obstacles. Mrs Fairbrother was a worthy woman, the wife of a large grocer who had made a considerable fortune by supplying H.M. vessels when put in commission. Her education was deficient, but she had the best and kindest heart in the world. Her thorough goodness did not allow those who knew her to admit that she was vulgar. The old lady had picked up what little she knew of history and geography from novels and plays, and her mind on such subjects was the veriest lumber-closet of disconnected facts and fictions. The only child, Jacquetta, had been well educated, and in manner and acquirements was far ahead of her mother. She was a true and good girl, and though the old lady's blunders were ridiculous, and—before company—embarrassing, she never laughed at them, never attempted to correct them unless it were absolutely necessary to do so, lest she should seem to assume superiority over her mother, and hurt the feelings of the woman she loved best in the world.

The gentlemen were the Baron de Montcontour, and an English friend, Mr Asheton. M. de Montcontour had been a good deal in England, and spoke English fairly well. He was an easy-going, amiable man, without great energy of mind or body. The Montcontour estates were small. He had a château on the Loire above Nantes, where lived his mother and aunt; his father had saved nothing, the property barely allowed its proprietors to live on it. It was advisable, if not necessary, that the young baron should adopt a profession to supplement his small patrimony. Accordingly he had studied law, and had taken pains to familiarise himself with English, because he saw that it would help him at Nantes, where a good many English were settled, whither English vessels came, and where some commerce went on between the two countries; where accordingly little difficulties sprang up occasionally which demanded the intervention of a lawyer familiar with both tongues.

Mr Asheton was the son of an English merchant at Nantes, and as the Baron had had some business connection with his father's house, the two young men came to know each other, and strike up a warm, if not very deep, friendship. They had just made a tour together of the Channel Islands, and were on their way home. There was a slight assumption of superiority and superciliousness in the tone of young James Asheton. He was *the* young man of the English colony at Nantes; a good deal of deference was shown him, his father was well off, he was of a marriageable age, and there were some dozen and a half young English girls at Nantes also marriageable. This is a condition of affairs not calculated to engender diffidence in a young man. He wore an eyeglass, and somewhat cocked his cap. He had fair hair, light whiskers, so fine that the soft air on the vessel blew them about, and he was constrained to stroke them back with his delicate hand, on which were several rings.

'What is that thing-a-bob sticking up on the coast yonder?' asked Mrs Fairbrother, pointing eastward, after the steamer had left Jersey.

'That ma'm, is Coutance cathedral,' answered Asheton. 'And, for a thing-a-bob, is a noble pile, in the early Norman style of architecture.'

'Is it in France?'

'Certainly, but on the extreme verge. An earthquake would send it over into debatable waters.'

'Well, that is odd,' remarked the old lady, 'because it is nearer Jersey than England; we can't even see our own

coast from here, and we can those of France.   How comes
it that the islands belong to us and not to the French?'

'The Channel Islands,' explained Mr Asheton, stroking
his whiskers, 'are the only remains of the Duchy of Normandy that are held by the British crown.'

'You know, mamma, that William the Conqueror was
Duke of Normandy before he became King of England,'
said Jacquetta hastily, afraid lest her mother should commit
herself.   The girl saw a twinkle in the young Englishman's
eye.

'My dear,' answered the old lady frankly, 'I know
nothing about it.   I have no head for the kings of England.
Indeed, I only remember about two of them, Edward who ·
picked up a lady's garter, and refused to stand on the Bible,
and Charles I who walked and talked thirty years after his
head was cut off.   Yes—by the way, there was another—
Alfred, who burnt some cakes.   It is enough for me, my
dear, to know and to love the name of our gracious Queen.
Confound their politics, Frustrate their knavish tricks, and
make them fall.   Amen.'

'What, ma'm, a Republican?   Wish to overthrow the
monarchy?' exclaimed Mr Asheton nibbling his whiskers.

'Fiddlesticks.   I mean the enemies of our great and
gracious sovereign lady Queen Victoria—and—make—them
—fall.'

Jacquetta drew her pretty lips together; a little tighten-
ing of her eyebrows might have been observed.   She did
not like the tone of the Englishman; he was laughing at
her mother.

'Madame has never been in France before? nor Mademoiselle?' asked the baron.

'O never, neither of us,' answered Mrs Fairbrother eagerly. 'And whatever I shall do if I find Aunt Betsy dead I don't know. Has one to send notice to the registrar? and what is registrar in French? And how about the will, taking inventory, and undertaker, and all that? They don't burn the dead in France, do they? I have read about such things; and I saw it done in a play once, only just as they were about to light the fire, the corpse blazed away out of a revolver at them and drove them away, and so saved the widow—but, no, I haven't got it quite right, it was an Irishman who took the place on the settee, that is what it was called, I think. I hope nothing of the sort is done in France.'

'Certainly there are no *suttees* there, ma'm,' answered Asheton.

'Well, I did not know. They are Catholics.'

'Let us hope, madam, your aunt will be alive,' said the baron. 'I would grieve to think that your first visit to my poor country should be made under sad circumstances.'

'One must be prepared, you know,' said Mrs Fairbrother. 'Whatever Jacket and I will do in a foreign land with all their queer ways, I'm sure I can't tell. Fairbrother ought to have come with us, but he couldn't leave the shop—business, I mean, couldn't or wouldn't—his foreman is a sharp man and honest. It is too bad, sending off us unprotected females like this, scrimmaging after a dead aunt, and neither of us knowing how to manage.'

'Where, if I may ask, did madame your aunt live?' inquired the baron.

'Near Nantes,' answered the girl for her mother, who

was too vague in her ideas of locality to give an intelligible
answer.   But Mrs Fairbrother replied as well, eagerly,

'At a place called Chanticleer.'   Then seeing her
daughter's lips move, she said, 'Now, I know I'm right.   I
can't be wrong.   I know it has to do with cocks and hens.'

'Yes, mamma, you are quite right—Champclair.'

'Champclair?' exclaimed the baron, and raised his eyebrows.   'May I presume to ask the name of the deceased
lady?'

'Oh yes, Mary Elizabeth Pengelly,' answered Mrs Fairbrother.   'Miss Betsy Pengelly.   She had been companion
to an old French lady with a blasphemous name, that is, a
name which should only be mentioned in the pulpit.   It
has to do with the broad road that leads to destruction.
My aunt got Chanticleer by the old lady's will when she
died.'

'Ah! my faith,' exclaimed the baron, 'Madame de
Hoelgoet.'

'That's it—Hellgate.'

'That is very singular,' remarked the young Frenchman ;
'as it happens, I know the circumstances, and you will
perhaps allow me the honour of assisting you in any way
that lies in my power.   On my desire to serve you, madame,
you may calculate.   Madame de Hoelgoet was a near
relative of my mother and of the aunt who lives with her at
her château, and,' he smiled, 'my mother has always felt a
little annoyed because Madame de Hoelgoet left Champclair
out of the family to a—what you call her—a companion.
But that need make no difference.   I do not feel with my
mother in this matter.   I have even heard that Madame
Pain-au-lait—excuse me if I do not give the name quite as

you pronounce it—deserved all she got. Madame de Hoelgoet suffered for many years from a most painful internal disorder, and Madame Pain-au-lait was devoted to her, and ministered to her through all, with unexampled devotion. No, for my part, I rejoice that she received her due, and my joy is doubled when I think that Champclair will pass now into such fair and excellent hands,' he made a bow to Mrs and then to Miss Fairbrother.

'Well, baron,' said the old lady with a pleased expression illumining her broad good-natured face, 'I'm glad you see it in that light, and express it so prettily. It shows you have a right way of looking at things, my lord.' Since she had heard that Montcontour was a baron, she insisted on 'my lording' him, to Asheton's great amusement. 'I haven't seen my Aunt Betsy for an age, but I've a notion what she did for the old lady with the Broadway name shortened her days.'

'M. de Montcontour and I live near Nantes,' said Asheton, 'and it will be a privilege, if you will suffer us to offer our services.'

'Bless us! I shall be most thankful,' said Mrs Fairbrother. 'I don't know how to manage anything. We've never had a death in our house, thanks be. I never had any husband before Fairbrother, and no other child but Jacket. It is bad enough in England, and the undertakers take such advantage of the situation. What they'd do in France to us strangers I shudder to contemplate. For my soul's sake I'm glad I'm not an undertaker.'

CHAPTER II

Mrs Fairbrother was not an observant person; she did
not suspect in the least the little play that was going on
about her, whilst she talked.   Both of the young men found
Jacquetta more agreeable to converse with than the old lady,
and each tried to involve his companion in conversation with
the latter so as to retain the society of the young girl for
himself.   Asheton proved restive when the good woman
linked herself on to him.   Through the corner of his eye
he could see the baron ingratiating himself with Jacquetta.
Therefore he took pains to refer the mother to his friend
for information on the necessary formalities attached to a
death and burial and the proving of wills; and no sooner
did he find the baron engaged in the explanation than he
spread an umbrella to inclose himself with the girl from
the other group, under the plea of cutting off from her the
glare from the sun and water, but in reality to raise a
stumbling-block in the way of his friend joining them.
However, M. de Montcontour was quite sensible of his
friend's intentions, and he extricated himself abruptly from
his discussion with Mrs Fairbrother by starting to his feet

and calling on Mademoiselle to cross with him to the other side of the boat where porpoises were tumbling in the water.

Asheton at once insisted on bringing Mrs Fairbrother over to the same bulwarks, to look at the porpoises, and he sat himself on the other side of Jacquetta to that occupied by the baron. The move was not absolutely successful, as he had the old lady on his left, and was obliged to talk to and listen, or pretend to listen to her. But he waited his opportunity to shunt her on the baron.

'Alphonse,' said he, when he saw his friend talking in a low tone to the girl, about something that seemed to interest her, 'Alphonse, Madame asks which hotel you recommend at Saint Malo.'

'Oh,' said the baron, completely concealing his disgust at the interruption, 'of course l'Hotel de France—Chateaubriand's native house. The hostess English, excellent wines, and a *table d' hote* famous everywhere.' Then to Miss Fairbrother, 'As I was telling you, the Guernsey lilies are not natives of the island, they were bulbs of African plants washed up from a wreck.'

'What about natives?' asked Mrs Fairbrother.

'The baron,' explained Asheton sulkily, 'was merely telling you that Chateaubriand was born in the house now a hotel. Chateaubriand, you know, who wrote *Atala*.'

'I know the march out of it,' said the old lady. 'It goes something like this, Tum—tiddletee—tum—ti!' and she hummed, and with her fingers drummed on the bulwarks. 'Do you know Chanticleer? I am afraid the drainage is bad, and that is what has brought my Aunt Betsy to an early grave.'

'Is she so very young?'

'Oh, well—about seventy. What sort of a place, now, is Chanticleer?'

'My dear madam,' said Asheton with eagerness, 'the baron alone can tell you. I have never seen it. I do not know where it is. I have not the smallest idea as to how the drains are carried. *He* knows all about it, has the map of the place in his head.'

That answered. The old lady let go the bulwarks and went behind Asheton and Jacquetta, and 'caught the bulwarks again beside Montcontour, on his right, and entangled him at once. Now was Asheton's turn with the young lady and he availed himself of it; he could be very agreeable when he chose, and he made an effort now and succeeded. The baron writhed in the meshes of the mother's talk, and it was some time before the chance presented itself to him of flinging her off on Asheton; but it came and he grasped it with eagerness.

'Come here, Jacques,' he called. 'Madame is asking if there is an English church service at Nantes, and wants to know the views of the chaplain. I cannot help her.'

'I am at Madame's orders,' said James Asheton stiffly, without showing annoyance, more than he could help.

'Ah, mademoiselle,' said the Baron, 'I was telling you, or about to tell you, that whilst on the Loire you should try to make an excursion up the river to Angers and Saumur. At the latter place you will see human habitations scooped in the rock, and families living in subterrains—what is the word?—caverns. Then, at Fontevrault you will see the monuments of Richard Sans Peur, and his Queen Berengaria. Mademoiselle will be staying some months at Nantes?'

'I do not know. Nothing is settled. We do not know whether my poor great-aunt is alive or dead.'

On arriving at St. Malo all four passengers agreed that the time had passed with marvellous rapidity since they had left Guernsey, and that the passage had been an agreeable one. There was but one drawback to it, thought each of the gentlemen, and that was that the other did not wholly engross the old lady, and leave to him an uninterrupted *tête-à-tête* with Jacquetta. Mrs Fairbrother liked both gentlemen, she hardly knew which she preferred. Miss Fairbrother did not say what she thought or felt, but she smiled and seemed happy, and not too depressed by the mourning for Aunt Betsy, whom, indeed, she hardly knew. The gentlemen passed the ladies' goods through the *douane*, and escorted them to the hotel, and insisted on carrying their umbrellas, parasols, and bundles of wraps and novels. Then they requested permission to call later in the evening and take Madame and Mademoiselle out on the ramparts to see the tide, which rises to a phenomenal height at St. Malo. The permission was readily granted, and three-quarters of an hour before the tide would reach its height the gentlemen appeared in the courtyard of the hotel, for the ladies.

St. Malo is a quaint old town built on an island and inclosed within walls. The houses are very high, rising five or six stories, and the streets are so narrow as to deserve no better designation than lanes. Indeed the town looks as though the builders had striven for a wager to crowd upon one little rocky platform above the waves, the greatest possible number of houses it could be forced to sustain. When the tide ebbs, the harbour that separates it from St. Servan is dry, but when it is in, that harbour has in it four fathoms of water.

Seaward the view from the ramparts is varied by an archipelago of white rocks bristling out of the sea, the larger masses crowned with forts and batteries. The sun was setting in the north-west, and sent a blaze over the rolling ocean, that seemed about irresistibly to swallow up the little town huddled on the rock with its feet in the water. The wind had freshened as the day declined, and drove the waves against the rocks, and lashed them into eddies of spray and jets of foam.

'The tide don't come in quite so strong in England,' said Mrs Fairbrother. 'I suppose the walls are built so high to keep it out of the town.'

'And as a defence against the English, madame,' said the baron. 'The town has twice been besieged by your gallant nation. To-day it surrenders at the feet of two fascinating invaders.'

'Oh, get along,' said Mrs Fairbrother, laughing. 'That's all blarney, my lord. But—by the way—was not this the town that Queen Mary said would be found written on her heart after death?'

'No,' said Asheton, with a twitch of the lips. 'That was Calais, lost to the British crown in her reign.'

'Ah! I hardly thought this could be it,' said Mrs Fairbrother, 'because the shops are so bad.'

Seeing that Asheton's face bore a puzzled expression, she hastened to explain herself. 'I mean that Queen Mary couldn't care much for such a place, where there's not a plate-glass front, nor a decent milliner's in the whole town.'

'Mademoiselle,' said the Baron de Montcontour to Jacquetta, 'the air is cool, allow me to fold this plaid about your shoulders.'

Whilst he was thus engaged, Mrs Fairbrother clutched the arm of Asheton, and said, in a low tone. Is it quite fair of me to avail myself of the help of your friend, lord Monkeytower, in seeing after my poor dear Aunt Betsy's affairs? You heard what he said. The property once belonged to his mother's family, and ought to have gone to Lady Monkeytower, instead of Betsy Pengelly. I daresay that her ladyship thinks Aunt Betsy unduly influenced her mistress—well, to make no bones over the matter—Madam Broadway—I can't call her as she was called in French. I've always heard the French are profane, and I believe it with this evidence. As I was saying, I daresay the family think Aunt Betsy behaved dishonourably, and persuaded her mistress. Yes, that is what I was about to say—Betsy we say was a companion, but she was a sort of lady's maid, only it sounds more respectable to say companion. Now I daresay the family think—'

'Quite so, I understand,' interrupted Asheton, who had not the patience to listen to the confused story. 'What do you propose, madam? to come to something practical.'

'Me! Oh I propose nothing; only feeling as they do, I don't know whether I ought to accept Lord Monkeytower's offer. It is very kind of him, but—I don't believe that her own relations went to see the poor sick lady when she was ill, except just to leave a card with a P.P.C. or R.S.V.P., or whatever the letters are. I don't know, I've never moved in society. Fairbrother is a grocer on a large scale. I don't mean that he is personally on a large scale, but I mean the grocery is. The Chanticleer property is no particular odds to me or Jacket, if my aunt has left it us, and Betsy was Jacket's godmamma. I may say to you that Fairbrother has done uncommon well in business, and laid by a lot of money, and might retire, if he were of a retiring disposition, which he ain't. Jacket will have twenty-five thousand pounds when she marries, and when her father and I are dead and gone, as much more ; so a little pinch of French dust and a shovel of French francs are no consideration to us, and we wouldn't be thought unhandsome by nobody. Leastways I wouldn't. I don't think Jacket considers it much ; if there was any sign that there'd been a bit of underhand dealing, not that I give Betsy the discredit of it—she was a right good Protestant up-and-down woman, and no quirks and crinkum-cranklums in her conscience. Lord! where was I got to ? I'm in a regular tangle.'

'You've got where you can't see the sunset,' said Asheton, sulkily ; he was looking over his shoulder at the baron, who had edged away with Jacquetta to a considerable distance on the rampart, and was pointing out to her the isle and fortress of La Conchée, that was steeped in the orange glory of the declining sun.

'I wouldn't do an unhandsome thing for the world,' continued the unwearied, unflagging Mrs Fairbrother. 'I wouldn't profit not a grain of mustard seed by any underhand and mean tricks, if Aunt Betsy were capable of 'em, which I don't believe. Still, she lived a lot in France, and you can't live among sinners and not consent to them, nor touch pitch and not be defiled. I'd rather give up our claim than have it thought by the Monkeytowers or any one else that we'd come into what we'd no good rights to. I daresay I don't express myself very clearly, but you can understand me. I'm a square woman, and I want to be always square. You can understand that—square, all round.'

'I understand,' said Asheton, biting his lips. 'Shall we push on further? The baron has gained a vantage point—for the view!'

'Certainly—but you will advise me.'

'O yes. You shall know my opinion when we get to Nantes.'

'Lauk-a-dear!' exclaimed Mrs Fairbrother, to her daughter. 'What gibberish are you talking, Jacket?'

'Oh, mamma, M. de Montcontour is so kind. He insists on my speaking French with him, so as to familiarise me with the language, and—he does not laugh at my mistakes.'

'Mademoiselle is incapable of a mistake, she gives laws to everything—to our language,' said the baron.

'My word! that's blarney again,' exclaimed the down-right old lady.

'I have been suggesting, madame,' said the baron, 'that as we are all going the same way, we should share a carriage and posthorses; the *voiturier* would conduct his own *voiture*. The *diligence* may be quicker, but it is less convenient.'

'And I replied,' answered Miss Fairbrother, 'that as we are hastening to my poor great-aunt, and do not know whether she is alive, we must not consider our convenience, but press on as expeditiously as possible.'

'If that concern we saw in the yard like a yellow wasp without a waist is what you call a diligence,' said Mrs Fairbrother, 'nothing on earth will induce me to travel in it. I never in all my life saw such a ramshackle conveyance. I wonder the Government are not ashamed to own it. Besides, it is dirty. I am convinced that the linings swarm with—well, fleas is too mild a term for the creatures. And as to its being more expeditious, I don't believe it. I saw the post-horses bring it in. They ought to have been at the knacker's years ago. My dear, I'm not going to be bitten and eaten for Aunt Betsy or anybody. I did not come to France to be cannibalised.'

Presently the sun disappeared and the air was chill. Mrs Fairbrother said it was time to go back to the inn. The gentlemen attended them and parted at the door; Asheton shook hands, but the baron only bowed low and took off and waved his hat with magnificent politeness.

As soon as the ladies had disappeared. 'Montcontour,' said Asheton, 'I am afraid we shall quarrel. You take unfair advantage of me. Do you know that this sweet girl is worth over six hundred thousand francs now and as many more in prospective?'

'If you had said a million, *mon ami*, I would have replied that you undervalued her.'

'A truce to your complimentary speeches. She can't hear you and they will not be repeated by me. It is a fact. The mother told me as much, and that old butter-tub is a truthful woman.'

'You mean this!—in cash, six hundred thousand francs!'

'I do.'

'Why, I'm not worth as much—that *gentile petite* would be precious without anything—but——'

'Yes, exactly, *but.*   What do you mean by that but?'

'There is a mother.'

'There is, Alphonse, a serious counterweight. She is a thoroughly good woman, honourable, kind-hearted, high-principled, but——'

'*Précisément*, Jacques—*mais*——'

CHAPTER III

Wᴎᴇɴ the two young men returned to their inn—not the
Hôtel de France—they went into the *café* and called for
café noir, at a little marble-topped table in a corner, and
lit their cigars.

'Jacques,' said the baron, when the waiter had with-
drawn, '*cette jeune fille me trotte en tete.*'

'*Moi aussi*,' answered Asheton; 'she is miles ahead of
the girls at Nantes. Besides—there is that twenty-five
thousand pounds sterling.'

'You must not think of her,' said the baron, hastily,
'you have been paying court to your English consul's
daughter—that beautiful blonde.'

'Ah, bah!—nothing serious.'

'You may think so, but the poor girl adores you.'

'Possibly,' answered Asheton, twirling his cigar, and
letting the smoke escape in a spiral from his lips—then,
after a pause, with an air of consequence, 'a man can't
help it if a girl likes him—cats may look at kings without
kings stooping to scratch their necks.'

'You will break the heart of the blonde, Jacques.'

'That is her affair. I have given her no encouragement. She is worth nothing, and this angel is worth fifty thousand pounds.'

'For shame, you are mercenary, you—with your father's purse to draw out of.'

'My father has a long purse, it is true.' Asheton threw one leg over the other, an arm over the back of his chair, and leaned back with his chin in the air. 'You are mighty eager to couple me with the consul's daughter, Alphonse.'

'I—oh, I care nothing about it; but she is a nice girl, and domestic and amiable; she would make you happy.'

'I hate tame cats.'

'She is very polished.'

'All the more slippery.'

'Oh, Jacques! you are false. I know you admired her.'

'Pardon. She admired me, and I respected her taste.'

'She is really very pretty.'

'Then take her yourself. That is enough of the blonde.'

The baron and Asheton continued smoking, then called for small glasses of yellow Chartreuse.

'It is of no use, Alphonse,' said Asheton, superciliously, 'your letting Miss Fairbrother trot in your head, let her leap the hedge and be out of the inclosure at once. You know very well that it is impossible for you to think of her.'

'But, Jacques, I do think of her.'

'Well, think, but with no ulterior views. Are you aware that her father is a grocer and wears a white apron —a common English grocer? You are a baron of ancient family; you are perfectly aware that your mother would never consent to such an union.'

'We are poor as rats.'

'And rats like the good stores in a grocer's shop.   Bah !
it is impossible.   In France you cannot marry without the
consent of your parents.   Think of your mother—of pro-
posing to her to take the niece of la Pain-au-lait, the maid
to Madame de Hoelgoet.   She would never, never consent.'

'Why do you talk of marriage ? May I not flutter
about the flower ?'

'A bee goes to the flower for the golden honey and
carries it off, but leaves the flower.   You cannot get the
honey without the flower.'

'I see what it is,' said the baron, losing his temper
slightly.   He was too well-bred and too easy-going a man
to be greatly put out, and show it.   'You want to carry off
Mademoiselle yourself, and kill the beautiful blonde with
chagrin.'

'I amuse myself,' answered Asheton, tapping his cigar
against the ashpan on the table, and then throwing up his
head again, and inhaling a long whiff of smoke.

'You must not trifle with this girl's affections as you
have with those of the blonde.   I will not allow it.'

'Halloo ! Knight Bayard, *preux chevalier !* I am to
leave the coast clear to you.   Well, I admit I have no
chance against a baron with a coronet of six pearls.
Especially when that vulgar old butter-tub thinks you will
make her daughter My-Lady.'

'There you are wrong, Jacques, it is I who have no
chance. Who in these liberal days cares for empty
honours ? Who asks to see your pedigree ? And who
that reads your pedigree believes in it ? No, my friend, it
is *you* who have every chance, not I. You are her

countryman, and you have good expectations from your father. Your nation is practical, it values solid advantages, not soap-bubble titles.'

'You, Alphonse, will render that gross mother and the girl many favours, will place them under a thousand obligations, if you help them with the settlement of the affairs of their aunt, and establish their right to Champclair.'

'You do not know that the Pain-au-lait is dead. If she survive, I shall be debarred the house. I cannot visit there whilst the maid-companion of Madame de Hoelgoet is in possession. My mother would not endure it. On the other hand, you will pass your days there dancing round the ladies.'

'The lady—I shall decline to dance round the butter-tub. Enough! Let the event decide.'

'In the meantime, what about the carriage and the journey in it? Who is to sit on the box, and which is to enjoy supreme felicity, basking in the sunshine of the eyes of mademoiselle?'

'Neither shall go on the box. We will both sit inside with our backs to the horses.'

'Yes—that is very well—but it will embitter the journey all the more, if one sits opposite Madame whilst the other is opposite that Angel.'

'We will change places at each change of horses. One will engage the old woman and leave the other free to prosecute his suit with the young lady. We will act chivalrously by each other in this matter.'

'It shall be so. Let us make a further agreement, which is to present the Angel with flowers and fruit?'

'To-morrow you shall offer flowers to your goddess, and

I will present cherries. The following day our *roles* will be reversed. Will that suffice you, Alphonse?'

'Admirably. It is three days' journey to Nantes, and I shall have two days in which to offer my floral oblations, to your one.'

'But I shall have two for cherries.'

'Do you think so basely of Mademoiselle Jacquetta as to suppose she will appreciate comestibles above flowers?'

'Consider,' said Asheton, 'she can only accept a limited number of roses and lilies, and almost an unlimited number of cherries.'

'Perish the thought,' said the baron, and shuddered. 'You judge her by her mother.'

'My dear Jacket,' said Mrs Fairbrother to her daughter that same evening, 'it is clear to me as starch that you have made a couple of conquests, and I'm not a bit surprised at it, for there never was a dearer girl than you.'

'Mamma!' laughed Miss Fairbrother, 'It is you who are the attraction; you talk so pleasantly and amusingly, whereas I am dull.'

'Nonsense, my darling, you say that because you think it will please me; I declare you have been infected by Lord Monkeytower with the itch of blarney. No, young men do not care for old women, talk they ever so sweetly. Which of the two do you like best?'

'Really, mamma,' said Jacquetta, laughing and colouring to the roots of her hair, 'this is nonsense, and it is the first time I've heard nonsense from your dear old mouth. I care for neither of them particularly, they are both pleasant companions on a journey, and may be useful to us. They are very kind and considerate.'

'Well, my pet, we shall see plenty of them, we shall be three days getting to Chanticleer'

'Mamma, I wish we were going in the diligence, we ought to travel night and day to Aunt Betsy.'

'My dear—not after having seen that fusty, dirty, blue cloth lining to the coach. You may be more charitable than me. I don't set up to be liberal. I am not going to gorge French fleas till they die of apoplexy. The carriage is ordered, and the horses and the driver. Three days, my dear—and two young men—umph, I say.'

'Oh, mamma!'

'It is all very well saying "Oh, mamma!" but I know the world, and you don't.'

If Mrs Fairbrother had been simply an ignorant, foolish, and vulgar woman, her daughter would not have turned out such a sweet and refined girl, notwithstanding the advantages given her, but Mrs Fairbrother was a woman with a vastly tender heart, high principle, and, though she talked like a fool, she acted sensibly. Her vulgarity was superficial—in her speech, not in her mind. There was no affectation in the woman, she was perfectly true. She had her pride—but it was a harmless pride—it was centred in her daughter. She, herself, made no pretence to be other than she was, and hated display, consequently she was not really vulgar. Her great blemish lay in this, that her tongue rattled quicker than her mind acted, and she said a great deal which had not been sifted by her judgment. Her daughter saw and valued her mother's excellent qualities, and overlooked, or was blind to her weaknesses.

The journey to Nantes was a pleasant one; the weather was favourable, the carriage was open all the time, the gentlemen were most agreeable, and the ladies were interested, astonished, and amused by the novelty of the sights that met their eyes. The two young men did what they could to entertain them. At Hédé the baron insisted on taking them into a peasant's cottage to see the making of buckwheat flat cakes; and then Asheton drew them into the garden of the inn to see angelica growing, from which the delicious crystallised transparent green sweetmeat is made.

The baron ran about after pinks and harebells, which attracted the admiration of Jacquetta, she had never seen wild pinks before. He composed bouquets for her of chickory and wild roses and snapdragon. Garden flowers were not to be had. But Asheton's cherries proved a failure; the roadside flowers were a little dusty, but the cherries purchased by Asheton were old and had maggots in them, so that Jacquetta was obliged to decline them after a first attempt.

At one village, whilst the horses were being changed, the ladies visited the churchyard. Jacquetta found her mother standing by a cross with tears in her eyes.

'Oh, Jacket! What a pretty idea. Do you see? This is a child's grave, and there is a glass-faced case under the cross containing the child's toys. I'll have something of the sort made for Aunt Betsy.'

'But—mamma—she——'

'Of course she had no toys, but she had a moustache-cup, not that she grew a moustache like a man, but she was very particular about her drinking out of her own cup; and when she was with us ten years ago, she took a fancy to a moustache-cup I had, and I gave it her. She said that none of the men or maids at Chanticleer would use and dirty that. Now I'll have a little case made, and a sheet of glass, and a crook, and hang up Aunt Betsy's moustache-cup on her tombstone. It will be quite beautiful, and moving to the feelings.'

When Mrs Fairbrother was back in the carriage, she said, 'There is one thing I have seen which is horrible. The idea of letting graves by leases for five, seven, or ten years, and then digging up the dead and chucking the bones into a common pit. I'll hire the ground as you call it 'in perpetuity' for Aunt Betsy. Let graves on lease, by paying!—and that where you have written up Liberty, Equality, and Fraternity! I can't understand it. You'll kindly manage that for me, gentlemen, will you not? I'll have Aunt Betsy properly tucked away in perpetuity.'

But Aunt Betsy was not dead. She received her relatives at her door on their arrival.

CHAPTER IV

DEAD! Prepared, disposed to be tucked in *en perpétuité*—
not a bit of it.

Miss Betsy Pengelly, or as her French servants and
neighbours persisted in calling her, Mdlle. Pain-au-lait,
had been very unwell with a bad influenza attack which
lowered her physically and in spirits so greatly that she
thought she was going to die. Then she wrote to her
niece Louisa Fairbrother, *née* Pengelly, that she desired to
see her before she died. The letter took three days going
to its destination, then Mrs Fairbrother had to wait two
days for the steamer, and so did not reach Champclair till
nine days after Miss Pengelly had written, and in those
nine days the wind had gone out of the east, the fountains
of Aunt Betsy's cold had dried up, and her recuperative
powers were so great that she was about the house and
came to the door when the carriage drove up with her
niece, great-niece, and the two gentlemen.

Dead! ready to be tucked in *en perpétuité* with her
moustache-cup dangling about her remains!—not a bit of
it. Having shaken off her influenza Miss Pengelly had

taken a new spell of life. She was delighted to see her niece Louisa, and her goddaughter Jacquetta, and much puzzled with the gentlemen, who were also somewhat perplexed what to do, when they found they were not required to organise an interment, and prove a will. The baron had the greatest difficulty to extricate himself, but he did it with perfect good taste, and Miss Pengelly was delighted to be able to meet on terms of civility one of a family she believed was implacably set against her. Asheton airily explained that he had come to escort the ladies as they were strangers. Miss Pengelly knew him by name, and had seen his fair whiskers and rings in the English chapel. She entreated the gentlemen to come in, and take some refreshment, but they declined. They must return to their homes, now that they had seen Madame and Mademoiselle in safety, but they asked and obtained permission to call in a day or two to inquire how the ladies were after the fatigues of their journey.

Mr Asheton did not wait for two days, he called on the morrow, and the day after that. The baron was less hasty, but he did appear at Champclair. He did not seem in spirits. In fact, he had told his mother nothing of his meeting with the Fairbrothers, and she had no idea whatever of his having been fascinated by a young English girl. The baron sneaked—literally sneaked to Champclair, and felt all the time he was there like a man who had committed a crime. The duty to father and mother is the paramount duty in a Frenchman's mind, that is the only commandment about the infringement of which he is super-sensitive. He would ten thousand times rather elope with his neighbour's wife, than disobey his mother about a trifle. Consequently the baron was not happy when he called, he knew he was doing wrong. His mother would have disapproved, had she been told whither he was going.

He did not venture to call again for a week, and then his uneasiness was not lightened when he found Asheton at the house, on familiar terms with all three ladies, as though quite an established friend.

'My dear Mrs Fairbrother,' said Asheton one day to the old mother when they were alone, 'I hope you will excuse my audacity if I venture on giving you a piece of advice. I believe my mother and the chaplain's wife are about to call on you—*would* you mind not saying anything about the—the—shop? It is not necessary to say that Mr Fairbrother is a grocer. If you would allow that he is a merchant, it will do.'

'But—he *is* a grocer, on a very large scale.'

'The scale makes all the difference, madam,' said Asheton. 'On a small scale he would be a shopkeeper, on a large scale—a merchant. Excuse my mentioning it. I would not do so, but that I was afraid it might stand in the way of your receiving social hospitalities whilst at Champclair. Miss Pengelly is not received, but you and Miss Fairbrother may be.'

'I won't hide the truth—Fairbrother *is* a grocer.'

'There is going to be a series of picnics and out-of-door dances, and other entertainments, and I think Miss Jacquetta would like to be present. The consul gives a party next week at Les Hirondelles, and I am sure Miss Jacquetta would immensely enjoy herself. But, my dear madam, if you let out with your refreshing frankness about the—the —the shop, she will not be invited. No one will call on you—you will be as much tabooed as if you had the small-pox.   Of course these social distinctions and all that sort of thing are rank folly and detestable and wicked—but my dear Mrs Fairbrother, we must take the world as it is.   We did not make it; the earth's crust is stratified.   However much displaced, contorted, broken by faults, the strati-fication remains as an integral element of its structure.   It is the same with the superincumbent social organisation, however disturbed by revolutions, the social beds remain.'

'Lawk!' exclaimed Mrs Fairbrother, 'I've heard of social gatherings and social teas, but I thought the great bed of Ware that accommodated twelve was the only social bed in the world.   The idea is not inviting.   I'll never get into a social bed myself, not I.'

Mr Asheton carried his point; for her daughter's sake the good lady refrained from allusions to the shop, but it went against the grain with her, her nature was so genuine, so candid.

James Asheton profited by his advantage over the baron, he was at Champclair nearly every day.   He took the ladies up the river; he made his mother and sister call on them, and through Mrs Asheton, the chaplain and his wife were got to call.   The chaplain had previously visited Miss Pengelly as one of his flock, but Mrs Chaplain had declined to do so—it was well known that she had been in a menial position; she was a fossil in a different social bed from that which contained Mrs Chaplain.   Asheton had plenty to say for himself; he had no occupation, his time was at his own disposal, and as he knew that his father though well off, was not likely to leave him much more than a flourishing business, he thought that twenty-five thousand pounds and a pretty girl would not come amiss. At the same time he had the awkward and difficult game to play of getting off with the old love before plunging in with the new. He had flirted a good deal with Miss Graham, the consul's blonde daughter, and it might lead to unpleasantness if he broke off his attentions to her too abruptly and transferred them too suddenly to the grocer's daughter. Accordingly he was careful not to be overpressing in his attentions to Miss Fairbrother, and at the same time he paid several visits to the consul's house, and was polite, cordially polite to the blonde. As he said to himself, he would let her drop lightly.

It was hard for him with his contemptuous, sarcastic spirit, to restrain himself from taking up Mrs Fairbrother when she made mistakes, but he did control himself because he saw that if he did this he would offend the daughter. He said nothing to his mother about his intentions, he merely observed to Mrs Asheton that the young lady was an heiress worth in all fifty thousand pounds. That was sufficient, his mother understood as fully what that meant, as if he had gone on his knee to her and asked her blessing on his projected union. Among savages it is 'bad form' to call things by their proper names, it is much the same among the cultured. Mrs Asheton went out of her way to be civil to the Fairbrothers, she had never fancied Miss Graham, not because Miss Graham was other than an excellent and accomplished girl, but because Miss Graham was one of sixteen children, and the consul had only three hundred a year on which to live, and could lay by nothing; also because she saw that James had no aptitude for business, and that if he were taken into the merchant's office, he would let the business slip away. James preferred amusement to work, and idleness to application. Consequently poor James must not be allowed to throw himself away on impecunious blondes.

Mrs Asheton gave a little party, to which the Fairbrothers were invited; at this she introduced them to other Nantes residents, among others to the consul and his lady, and Mrs Graham, without a suspicion, invited both to her *al fresco* entertainment at Les Hirondelles.

Mrs Fairbrother would have liked to return to 'her old man,' but she saw that her stay gave pleasure to Aunt Betsy, and that it was good for her daughter, who was seeing a fresh bit of the world, improving her French, and had made one or two captures. She talked the matter over with Aunt Betsy, who said that her leaving was not to be thought of; the baron belonged to one of the best families of the Loire; though the family was poor, it was thought highly of. The late baron had been esteemed as a man of unblemished honour and respectability, and Madame la Baronne, though she was unkind and spoke harshly of her —Aunt Betsy—yet belonged to one of the first aristocratic circles of Brittany, the De Pleurans. As for Mr James Asheton, he was the son of a good substantial merchant, a decent young man, but thought to be a bit of a flirt. It must be left to Jacquetta to choose between the young men. Certainly, in her native town, she would stand no chance of marrying any one so much above her in station as either the baron or Mr Asheton. Certainly Louisa must not be obstinate and go back to England, and spoil her daughter's chances.

The two old women talked over these chances together a

good deal, but the person most interested, Jacquetta, gave them little thought. She was very happy at Champclair, intensely interested in all she saw; the novelty was not worn off, and when her mother spoke of returning home, she begged so earnestly and prettily that the holiday might be prolonged, that Mrs Fairbrother yielded at once, and wrote to Fairbrother not to expect either of them back for months. Did she like either of the young men? Certainly she did—she did more—she liked both, and liked Asheton best. The French manner, the high-flown compliments, of the baron oppressed her, and made her fancy he was unreal. But Asheton she thought was straightforward, perhaps a little too sharp in snapping up her mother; he was an Englishman, and so went out of his way to be uncomplimentary. She knew the worst of him, he wore that on his outside.

Les Hirondelles was a pretty little place about five miles from Nantes; it was a chateau with charming woods, walks, terraces and gardens, that was not inhabited by the owner, and was not let. The owner lived in Paris, and visited Les Hirondelles occasionally. With that queer, keen way which Frenchmen have of making money when and how they can, and without an idea of thereby compromising their dignity, the count who owned Les Hirondelles kept up the woods and gardens as a sort of show-place for the Nantois, who were charged fees for admission, and who might hire the place for the day, for giving entertainments at it. They might take the gardens for an afternoon for fifteen francs; if the weather were wet, and the company wanted the use of a room or two in the chateau, that was charged heavier, twenty francs. The charges were not high, but there were a good many extras, and it was thought in Nantes that the count made a good thing out of Les Hirondelles.

'Are you going to Consul Graham's affair, Alphonse?' asked Asheton.

'But yes.'

'No use, Baron. You are only gathering heartache. I don't think you will succeed.'

'Jacques! You certainly will not be so heartless as to use the *soirée* given by Madame Graham as an opportunity for throwing over her daughter for Mdlle. Fairbrother?'

'You are too precipitate, Alphonse. I have said nothing.'

'But I see you are digging your approaches very diligently. You have not the difficulties to contend against which crush my spirit, and make me almost despair. You cannot conceive how I admire her. I am as one distracted.'

'You have no chance,' said Asheton decisively.

The party at Les Hirondelles was fortunate in weather. The evening was lovely. The Fairbrothers drove thither in a hired carriage, and when they arrived the baron and Asheton were in waiting to help them to dismount. Jacquetta had to select to which she would give her hand in descending; she gave it to Asheton, who cast a glance of triumph at the baron. But the girl did it, not as a token of preference, but out of respect for her mother. M. de Montcontour was the superior in rank, and therefore ought to assist her mother.

The pretty gardens were full of flowers, not rare flowers, but those that are showy. The roses were beautiful; and the Hibiscus bushes which in England produce a blossom here and there, were covered with bloom. Our dull skies do not favour the flowering of plants, but the development of leaf. The beech and lime trees were young. One does not see abroad the old and splendid park trees that adorn the English landscape. These were plaited, and formed bowery walks and mazes, in which the young people wandered, and lost themselves, and seemed like moving flowers in their bright summer dresses. There was music, a piano was being played in the *salle*, and the windows were open. Dancing was to go on either on the terrace under the windows of the *salle*, or in the great room itself. Every one knew that the use of the *salon* had cost the consul twenty francs, and the use of the piano ten francs.

The notes of the piano sounded feebly on the terrace, and the dancers there must trust to imagination for the tune, but they could hear enough to give them the time. The gravel moreover was not good to dance on, whereas the floor of the *salle* was waxed and polished. Nevertheless, a good many couples preferred to dance out of doors.

Jacquetta was within; she had been waltzing with the baron. When she withdrew her hand from his arm, she went to one of the windows and leaned out. She saw her mother at the further side of the terrace talking to Mrs Asheton. Under the window stood James Asheton with the blonde Miss Graham. They had been dancing on the terrace; a flight of five steps below the great hall. As Jacquetta leaned on the windowsill she was above their shoulders, and could hear all they said.

'Who is that lady with your mother?' asked Miss Graham.

'That—oh!' answered James Asheton. 'That buttertub is a Mrs Fairbrother.'

'You came from Saint Malo with her and her daughter,' said Miss Graham, in a tone that displayed some jealousy.

'Oh, yes. Never amused myself better. The old thing is a fool. I must tell you some of her blunders—she is as ignorant as a horse—the social bed, that is her last.'

Then Jacquetta coughed, and Asheton turned round, caught her eye, saw her colour, and was confounded. He could not apologise, for in a moment she was gone. She had run down the steps from the *salle* on to the terrace, and had crossed to her mother, and seized her hand.

'My dear Jacket, what is it? you are squeezing my hand, what is the meaning of this sudden gush of affection?' She looked at her daughter, whose temples were spotted with red, and tears were in her eyes. Jacquetta could not speak, her lips trembled. Had she spoken, her eyes would have over-flowed.   .

'Is there anything the matter?' asked Mrs Fairbrother.

'Oh, no,' answered Jacquetta with an effort. 'Let me take your hand, mamma, and walk with you the rest of the evening, dear, darling mamma. Oh, how I love you.'

'But what *is* it?' asked Mrs Fairbrother.

That she never learned. Her daughter never told her.

Jacquetta did not know what the mistake was about the social bed, and her cough stopped the narrative on the lips of James Asheton, and prevented its becoming public property that evening.

Presently the baron met Asheton, and the latter with a rueful countenance said, 'I've made a ghastly blunder. I have done for myself, Mademoiselle Jacquetta will never speak to me again.'

'What have you done?'

'Done!—I've made fun of her mother in her hearing.'

'*Mon Dieu*, Jacques! That is fatal.'

'Now, old friend, the coast is clear for you. I have lost my chance for ever. Go in and conquer.'

'Oh, Jacques, I wish the difficulties were surmountable, but you know as well as I do that there are *les couches sociales.*'

'For heaven's sake not a word about social beds, I have heard too much about them. It is they that have been the unmaking of me.'

Two days after the party at Les Hirondelles the Baron de Montcontour appeared at Champclair in a new glossy cloth coat, evidently assumed for the first time. There was not a speck of dust, not a hair on it, no rain-drop had taken off its first gloss. His hat also was distinctly worn for the first time. When he removed it the creamy kid lining was as clean as a lady's ball-glove. His waistcoat was white, starched, and the creases in it just as it had come home folded from the wash. His trousers were lavender, his gloves ditto. From immediately below his waistcoat to immediately above the top of the bootleather on both legs descended a perfectly irreproachable crease in the trousers, the result of mingled tenderness in folding, and firmness of pressure when folded.

When the baron removed his hat an odour of otto of rose was diffused through the room from his neatly trimmed and curled hair, which had been recently treated by a *coiffeur*.

That this elaborate get-up meant something, and that something serious, could not be doubted ; Miss Pengelly saw it at once, Mrs Fairbrother sniffed it, and first the unmarried lady had to leave the drawing-room to order the cook-housemaid to get refreshments, then Mrs Fairbrother remembered she had a letter to write, and she apologised to M. de Montcontour for withdrawing. The baron was left in the sitting-room with Jacquetta, who became alarmed, and gave an appealing look to her mother to stay—and with Ponce, Aunt Betsy's fat black pug, which, with its eyes nearly starting out of its head, sat like a heraldic monster on a gate-post, upon a stool in the middle of the room, looking knowingly, interestedly, first at the baron, then at Jacquetta

When Mrs Fairbrother entered the little back room to write her letter, she found Aunt Betsy there; she had given her orders to Jacqueline her factotum, and had not returned to the drawing-room.

'Well, my dear,' said Miss Pengelly, 'he's come at last to do it.'

'I think so, auntie.'

'I'm positive. I know the ways of the country. He has never worn that hat, those gloves, that coat, and perhaps the other things, before. Did you see also that his shirt front bulged out?'

'No, I didn't.'

'It has been double starched; mark my words he means to do it. Do you think Jacket will accept him?'

'I don't know,' answered Mrs Fairbrother. 'I thought she liked young Asheton best; but they had a tiff about something at the Rundles t'other day, and she has not told me what it was about, nor has he called since.'

'I hope she will,' said Miss Pengelly, 'it would be a great comfort to me. I don't like the Montcontours to feel hurt about my getting Champclair, and this might make all right again, as I shall bequeath it to Jacket. Where is Ponce?'

'I left him sitting on the stool.'

'Did you call him?'

'Yes, but he would not come; he just stood up and sat down on his tail again. The young people will not mind his presence. He is only a dog.'

'Only a dog, yes—but such a dog. I won't have Ponce disparaged. Take care that I don't leave Champclair to him.' Miss Pengelly laughed. Then she added, 'Well, if Ponce wants to leave the room the windows are open.'

'Do you think that Jacket would be happy with Lord Monkeytower? She would have to live out of England and it would be a great privation to us not to have Jacket near us, and it would also be a sore trial to her, she is such an affectionate girl, so fond of me and her father. Dear child, I don't like to think even of parting with her.' The old lady's eyes filled with tears.

'Nonsense, Louisa,' said Miss Pengelly, 'I have lived a great part of my life in France, and like it well. I dare say I would find it dull in England if I were to return to it. One can live anywhere and be happy if one does one's duty and has a clear conscience, and the digestion be all right You will have to get Fairbrother to retire from business and come and live near Nantes. There we shall form quite a colony and dictate to the consul and the chaplain.'

'I don't understand Frenchmen,' said Mrs Fairbrother, sadly shaking her head. 'It is like poultry. I got some Aylesbury ducks once and thought they wanted water, most ducks do; but though these were ducks they didn't care for water, and Brahman fowls I overfed with heating diet, they wanted different treatment from Hamboroughs and Dorkings.   It is so with human beings—there are different breeds and they have different ways, and ought to be understood. They lay differently, and some are good sitters, and some ain't. I mean fowls, not human beings. I know nothing of Frenchmen; never saw one out of a menagerie before I came abroad.'

'The baron is a worthy young man, I have not heard a word against him, and he belongs to a family which has never produced a black sheep.' Suddenly in at the window bounded Ponce, and danced, snapping, barking, wagging his stump of a tail, round his mistress. His goggle eyes twinkled with excitement, his fat glossy sides quivered.

'My dear!' exclaimed Aunt Betsy. 'Oh, Louisa! She has accepted him.' Then the two old women flung themselves into each other's arms and burst into hysterical weeping.

The door opened, and Jacquetta appeared in it, also with tears in her eyes. But Ponce danced and barked, and snapped at his tail, full of delight, and his protruding eyes sparkled with intelligence and expressed his grasp of the situation.

Ponce was premature, so was Aunt Betsy. Jacquetta had not exactly accepted the baron, but she had not refused him. She had referred him to her mother for a final answer. Now she came to beg Aunt Betsy to go to M. de Montcontour and to let her consult her mother about the offer.

Miss Pengelly rushed into the drawing-room with both

her hands extended, Ponce running after her. She seized the baron's hands and shook them, and shook at the same time the tears from her eyes.

'I am so glad, dear baron! All comes right in the end in the best of worlds. I do assure you I was most surprised when I learned that Madame de Hoelgoet had left me Champclair, I never, never urged her to do anything for me. I did my duty to her, and received my wage. If I thought about receiving anything more, I expected only maybe a couple of hundred francs as a little remembrance —never, never that I should have Champclair. Do me justice. It has hurt my feelings inexpressibly that Madame la Baronne, your mother, should have supposed otherwise. I am incapable of acting unjustly to and taking an unfair advantage of a fly. And now all will come right; for I shall leave Champclair to Jacquetta, and so it will return to the family. Madame la Baronne will no longer feel hostile towards me. Your mother consents to the union?'

M. de Montcontour's beaming face became grave. 'Alas! Mademoiselle, that is my difficulty. I have not asked my excellent mother's consent. She does not even know of the existence of Mdlle. Jacquetta. I will break the news to her softly, she will bow to my wishes. She will see that her refusal will drive me frantic. She will learn that the happiness of my life depends on this union; when she sees Mdlle. Jacquetta every prejudice will vanish.'

'Tell Madame your mother,' said Miss Pengelly eagerly, 'that our dear Jacquetta is called after the late Madame de Hoelgoet. I was her godmother, and when she was baptised I insisted that the child should receive the name of my dear mistress, not mine; I am, and always was, a nobody. Tell Madame la Baronne also that Madame de Hoelgoet took a great interest in our dear Jacquetta and used to ask after her, and sent her once a silver egg-cup, because she said she felt, in giving her name to an infant, as if she, and not I, had the best claim to be considered her *marraine*.'

'I will say everything I can to break down her objections. I think I will go away to Saumur, and write thence to my mother. I could tell her all so much better in a letter. I am nervous in her presence.'

'*Mon Dieu*! you must do nothing of the sort. It is not right. Go home at once, as you are. When Madame sees you thus dressed in new clothes, a white waistcoat and a stiffened shirt front, and smells your hair, and all the rest, a cold feeling will creep down her spinal-marrow, and she will know an event of the utmost importance has happened. She will ask you what has taken place. Then, like a man, speak out.'

'Mademoiselle!' exclaimed the young baron, 'you are right. The ancient Germans sought counsel at the mouths of priestesses, 'and when they said the word they rushed headlong to battle. You inspire me. I will go before my mother and aunt at once. I will tell them all, whatever be the consequences to myself.'

Next day the baron returned, looking much depressed; his very clothes hung limply about his form, he was like a peacock that had been exposed to rain. With great difficulty and much hesitation he had told his mother everything in the presence of her sister, his aunt, Mdlle. de Pleurans. Madame de Hoelgoet had been a de Pleurans before her

marriage, and Champclair had been her own property—
Pleurans property.

'Well my dear baron?' asked Miss Pengelly.

'I am in despair,' he replied. 'What is to be done? I
cannot live without Mdlle. Jacquetta, and my mother
absolutely refuses her consent. She even threatens me
with her curse. I dare not repeat her words. She is a
strong-minded woman. When she learned the whole truth,
she looked perfectly calm. I, on the other hand, was
profusely agitated; and she said I might stretch her on the
rack, I might tear her flesh off with red-hot pincers, but
never would she consent to my taking to wife the—the
daughter of—excuse me, I cannot repeat all her words.
They went through me like knives. I went further than I
ought, I even alluded to Mademoiselle's fortune of over six
hundred thousand francs, I said that in the end it would be
over a million. I told her that through this union Champclair would revert to the family, but everything was in vain.'

'Did you mention the egg-cup?'

'I did mention the egg-cup,' said the baron, with a
quivering voice. He had hard work to do to restrain his
tears. 'Even that did not move her. She is an obdurate
woman—but heroic, truly heroic! She would rather we
sank lower in poverty than we are, she said, than have her
son recover the family splendour through a *mésalliance*.'

'My great-niece will never consent to take you without
your mother's consent.'

'I know that,' said the dispirited young man; he sat
with his new hat in his hands, between his knees, and he
looked down into it, much as King Richard II looked into
his crown before resigning it, 'like a deep well' in which

his sorrows sink, 'full of tears am I, drinking my griefs.'

The pale primrose of the lining-band was already discoloured. His head must have perspired a good deal, and the day was not warm. There must have been much agony of mind to have so discoloured the lining. And now a sparkling tear fell from his eye into the depths of the crown upon the name and address of the maker. Miss Pengelly was moved. She went up to him, and took his head between her hands and kissed his brow.

Ponce also came to him, and stood up, and put his fore-paws on his knee, and whined, and looked up with intelligent eyes into his face, and then licked his own muzzle.

'Go down, Ponce. Do not interfere,' said Miss Pengelly; then to the baron, 'Monsieur, would you desire to see Jacquetta to-day?'

He shook his head. 'The desire, my dear Mademoiselle, is ever here,' he touched his heart, 'but to-day I must not. I could hardly endure it in my present condition of mind. I feel desperate. To live without my angel would be purgatorial torture. I cannot face such an eventuality. I must and will have her, or perish. I will make one more appeal to my mother—one final and terrible. If she still refuses me—then nothing will remain but——'

'But what, M. de Montcontour?'

'Do no not ask further, Mademoiselle. Enough when I say that I cannot live without *Her*.'

'Oh, baron!' exclaimed Miss Pengelly, starting to her feet and turning pale, 'do nothing desperate; be governed by reason, be prudent.'

'Reason, Mademoiselle, is overwhelmed by passion.

Prudence is beyond by attainment. I feel as if I were caught in an eddy, embraced by a whirlwind, and swept along in a vortex, whither I know not, but I see that destruction lies in my track.'

'M. de Montcontour!' Aunt Betsy held his hand, Ponce laid hold with his teeth of the back of his trouser leg at the heel, and stiffened his spine and four little legs, so that as the baron left the room he dragged the dog along the polished floor after him. Ponce would not let go till he had reached the door.

'Oh, M. de Montcontour!' cried Miss Pengelly.

The baron walked away without turning his head. He was deadly pale.

CHAPTER VI

M. DE MONTCONTOUR returned home. He ate nothing at dinner. He scarcely spoke. His face was pale and drawn, and though he tried to conceal the state of agitation in which he was, his mother and aunt saw that his hand shook.

Neither of the ladies was in good spirits, but Madame de Montcontour affected a buoyancy she did not possess, and talked gaily of excursions in the neighbourhood, and of economies in the farm. Her son was not deceived, he knew that this was put on to disguise her inner trouble. The baroness loved her son, and was very proud of him. Indeed, he was the idol of her worship, and she would not suffer her idol to cast himself down from his pedestal. She had talked the matter over with her sister. She had known for some time about his visits to Champclair, she had even heard of his journey from St. Malo with the ladies, and her suspicions and fears had been roused. She had called on Mrs Asheton, and from that lady had heard about the Fairbrothers. The father of the young demoiselle was a grocer, and the mother was the niece of Mdlle. Painaulait, who had been the servant of Madame de Hoelgoet. Mrs

Asheton concealed nothing, she insisted on the vulgarity of Mrs Fairbrother, and when asked about the daughter, shrugged her shoulders. It was to the interest of Mrs Asheton to set the baroness against Jacquetta, because Mrs Asheton, as a good mother, wanted the girl for her own son, and knew perfectly that the baron was his rival. Accordingly, when Alphonse announced to his mother that he desired to marry Mdlle. *de* Fareboutier, as he rendered her name, craftily inserting the *de* as a hope of disguising to his mother the plebian origin of his affianced, he found that the lady was perfectly acquainted with the antecedents of his beloved, she scorned the assumption of *de*, and asked if he had not mistaken the end of her name, and that it was *boutiquier* not *boutier*.

Her son withered under the sarcasm of his mother. He made a pathetic appeal, with much poetry of elocution to her maternal feelings, which entirely failed in its desired effect. Mdlle. de Pleurans threw in her remarks, she sneered at the niece of the Painaulait, because she was the niece of that infamous woman who had 'assassinated her mistress and plundered her carcase.' This was an exaggeration, as the baron ventured to point out; the Painaulait had not been guilty of the crimes imputed to her, Madame de Hoelgoet had died of an internal disorder as had been attested by her medical attendant.

'Feed to say so by the Painaulait,' interjected Mdlle. de Pleurans.

'Pardon, *ma tante*, it was well known that the disorder was ravaging Madame de Hoelgoet for months, even for a year and a half, before it terminated fatally.'

Then Mdlle. de Pleurans changed her attack.

'Because you cannot recover the property of your family by any other means, you stoop to put your coronet and our unblemished arms under the dirty foot of the menial who robbed us. It is infamous. *Sainte Vierge*! that I should have lived to see this day!'

'Again, pardon, aunt. I have not offered my hand to the Painaulait, but to the beautiful and accomplished and virtuous Mdlle. de Fareboutier.'

'If you utter that *de* again in connection with the name,' said Madame de Montcontour rising with dignity, 'I leave the room.'

She looked coldly, disdainfully, at her son.

'Alphonse, contemplate these portraits of your ancestresses.'

'I do, mother, and think they were very ugly women.'

'Alphonse, they were all titled ladies with pedigrees back to Adam, and historic names.'

'We are poor, mother.'

'But—noble,' she said sternly.

After a pause she laughed harshly, and said with curling lips, 'Mademoiselle is an heiress. We shall see the lilies of Montcontour quartered, quartered for eternity, with three pots of Dundee marmalade, in chief—a cheese-scoop. Remember, my son, if she were not an heiress, her detestable modern arms—evoked from Heaven knows where—might pass away into nonentity, and be forgotten, but the arms of an heiress continue, quartered, in permanence, a perpetual glory, or an indelible stain.'

During dinner, after the baron's return from Champclair, he said in a broken voice to his mother, 'It is possible that

Jacques Asheton may call on me this evening. If so—
entertain him; say I am unwell, and cannot see him.'

'Yes,' answered the baroness, 'we will do so.'

When the servants retired, he took some Pistachio nuts,
cracked them, and said, 'Mother, for the last time I ask
you to re-consider your determination.'

'Alphonse, I will never consent.'

'You, my mother, would wreck my whole existence.
You, who gave me life, would take it away. You have
been to me my Clotho, even you will be my Antropos—
cutting the thread you began to spin.'

'What do you mean?'

'I mean this—that if I do not obtain Mdlle. Fareboutier,
life has for me no charms, it is a horrible gulf of blackness
irradiated by no star. My Jacquette is everything that is
amiable, virtuous, noble, and beautiful; it is you, mother,
who taught me to love virtue and admire the ideal in
woman. It is because I have been thus inspired by you
that I aspire to Mdlle. Jacquette. You have taught me
to look for a saint, and when I behold the saint, you forbid
me to worship her.'

'*Fi-donc*! She is no saint, she is a Protestant,' shrieked
Mdlle. de Pleurans. 'Will you taint the blood of your
house with the poison of heresy, as well as mix it with the
treacle of the shop!'

'Remember this, mother,' said the baron solemnly, 'if
you refuse to allow me to marry the woman I adore, I
shall never marry. I shall expire, the last of my race and
of my name.'

'It is well—expire with honour.'

The baron became as pale as one of the almonds on his

plate. He stood up and bowed to his mother. He said not another word but walked to the door, there turned, looked wildly at her, bowed again, and withdrew.

'Josephine,' said Mdlle. de Pleurans, after the silence of several minutes, during which the ladies listened to his retiring step on the stairs, 'have you not expressed yourself too strongly? What if he were to take you at your word?'

'How so?'

'He threatened to put an end to himself; and you bade him do so.'

'I did not understand his words thus; you exaggerate.'

'Not at all. Remember his expression. "I will perish, the last of my race and name"—and you replied, "So be it — perish with honour."'

'*Mon Dieu*! I did not think that.' The baroness became alarmed, and trembled. 'He meant that he would go to Algiers, and if necessary, die for his country in war.'

'That is possible, but his words might be taken otherwise, and he might understand yours as conveying an order to him to terminate his blighted life.'

'Merciful heavens! Celestine! Take off your shoes and steal after him. He has gone to his own room. Listen at the door. Peep through the keyhole. Try the lock. If he has fastened himself in, he means something terrible. I dare not go—my tread is too heavy. You, run.'

The aunt did as requested, and the heart of the baroness beat with alarm. Her poor Alphonse was more enamoured than she had supposed; it was really true that life would be a blank to him without that grocer's daughter. Why had she been so abrupt with him? Why had she not dealt more skilfully with him—and used her ingenuity to break through the engagement later on, instead of forbidding it bluntly at the outset, when he was in the first fervour of his passion?

'Well—oh, Celestine! what is it?' Mdlle. de Pleurans reappeared at the door, with her finger to her lip.

'He has locked himself in,' she said, with a ghastly face.

'Run, run back,' exclaimed the agitated mother. 'Run and look through the keyhole. If you see anything suspicious, come and tell me. Perhaps he is only going to write her a letter—perhaps he is only going to shave.'

The aunt again disappeared.

In the meantime the baron was pacing his room with folded arms. He had a large room with long windows that commanded the garden. Between the windows was a rack on which hung a gun, a sword, and a couple of pistols; also some riding-whips and a pair of spurs. Over the marble mantelshelf, at the end of the room, was a mirror.

The baron, as he paced the room, came up to the looking-glass, and considered himself in it. He saw how pale he was. He saw the red line marked on his white brow by the pressure of the new hat. The leather must have had some improper dressing, for it had drawn his flesh like a blister, and made it very red. An hour and a half had passed since he had removed his hat, yet the red line remained.

The baron went to the window and looked out. Far away, behind yonder belt of poplars, at a distance of about three miles, was Champclair, the place, to which all his thoughts, all his ambition turned. There, where that dense osier-growth was visible, lay the Loire, that river which had been choked with the body of royalists in the Reign of Terror. His grandfather on his mother's side had perished in one of the Noyades. None of his family feared death. The sky was very blue; not a bird was in it—yes, there was a magpie, not high up, but in the garden, darting past the *arbre Judas*. One magpie for sorrow. For sorrow! what sorrow was his! A sigh escaped his bosom. Again he paced the room, and again looked at himself in the glass. He started. It seemed to him that his dark hair was turned white in places. No wonder! He had heard of men condemned to death whose raven locks had been bleached in a night. Why not his? He had suffered mortal agony, and a night and a day of inexpressible desolation.

He ran and got himself a hand toilette-glass, and held it behind the back of his head, then at the side. He had been mistaken. The side-light from the windows on his smooth and glossy hair had given a pale reflection. On closer examination he found he had been misled by appearances. His hair had not changed a tint.

Then he flung himself at full length on his sofa, and clasped his hands over his eyes to shut out the light that poured in on him through the windows. He drew up his right leg till it was bent as much as it could bend, whilst the left was extended, and the foot drooped like a fuchsia-blossom over the edge of the sofa. Then he thrust out the right leg and drew up the left. And all the while, Aunt Celestine was watching him, with her eye glued to the keyhole.

He took his pocket-handkerchief from his tail pocket, and to do this, had to turn over on his side on the sofa;

then he resumed his position on his back, and threw the handkerchief over his face, and placed his right hand on his heart. Now both his legs were extended, and both feet hung limply over the end of the sofa, for his body was longer by twenty-five centimetres than the sofa.

Aunt Celestine's heart beat, and she trembled so violently, that she shook the door, but her nephew did not hear her. He might have been a dead man lying thus. If Aunt Celestine had not seen the white cambric over the nose distend itself with his breath, and then contract, she would have believed he was dead, that his noble heart had broken out of sheer grief.

But no! he certainly was alive. He leaped from his prostrate position, and went again to the window. The garden was large but badly kept. He could not afford a proper gardener, and could not afford to let the man who did the garden stick to it. The walks needed weeding, the flower-beds were untidy. There was a summer-house, covered with *Caucoras japonica*, untrimmed and falling away from the trellis. There was a fountain in a pond in the garden, but the water was stagnant, choked with green slime, and the jet no longer played. The pipe was out of order, and he had not the money available for relaying lead pipe. There were statues in the garden, by the fountain, a nymph with a pitcher. The nymph's nose was broken off. He had himself stuck on one of putty, but the frost of winter had taken it off again, and another had not been fitted. Money was needed. At the top of the pavilion, which was shaped like a Chinese pagoda, were glass bells, white and red, and yellow and blue. In the autumn a storm had broken half the bells, and he could not afford to replace them. How romantic it was to sit in the pagoda when a soft breeze blew and to hear the glass bells tinkle. How Paradise-like it would have been to sit there with Jacquetta, eating ices, and feeling that he had several five-franc pieces in his pocket, listening to the glass bells chiming a song of love overhead.

On the terrace was a pedestal on which had stood a glass globe, a metre in diameter, silvered inside so that it acted like a concave mirror. Any one who looked at himself in it saw his nose like the proboscis of an elephant, and his ears the size of cowrie-shells. A mischievous *gamin* had thrown a stone at it five years ago and broken it, and he had not been able to replace it since. Oh the loveliness, the exquisiteness of the thought, that if Jacquetta had been his bride, he might have been able to put another glass-silvered globe on that pedestal, and take her soft, delicate hand in his, and lead her up to it, and show her how it exaggerated her nose and diminished her ears !

The poor baron could not bear the thought. He closed his shutters and turned the strips of wood in the jalousies so as to exclude the view of the garden and the dazzling light. Then he took down one of his pistols, and polished it, then loaded it, and put a cap on the nipple. No Mont-contour, no De Pleurans had shrunk from facing death.

Then the baron walked the length of his room once more, and stood gravely before the mirror over the mantel-piece, and contemplated himself in it. His face was grey, it was not white as before, but grey. It was grey because the room was partly darkened by the closed shutters.

He heaved a bitter, long sigh and raised the pistol.

Aunt Celestine had seen him contemplate the garden.

She had seen him take down, load and prime, the pistol. Then she rushed down stairs to Madame de Montcontour.

She found James Asheton with her. The young Englishman had just called, and Madame la Baronne was hastily explaining to him the cause of her anxiety. In dashed Mdlle. de Pleurans with her eyes distended and her hands raised 'Josephine! he has darkened the room! He has taken and cocked the pistol!'

The baroness was frozen with terror. Even Asheton was mute with dismay. Aunt Celestine stood in the door looking from one to the other.

. At that moment they heard an explosion—the report of fire-arms. The baroness and Mdlle. de Pleurans screamed, Asheton rushed up stairs. He knew his friend's room. He knocked at the door. No answer.

Then up came Madame de Montcontour and Mdlle. de Pleurans wringing their hands, weeping; then the servants in dismay, whispering.

Asheton tried the door, it was locked. He put his knee to it to force it. 'Run!' he called to the gardener. 'Put a ladder against the window; get in that way,' but he could not wait for this to be effected, he ran against the door, struck it with his whole weight, and burst it open.

In the darkened room, seated on the end of the sofa, with the pistol still in his hand, with his other hand over the back of the sofa, and his head resting thereon, was the baron, motionless, and the floor was strewn with pieces of glass, that crushed under the feet of those who rushed in. The atmosphere within was charged with the smoke from the pistol.

Madame de Montcontour flew to her son, cast herself on her knees by him, caught his hand, wrenched from it the pistol. 'Alphonse! speak, my soul! You have not blown out your brains!'

He did not answer; perhaps he could not. His hand was warm and flexible. The tears of his mother flowed over it.

'Alphonse! I withdraw the refusal. If you still live—take her.'

Then the baron slowly raised his head and said, 'Mamma! you have resuscitated me!'

'He lives! He breathes! He speaks!' The good woman nearly fainted.

'Let all leave the room,' said Montcontour slowly. 'All, that is, but Mr Asheton.' He spoke with an effort. He was obeyed, with awestruck faces the servants stole away. They had trodden on the threshold of a great family mystery. The mother and aunt retired with raised hands and streaming eyes, blessing Providence which had miraculously interfered to save the life of their dear Alphonse.

When they were gone Asheton said gravely, 'What is the meaning of this? What have you attempted?'

'To shoot myself.'

'But why?'

'My mother forbade the union.'

'You—you deliberately took aim at yourself?'

The baron nodded.

'Where, at your heart?'

He shook his head.

'Where? At your head?'
Again he made a sign of dissent.
'But where then—at yourself?'
'Yes, at myself,' solemnly.
'But *where*?'
'In the glass.'

CHAPTER VII

So it was settled. The Baron de Montcontour was permitted by his mother to marry Miss Fairbrother; but that was the extreme limit of concession. The baroness would not call on the Fairbrothers, nor invite them to the Chateau de Plaissac, that was inhabited by herself and Mdlle. de Pleurans, along with her son, the owner.

Now, Madame de Montcontour spoke to her friends of the intended marriage, and when she did so always mentioned her proposed daughter-in-law as Mdlle. *de* Fareboutier, whereat her acquaintances and friends sneered behind her back, as she had sneered at her son when he added the *de*.

Mrs Fairbrother and her daughter returned to England, The *trousseau* of the latter had to be prepared. The wedding was to take place at the home of the bride. The father expected that, and Miss Pengelly admitted that it would never do to have Jacquetta married from Champclair, it would put the baroness in too unpleasant a situation. She might be willing to accept Jacquetta, but could not be expected to stoop further.

Mrs Fairbrother could not see why if the baroness yielded in essentials she should stick at immaterial matters. 'If she will accept Jacket as her daughter, why don't she come and see me and her? That may be French ways, it is not English. When we eat humble pie we eat it all and don't niggle at the pastry.'

Mrs Fairbrother had other things to think of than the pride of the baroness when she was at home, though once or twice the good woman did grumble over it. For instance, when Fairbrother asked what sort of a house Jacket would have, whether the house was nicely furnished, 'Bless you, Thomas,' answered his wife, 'I've not seen it. It does seem mean of the baroness not to have asked me there to take a look around. I should have liked to look at the nest which is to contain our dove. But, Thomas! French people ain't on the outside like English people, yet inside I take it all are much the same; we all come from Adam. I thought at one time black sheep had black flesh and white sheep gave white mutton, but there's no distinguishing the meat when the wool and skin are off.'

Poor Mrs Fairbrother did her utmost to put a good colour on the engagement. She was not in the best of spirits herself. The prospect of parting with her child troubled her, and she had less confidence in the future than she professed. Whilst at Champclair she had been encouraged by Miss Pengelly, who was delighted at the prospect of having her niece settled near her, and of reconciliation with the de Pleurans ladies. Old Fairbrother was proud of the idea of his daughter marrying a baron, and he vowed he would give up business and establish himself near her.

'Let her get married and comfortable into her house first, old man,' said Mrs Fairbrother, ' then we'll go. Give 'em a twelvemonth.'

Jacquetta was to be well furnished for her wedding. Her pocket handkerchiefs were embroidered with coronets, she was allowed to have as many dresses and bonnets as she chose. Mr Fairbrother gave her *carte blanche* to buy what she liked. He had plenty of money and spent little on himself. Everything he had was for his daughter, and would be hers eventually—as much of it now as she wished. Let her put both hands into his purse, he said, and grab as much as they would hold.

At last the wedding took place, first celebrated in the parish church, then at the Catholic chapel; Madame de Montcontour had insisted on this latter, the baron himself was indifferent, he would have been content with the earlier ceremony; but he would not go against the wishes of his mother, and Jacquetta was ready to do anything to ingratiate herself with her future mother-in-law.

The bride and bridegroom spent a happy month in the Channel Islands, and Jacquetta learned to value her husband for his many good qualities. He was most attentive to her, kind, simple-minded, and desirous of pleasing; easily amused and- interested, full of conversation, and taking great delight in familiarising her with his native language. His weaknesses, absurdities, affectations were all superficial, at heart he was a good and upright man, perhaps a little narrow, and rather unselfreliant, but incapable of doing a dishonourable act, and always ready to think kindly of others. Jacquetta thankfully acknowledged what she saw ; she wrote to her parents that she was very happy,

and found reason to daily admire and love her husband
more. The good old couple wept over her letters and the
mother kissed them. And each, in prayer, every night and
morning humbly asked that dear Jacket's happiness might
continue, and both talked of and laughed at the prospect of
closing the shop and retiring to the banks of the Loire for
the rest of their days.

'And, mother,' said Mr Fairbrother, 'who knows, Jacket
may want you near her some day when a mother is the best
nurse and truest friend that can be called in to a young
wife.'

One bright autumn day the carriage that contained the
bride and bridegroom drove up to Plaissac, and the servants
came to the door.

Jacquetta looked with colour spots in her cheek for her
new mother. She was not on the threshold to welcome her.
She was not in the entrance hall.

'Where is madame, my mother?' asked the baron un-
easily, looking about him.

'Madame la Baronne,' answered a servant, 'prays that
she may be excused appearing, she has *une migraine*, and
is in her room ; but everything is ready.'

'And my aunt, Mdlle. de Pleurans?'

'She also is indisposed, and is attending on Madame la
Baronne.'

Neither showed that evening. The baron affected a
cheerfulness he did not feel. He apologised for his mother.
She suffered acutely when she had a *migraine*. It was impossible for the mind of man to understand the greatness
of her sufferings when indisposed. He would go into her

room himself and ask to be allowed to introduce his wife to her there. Accordingly he went upstairs, and was admitted. He returned with heightened colour. 'Mamma offered a thousand—a million apologies, but she was really very bad. She had been obliged to take camphor pilules, she could hardly hold up her head. She entreated Jacquetta to compassionate her, and suffer her to make her her compliments on the morrow. She was desolated that this *migraine* had come on her at so inopportune a moment,' &c., &c.

Jacquetta saw that her husband was hurt and annoyed, and that he was making the best of a bad business. She tried also to put a good face on it, but when they were together in the pagoda, under the broken glass bells which clinked dismally overhead, she burst into tears.

. 'My dear,' said the baron, 'why do you cry? You are tired with your journey. You are overwhelmed with the novelty of the situation. You had better go to your room, and rest there awhile.' He knew why she cried, but he pretended not to.

'Yes,' she said. 'All is so strange to me, and I cannot at once realise that this is to be in future the centre of my sphere, the sun-home round which all my thoughts as planets must move; from which I must try to exercise all my attractive powers.' She smiled sadly. She thought that already she was exercising a repellent force.

She went up to her room. The chateau was not fully furnished, not as an English house, even among the middle classes. There were no deep pile carpets, no inlaid or Japanese cabinets, no pots with flowers about. There were pictures, family portraits, dingy, with old frames that had not been regilt for a century and a half, or two.

Her room seemed void of comforts. There were a couple of chairs, a washstand, no dressing-table, no carpet ; only a little mat by the bed. The fireplace was closed with a board, papered with a rude picture of an ultramarine sea, under an ultramarine sky, with a ship on the former, and a boat and fishermen in vermilion caps. Over the mantel-piece was a mirror, dingy, in a more dingy frame. There were no ornaments on the shelf, there was not a vase or specimen-glass with flowers anywhere, giving token of wel-come.

The window curtains were of muslin, tied back with scraps of pink ribbon. The bed and the washstand were of walnut.

Her own room at home had been so cosy. She had little pictures everywhere, a pretty paper on the walls, covered with rosebuds, and the freshest, crispest, gayest chintz, for her bed furniture and window curtains. Her chimney-piece, and her dressing-table had been crowded with orna-ments.

Alphonse saw that his poor little wife's heart was full, he took her hand, stroked it between his own, then raised it to his lips.

'We do not live in the luxury to which you have been accustomed, dear Jacquetta, but——'

'Oh, my husband, I do not ask for luxury, only for love.'

'You have mine.'

'Yes,' she answered, and forced a smile. 'But I would have that of your mother and aunt !'

'That you will conquer.'

'I will try.'

At eight o'clock next morning the servant tapped at her door, to announce breakfast.

'What—already!' exclaimed Jacquetta. It is very early. I am hardly dressed, I—I thought——' She looked at her watch, 'It is only eight o'clock!'

'Madame la Baronne and Mademoiselle have already been to the parish church to mass,' said the servant—an old servant—somewhat grimly. She shared her mistress's prejudices against the English girl, the heretic, the *bourgeoise*, brought into the house. Then Alphonse came in.

'We are early here, my cherished one,' he said. 'You will try to be quick so as not to keep my mother waiting. It is my fault, I ought to have told you the rules and hours of the establishment. I will go down stairs and delay the breakfast—if possible. I will explain, I will take all the blame on myself. I know you will be as expeditious as possible.'

He did so. Presently he came up again, looking agitated. 'Are yeu ready, my angel?'

'Nearly, Alphonse, but surely your mother will excuse me—the first morning after my arrival. I was tired, and did not expect breakfast before nine o'clock. At home we breakfasted then.'

'I have explained, but my mother has been accustomed to a clockwork life. Are you nearly ready? I will run down and tell her you will descend in one minute.'

Shortly after, he reappeared. '*Chérie!* are you ready? I am sure you will do. You look exquisite.'

'One minute, I must put on my cuffs.'

'Oh, you will do superbly without.'

'I cannot come down without my cuffs.   There, Alphonse, I am ready.'

He held out his arm, and made her descend the staircase on his arm, as if he were taking her to dinner, and entered the room thus, where breakfast was laid.   Her mother-in-law and the aunt of Alphonse were there, standing and looking sternly at the coffee-pot and milk jug.   Neither took a step forward to welcome her.   Alphonse led his wife to them, and the poor little English wife put up her fresh cheek to the old baroness for a kiss, but her mother-in-law drew back.

' My son—the coffee is very cold.'

'So,' said the aunt, 'So is the milk.'

Alphonse coloured.   '*Ma mère*!' he said with some heat.

'I beg you pardon, madame,' said the dowager with a curtsey.   'I was looking at the coffee-pot and did not observe you.'

'I entreat you pardon,' said Mdlle. de Pleurans, also with a curtsey.   'My attention was so engrossed in the milk-jug that I also did not observe you.'

' And now that you do observe her, my mother, my aunt, what have you to say ?' exclaimed Alphonse.

'Madame,' said the dowager, looking at Jacquetta, with a frosty, hard eye, 'I regret the coldness of everything. I am desolated that the coffee and the milk, and—and a great deal beside, are so cold—so very cold, as you may have perceived, but—*we* are not to blame, not we.'

CHAPTER VIII

AFTER a breakfast by no means pleasant, at which the baron laboured to sustain a flagging conversation, and to drag his wife into notice, she took his arm and they walked together in the garden.

As they approached a pedestal that sustained nothing, Alphonse said, 'My dear Jacquetta, I believe that the ambition of my life approaches satisfaction. I have for several years desired to see this pedestal support once more a globe of glass, silvered inside, which shall be, in fact, a globular mirror, reflecting every surrounding object in the most extraordinary and distorted manner. If you approach it, your nose will assume dimensions perfectly colossal, whereas your extremities will be reduced to points.'

'My dear husband,' said Jacquetta, who had not been listening to what he said, 'how long does your mother remain in the house?'

'How? What?'

'And your aunt? When do they leave?'

'Leave! What do you mean?'

'I suppose now they go elsewhere; it would have been

better had they vacated the chateau before our arrival, as they evidently have made up their minds not to like me.'

The baron shivered as if touched with a sudden frost.

'Of course she remains—I mean, they remain; the one is my mother, the other is my aunt.'

'But—now I have come here, your mother assuredly leaves.'

'Leaves! *Mon Dieu*! Turn my own mother out of doors; it would be a crime, infamous and scandalous.'

'But she has her own house into which to retire.'

'She has no house.'

'Then—lodgings.'

'Lodgings! *Ma foi*! I am hot. *Je transpire*.'

He took out his handkerchief and wafted it before his face to cool it. He looked very hot.

'But,' said Jacquetta, 'now I am mistress here.'

'You! My mother!—that is! I am in despair.'

He was clearly frightened—horror-struck at the unheard of proposal, to turn his mother and aunt out of the chateau merely because he had brought a wife into it. 'You do not understand. My mother came here—to Plaissac, when she married my father. She became a mother here —I was born here. The place is endeared to her by the most loving, the most sacred associations. To turn her out! *Sainte Vierge*! It would be a frightful scandal.'

'But how can we get on together? She *will* not like me.'

'Good heavens! You *must* get on together. You can eat at the same table, sleep under the same roof. You do not say, she must clear out of this world because you are in it.'

'No, that is altogether different. I cannot live under the same roof with her, if she refuses to treat me with common civility.'

'Ah! I know my mother well. Be tranquil; she thinks it is due to her dignity to act with coldness, but you will find out that after a while she will be good to you.'

'I cannot endure this. If I remain here I shall be utterly miserable. Oh, why did I leave my dear father and mother, who loved me so tenderly!'

'Be reassured, my cherished one! You see everything in wrong proportion as if you looked into a silvered globe such as once stood on that pedestal. Be at ease. Assure yourself. Though your nose may look like the proboscis of an elephant it is moderate in size—quite small. It is so with everything. You are mistaken. This trouble is not a mountain, it is a molehill.'

He tried hard to comfort her. He said every kind thing that came into his head.

'I will go this afternoon and see Aunt Betsy,' she said after a while; 'and you will come with me, Alphonse. We can, of course, have the carriage.'

'Yes,' answered the baron, 'I will ask mamma.'

Mdme. la douairière looked very glum when her son mentioned that the carriage was wanted.

'What for?' she asked.

'Madame,' said Jacquetta, 'I desire to pay a visit to my aunt, at Champclair.'

The dowager's face darkened more than before. 'I object to your going there,' she said. 'Before you were married, it was inevitable—now you belong to us, and no longer to the society of inferiors.'

'Madame,' answered Jacquetta, 'I intend to call on my aunt. I belong to her by ties of blood which I cannot and will not forget.'

'This is a tone that ill becomes you, madame!'

'Excuse me, mother-in-law, I know my duty.'

The old lady was staggered by the resolution of her daughter-in-law, accustomed as she was to implicit obedience on the part of her son.

'If you must go, I suppose you must; but understand, I object to seeing the Pain-au-lait here.'

'I shall be grieved, *belle-mere*, that you should be confined to your room when not indisposed.'

'How do you mean?'

'I mean, madame, that of course my aunt will visit me here, and if you decline to meet her, it will be your care to keep out of her way.'

'*Mon Dieu!*' gasped the baron. '*Comme je sue!*'

The dowager said no more. The carriage was ordered, and came round—a wretched turn out—a yellow landau with a coat of arms and baron's coronet on it, but the paint off the wheels, the leather blistered, chipped, and dull, the harness unpolished, no bright brass or silver in the mountings, the horse a gaunt, shambling creature that advanced at a dance, throwing out its rough feet sideways. The driver was the gardener, who also cleaned the knives and boots, with a copper-coloured face, and the shabbiest livery. He held the reins with both hands, and his hands were not encased in gloves.

'Has he no gloves?' asked Jacquetta.

'Oh, yes! Jean, you have a pair. Put them on whilst going through the town.'

Jacquetta could not help laughing in spite of her trouble. 'My dear Alphonse, we will change all this in time. Of course, I have plenty of money, and if my dear papa and mamma come to see us, they will expect a proper baronial turn out. Why—even the surgeons with us drive better carriages and horses, and have more stylish servants than you nobles.'

'We have been very poor,' said Alphonse.

'Yes, dear husband, but now we are rich.'

Aunt Betsy was wild with delight at seeing her niece, and thanked her over and over again for coming at once to visit her.

'You only arrived yesterday evening, and you drive this first day to see me! That is kind. What did the dowager baroness say?'

Alphonse was not present just then, he was in the garden talking to the gardener, so Jacquetta told her aunt about her little fight with the old lady. 'I have carried my point, and I will not give way,' she said. 'I know my right as a married woman.'

'My gracious, Jacket! I had no idea there was so much spirit in you. Come and visit me when you like, but I will not go to Plaissac.'

'Why not, aunt?'

'Because I do not want further to offend the baroness. Perhaps when I am dead and you have Champclair, she will not feel so bitter against me.' The good old Pain-au-lait was a humble creature, not at all pushing, and she looked with profound admiration at the family of her late mistress and benefactress. 'No, my dear, don't take it ill of me. I know what I am. I'm an old servant, and not a lady. Come and see me, and you are always welcome; but I'll not intrude on the baroness and Mdlle. de Pleurans. You may tell them so. Also, my dear, don't try to fight them, you will gain nothing by it. As the newspapers say, you can't fight away from your base. See how the baron reverences these ladies.'

It was clear that her residence in France, and with Mme. de Hoelgoet, had imbued the Pain-au-lait with the modes of thought and views of those with whom she had associated.

When the baron and Jacquetta were in the carriage again on their way back, 'You will be submissive to my mother?' he pleaded; 'she always has been mistress in Plaissac, I mean, ever since her marriage. Only Revolution dethrones queens. She has been head of the house— only in the Reign of Terror do royal heads fall—you—you will not inaugurate a Reign of Terror?'

'May I rule in the gardens?'

'Oh, yes; my mother does not care about the gardens.'

'And I will begin my rule there by ordering a silvered globe for the vacant pedestal. We drive through Nantes. We will stop at a glass shop.'

'My angel! my queen!' He clasped her hands and kissed them, he would have knelt to her in the carriage had she suffered it. 'We will carry it home. You will see your nose in it—colossal, and your extremities reduced to the *pattes* of flies.'

As proposed, so done. At the shop it was suggested that the glass globe, a yard in diameter, should be sent to the chateau, but of this the baron would not hear. He was like a child with a new toy. He was impatient to have the pedestal re-occupied. He knew how dilatory they were in shops. Time was of no object to the messengers. Besides, the globe might be broken. In the carriage he and madame could sustain it between them. The weight was not excessive, and they could amuse themselves on the way, looking into it.

Accordingly the baron and young baroness got into the carriage, and the globe was handed to them, and they found it quite possible to carry it. The driver was ordered to go '*doucement*,' and through the streets of Nantes, and along the road to Plaissac, the horse danced, much as though he were performing on a tight-rope, and the coach·man with his red hands held both reins—he had pulled off his white cotton gloves on leaving Nantes—and talked to the horse. In the carriage, the baron looked over the top of the enormous globe at Jacquetta 'My angel! I see you.'

'Yes, Alphonse,' she answered. The carrying of the great glass ball was fatiguing. 'I also see you.'

'I hope you are not exhausted. We shall soon be at the chateau.'

'No, Alphonse, I can carry the globe very well, so far.'

'Can you see yourself in it?'

'Yes, Alphonse.'

'And what do you think now of your nose?'

'It is as you said, colossal.'

She could hear the baron laughing on the other side of the ball, and by the motion of his knees, saw that he was thrusting his body and head forward, then withdrawing them, so as to observe the development and reduction of his nasal organ in the mirror according as he altered his distance.

On entering the gates of the chateau and driving up to the door, the coachman cracked his whip, and the baron shouted 'Maman! maman!'

The heads of the dowager and the aunt appeared at an up-stair window, and the old baroness shouted from it to her son to know what he wanted.

'See, see! I have a reflecting globe for the pedestal. My angel, my cherished one, has given it me. It came very expensive, but she paid for it. I am so happy, oh, so happy! Come down, mamma and Aunt Celestine and help to remove the globe. I will allow no hands but those I love to touch it. Think, mamma! My father gave you this when you married—I mean the other globe—and now my charming Jacquetta presents me with one to replace that broken by the detestable *gamin*—may he be thunderstruck!—on this most auspicious day.'

The two old ladies came down and assisted in removing the globe. Then all four, standing round it, with their hands under it, moved along the terrace in the direction of the vacant pedestal.

Inevitably their hands touched under the ball, that of the dowager rested on that of Jacquetta.

The situation was really comical, the four had to step very cautiously. The baron went backwards, looking over his shoulder to take his direction.

'Keep pace,' he said. 'Gently, gently, or it will fall.'

Then the dowager baroness laughed. 'Celestine, are you not ashamed of your nose?'

'But, Josephine, yours is as prodigious.'

'And so must be that of Alphonse,' said madame.

'And that of Jacquetta,' said the baron. Now, then, cautiously—very cautiously, lift the globe into its place.'

When the great silvered ball was planted securely on its basement, the baron said :—'See, ladies ! A shining world of happiness was disclosed to the eyes of my mother when my poor father brought her here. That fell to pieces, apparently destroyed for ever. But no ! Another shining glittering, yet fragile world of happiness, and love, and transport, appears before our eyes to-day. To-day it is my darling Jacquetta who gives it us. It is very beautiful ; it shines like the sun, but it is very fragile. It will inevitably go to pieces unless—we unite hands and bear it together. Let us embrace.'

It was impossible to hold out against his good-nature, and the situation had been so grotesque as to shake the resolution of the baroness-mother, who had measured weapons with her daughter-in-law, had come off the worst, and rather respected her for her spirit.

'Very well,' she said, 'let us embrace.' But the embrace resolved itself into a cold touch with the lips on the brow of Jacquetta.

CHAPTER IX

Tᴛᴇ relaxation was but momentary, the reconciliation
temporary, as poor Jacquetta discovered when she sat down
with the old ladies to dinner. They had retreated into
their cold reserve. They scarcely spoke. The dinner
might have been taken as a poor copy of that of Sintram's
father. The old Norse baron set suits of armour round his
stone table when he had no other guests, and caroused with
them. It seemed as if this French baron had invited two
mummies to his table. The old women looked as dry and
brown and stiff, and were almost as silent.

This state of affairs could not continue. Whether due to
the remonstrances of Alphonse, or to the baroness's sense
of the impossibility of maintaining the estrangement in all
its frostiness, or to the fact that, when visitors came, she
was obliged to dissemble her dissatisfaction and behave
with civility to Jacquetta, or, lastly, to the effect of the
bride's beauty and neatness and sweetness of disposition, it
came about that a tolerable *modus vivendi* was established,
The dowager and the aunt spoke to Jacquetta at table, and
saluted her morning and evening with courtesy, but they

never showed her the slightest affection, never allowed her to feel that they had taken her into their confidence and affections.

Jacquetta was obliged to be satisfied with this. There was no longer any show of insolence, nothing positive which she could lay hold of as a grievance to complain about, but they studiously shut her out from all intimacy with themselves, and made her feel lonely.

Jacquetta had an English girl's energy and activity of mind and body. She could not lapse into doing nothing. She craved for some occupation. At first there were numerous calls. Visitors came to pay their respects, and she and her husband had to return these calls, but when this was over the time began to hang heavy on her hands, and she asked for something to do.

The garden, she had been told, was a field in which she might exert herself without running counter to the prejudices of the dowager. Accordingly she began vigorously to take the garden in hand. She had the beds weeded, the plants trimmed, staked, and pruned. She ordered a conservatory to be run up, and inspected the construction. Then she stocked it. But winter was drawing on, and in winter the garden is not interesting. Still, for a fortnight she was engrossed in bulbs, superintending the potting of tulips, hyacinths, polyanthuses, and lilies.

Then she resolved on re-furnishing the drawing-room. Here she was treading on dangerous ground, but she was firm, conciliatory, at the same time, and showed so much taste, that the old ladies, though they grumbled, were unable to oppose her. The money spent was her own, and they knew very well that everything connected with the place was shabby.

Next came a charming victoria and a beautiful pair of horses, the harness silver-mounted, with coronets on the blinkers, breast-plates, saddles, and an English coachman sent out from home, her father's present. The coachman was a married man; he brought also his young wife, who could act as lady's maid to Jacquetta, and a young brother as groom.

When the two old ladies drove out with the young baroness in this splendid equipage with two livery servants on the box, in all the trimness of English appointment, the old ladies sat as stiff as pokers, and their hearts were puffed up with pride. Actually, Jacquetta had insisted on giving both ladies the places of honour, and on sitting with her back to the horses. Mdlle. de Pleurans had protested, but she accepted the offer, and as the new carriage drove through Nantes, the old ladies bowed condescendingly to their acquaintances whom they met. After this they were a shadow more gracious than previously. No stranger would have perceived the difference, but Jacquetta, by considering their conduct on this day with that of previous days, could see an improvement. They were, however, too proud to allow the change to be emphatic, it was enough that it was perceptible. Alphonse now abandoned all thoughts of following his profession as a lawyer. His object in taking it up was no longer an object. There was no occasion for him to labour at a profession. He had means at his disposal without it.

Now he began to be interested in his estate and farm. Hitherto things had gone on in a hand-to-mouth fashion, because he had not had the means for putting the property into order; for repairing the dilapidated farm buildings, and building new conveniences. He began to read books on agriculture, and to think he would make of Plaissac a model farm. Everything should be on the most modern system. He was enthusiastic about English farming. He must have Guernsey cows, and South Down sheep; the poultry reared by the peasants were of an inferior description, more bone than meat, and desultory layers. He would have the best sorts over from England. He was out all day, trudging about the farm, and displaying to the astonished peasants a great deal of book-learning about draining, and manuring, and rotating of crops, and breeding of cattle. What he read one evening, whilst smoking, he retailed to the wondering men next day, and forgot on the third. He had the idea that he was going to quadruple the value of the estate; but to do this he must first sink capital in it. So he began the sinking process, which is a very easy one. Fortunately he had a Frenchman's natural shrewdness and caution about money, and though he schemed and talked about a great outlay, he did not spend very much, and what he did spend was not wasted. Indeed, everything on the estate was fallen into such a condition of ruin that necessary repairs had to be undertaken and finished before improvements could be begun ; though not, of course, before they could be talked about.

The baron was out all day. Jacquetta saw very little of him. She was left alone in the house. She could not spend much time, in the winter, in her greenhouse and gardens, nor drive about when the weather was unfavourable. She went at least once a week to her Aunt Betsy, and Betsy shook her head. She thought her niece was dispirited, was not looking well. Jacquetta did not complain, but she was silent and had lost her sparkle. No wonder. It was dull at Plaissac with those crabbed old women who were civil but not cordial. The English community at Nantes was not large, and Jacquetta did not take a fancy to any of those who helped to compose it. Mrs Asheton she did not much like. The lady could not forgive Jacquetta for having quarrelled with, and thrown over, her son. An unintelligible feeling kept Jacquetta from making a friend of Miss Graham. She knew that the opinion of society at Nantes gave this blonde beauty to James Asheton. Jacquetta was thoroughly true in heart to her husband, but she did not forget that Asheton had been her admirer, and she really had liked him better than the baron, till he made the fatal mistake of ridiculing her mother. Was there, far down in her heart, a fibre of unacknowledged jealousy? Shd did not suppose there was, but she could not like Miss Graham.

Towards James Asheton, Jacquetta acted with ease and tact. She let bygones be altogether bygones. She spoke to and greeted him frankly, and not by word or sign gave him occasion to think that she remembered his mistake. She did not see much of him. He was sulky at having forfeited her. But when he was in her presence, and the consul's daughter was also there, he was unusually civil to the latter. He resolved to show the young baroness that he was heartwhole; he would let her suppose that his attraction had been, all along, elsewhere—that she had deluded herself if she supposed he had at one time cared for her.

One day Jacquetta put her hand on her husband's arm,

and said, 'Alphonse, you are not going on the farm now.
You will come with me to the presbytery, I want to call
upon M. le curé and his sister. I do not know her, but I
am told she is very good.'

'Oh, yes, she is good—but *dévote* and narrow.'

'You will come with me?'

'Certainly, Jacquetta, you have but to order and I obey.

The curé was a worthy man, frank and cheerful, a little
blunt in his manner, but very kindhearted. He was to be
seen in all weathers about his parish, with his cassock
tucked up under his girdle, exposing his coarse cloth
trousers, very old and discoloured, and his great shoes with
thick soles. Under his arm or in his hand he carried his
red-edged breviary, the red rubbed off wherever the thumb
went, and the cover discoloured with wet. He had been
in the parish for a great number of years, and was respected by all, even by those men who sneered at ¡priests
and professed to live without religion. His house was
kept by his sister, a poor little deformed creature, no higher
than a child, but full of energy and practical good sense.
She had a harsh, shrill voice, but the gentlest and sweetest
of spirits, was devoted to her brother, and proud of the
parsonage, which she kept beautifully neat. She always
looked at the bright side of things, was ready at all times
to do others a service, and was so humble that the least
attention shown to her overwhelmed her with gratitude.
The poor little hunchback suffered a good deal of pain in
her spine, but she never murmured; her face was plain in
feature but full of the light of a patient and loving spirit.
By some unfortunate fatality she had been christened
Gracieuse, a more inappropriate name could not have been

chosen for her, but when she was an infant her deformity was not suspected, it had come on gradually with advancing years.

The parsonage was not a large house, it had one good room in it that served as reception and dining-room, very plainly furnished, and a library in which the curé kept his small collection of books, all professional except a *Quintus Curtius* in Latin, the only book of light reading he possessed. The *salle* had no carpet of any sort in it, and the walls were adorned with a couple of coarse sacred pictures, a portrait of Pius IX, and a statuette of Notre Dame de la Salette. The curé dined on Sundays, at least once a month, at the chateau, so that Jacquetta knew him ; but she had never been to the parsonage before. She was aware that he had strongly disapproved of the baron's engagement ; he and the two old ladies had discussed it together ; but she did not know that when the marriage had taken place he had given the dowager sensible advice, '*Allons !* it is done. Make the best of it.'

He was very pleased to see the young people, and he thanked the *châtelaine* for calling on him. He made conversation whilst his sister hurried from the kitchen to change her gown and brush her hair, and put on a clean cap and apron before appearing. When poor Gracieuse entered, and had been introduced to the baroness, the curé asked Alphonse to come out round the garden with him, he wished to show him a tool-house he had erected, and a potting-table of his own invention. When they were alone together, 'Well, now !' said the curé, 'how does your mother treat your wife ?'

Alphonse shrugged his shoulders.

'My friend, we must make allowances for the prejudices of old people. I, myself, maybe, am not without my prejudices; but—the young baroness is charming. Here and there, in nooks and corners, under hedges and walls on north sides, the frost lingers long after the spring sun has begun to laugh at the earth and bid it break into flower, but in the end—everywhere—the frost disappears. It is a matter of time. You must be particularly attentive to the young lady, she will find the chateau dull, and she has only you to look to to enliven it. Come, you have seen my potting-table, let us return to the *salon*.'

In the meantime Jacquetta had approached the object of her visit.

'Mademoiselle,' she said with her broken French, which had a certain charm and sweetness in it when proceeding from her mouth, accompanied by her pleasant smile, 'I have come to you with a petition. Time hangs heavy on my hands. In winter there is not much I can do in my garden. I am of an eager spirit, I must do something, and I have come here to ask you if it be possible for me to execute what I have in mind.'

'But, madam, you have only to command me.'

'Pardon, I have to entreat you. It is a very, very great favour I ask. Without your help I can do nothing.'

'I place myself at your disposal, Madame la Baronne.'

'Mademoiselle, in England of late years it has become quite the custom at Christmas to have trees covered with lights and presents for children. We generally there give a Christmas-tree to the poor little ones of a parish. I have a desire at the approaching festival to have such a tree. I see that the peasants hereabouts are very poor, and some

of the children have not warm clothing for the winter.
Do you think we could set to work and knit them socks
and worsted shawls, and make little jackets, and cut out
flannel petticoats?'

'Oh, madame! madame la baronne?' The cripple held
up her hands and her eyes filled with tears. 'The good
God put this into your heart!'   .

'But,' continued Jacquetta, 'I can do nothing without
you. I will supply the flannel, and the wool, and the
cloth, and the buttons—in fact all the material, if I can
persuade you to help me in making the little garments—if
I *might* come here twice a week in the afternoons or even-
ings and work with you.'

'Oh, madame! madame la baronne!'—and the poor
hunchback came to her from her chair and fell on her
knees and kissed her hands. 'M. le curé will pray for you.'

'Do not, in pity do not,' said Jacquetta, alarmed and
withdrawing her hands. 'It is only that I want to do
here what we do at home, and keep up old associations. I
must ask of you to intercede with your brother, M. le curé.
I do not quite like to have the tree at the chateau; I would
rather you had it here, if you and M. le curé would not
greatly mind.'

'Mind? Oh, *mon Dieu!* mind! It would be the
happiest day of our lives.'

'Then it is settled.'

'Settled! oh, I am bewildered. Who are to come?'

'All the children of the parish.'

'But—it is too much—all to receive presents!'

'Why not? I should much like it. If you do not
mind.'

'Oh, we shall be too pleased. But, madame, if the Christmas-tree be in our *salon* and not at the chateau, the stupid children will suppose that we give it, and you will not be sufficiently thanked as the giver.'

'But it will be yours as well as mine. I shall find a little material, but you will furnish the room and have all the trouble.'

'Ah, bah! that is nothing. You will have the merit.'

Then in came the curé and Alphonse. The sister, unable to restrain herself, in her shrill, ear-piercing tones screamed the news to her brother. The curé listened and nodded his head. 'It is well. It is a good thought. I thank you, madame, in the name of my parishioners, and of my sister, and of myself. I see, *mon ami*,' he turned to the baron, 'that your wife is dispelling the frost everywhere, driving it out of the nooks of old cold hearts that look to the north. Come, let us hope, let us be sure, the violets will bloom where now lies the ice, everywhere, everywhere, *mon ami!*'

CHAPTER X

THE dowager and the aunt must have heard of the proposed Christmas-tree, but they said nothing concerning it Jacquetta had intended to ask them to help her in making clothing for the poor children, but her courage failed, she dreaded a rebuff. They, on their side, were piqued because not associated in the preparations, and failed to see that their own repellent behaviour took from Jacquetta the courage to ask them to unite with her. The Christmas-tree, instead of proving a means of drawing them into fellowship and goodwill, was made a grievance. The young wife was trying to bribe the parishoners to think more of her than of the dowager and Mdlle. de Pleurans. Of course with money a great deal can be done. If folks have the bad taste and bad feeling to use their money for this purpose they will always get a following, always obtain popularity; but what is a purchased popularity worth? How M. le curé could lend himself to advance the crafty designs of the young baroness passed the comprehension of the two ladies. No doubt the Pain-au-lait had been asked to contribute. She was to be allowed to have a finger in the matter. The plot was clear as daylight. Jacquetta and the Pain-au-lait desired to dethrone the ladies who had previously been looked up to as the benefactresses of the parish second only to the Holy Virgin.

The old ladies became more stiff than before. They talked to one another at table, or when they were in the parlour with Jacquetta, about affairs that interested them and made oblique stabs at her. She, poor girl, was a complete stranger in her husband's house. She had only the coachman's wife about her, to talk to concerning England. But Jacquetta was not so foolish as to make a *confidante* of a lady's maid. Sometimes she took up her pen resolved to tell her mother plainly how wretched she was. 'They think me happy,' she said. 'I shall only make them miserable, and they can alter nothing,' So she tore up her letter. To Aunt Betsy she said a little, but very little. Aunt Betsy was an excellent old woman, but not much of a standby. She had small judgment, and was incapable of offering advice. When Alphonse came in from the farm, or from shooting and hunting, both which amusements he had taken up, he was very kind to her; but he was tired out, he went to sleep in his arm chair or on the sofa till supper. When he talked to his wife it was about his pursuits. Jacquetta did not complain to him, and he asked no questions. He preferred not to enquire into the situation as he was incapable of altering it.

At last winter set in with severity. One morning the landscape was covered with snow. Alphonse was unable to go out. Jacquetta was glad to keep him at home that she might have some one to talk to ; but he was dull and impatient at the weather. He had difficulty to stifle his yawns in her face. The days seemed interminable. Jacquetta read to him and sent him to sleep; talked to him but without enlivening him; played to him, but he had no genuine love of music. He said that all English music was alike—songs, hymns, dance-music—it was the same tune; German music was heavy, intricate, unintelligible. Finding at last that she was unable to amuse him, she abandoned the task as beyond her powers.

Now the real goodness of the dowager came out. She was indefatigable in supplying the necessities of the poor. She had soups and simple puddings made for them, and they were allowed to come into the kitchen of the chateau as much as they liked to warm themselves at the great fire. This somewhat interfered with the work of the house, but it was all the more charitable, because it gave real inconvenience to the household. The dowager trudged about in the snow visiting the sick, and carrying food to the infirm unable to come for it themselves. To some extent, no doubt, the old lady was actuated by a spirit of rivalry. She would not be outdone by her daughter-in-law. But it was not so altogether. She always had been charitable; the poor had always looked up to her for assistance; and on her very limited means she had assisted them. Now everything in the castle was on a more liberal scale, and the dowager baroness was not in the least ashamed to give in greater profusion out of what was purchased with Jacquetta's money. The poor overwhelmed her with thanks which she accepted as her due; though the good *bouilli* and *bouillon* which were substitutes this winter for the bread soup of last, were paid for by the disliked and much-abused daughter-in law.

Jacquetta had acted very differently about the Christmas-tree. She had requested the curé's sister to manage that, *lest* invidious comparisons should be made between herself and her mother-in-law, in her own favour.

One day the baron drove into Nantes and returned with Asheton. He was unable to endure the dulness of the winter days alone longer, and had gone for his friend, had insisted on his packing his portmanteau, and coming to stay with him at Plaissac.

Jacquetta was surprised, and not particularly pleased; but this feeling of annoyance rapidly wore off, for the young man was pleasant, Alphonse brightened when he had a male companion with whom he could play billiards and smoke and talk about shooting and other sports. The old ladies, moreover, put on a semblance of amiability whilst a stranger was present, which they thought unnecessary at other times. Young Asheton talked English with his countrywoman, and it was a joy to her to be able again to speak with an educated person in her own tongue about the literature of her own land. Without a muscle twitching in his face, Asheton asked after her mother, and spoke of the pleasant drive from St. Malo, of the old lady's surprise at the novelties she had seen. Was Mrs Fairbrother well? When had she last written? Was she coming out to Nantes in the summer? He had been once or twice to call on Miss Pengelly since the breach with Jacquetta. This had pleased Jacquetta, and he was able to talk about her aunt and Champclair, with happy ignorance or indifference to the fact that Champclair was, with tacit consent, not spoken of in Plaissac, before the old ladies. Then it came out that Asheton knew a girl who had been a schoolfellow of Jacquetta's at Cheltenham, and had heard her stories of the comical old Misses Woodenhead, the spinster proprietresses of the establishment for young ladies. Asheton knew intimately the brother of this girl. He had visited him at his home in Sussex; Jacquetta was eager to hear all about this home. Her bosom friend had often described it to her, and now here in her exile she met an acquaintance who had been there. The world is not very large—England certainly is not—and we are always jostling against those who have jostled our friends.

Poor Jacquetta had been without English books. She had not seen the last novels, James Asheton had them—his sister had received a box of books from England. He would walk into Nantes and fetch them. When Alphonse was present he also talked English, though usually with his wife he spoke French. He had insisted on this, as it was good for her to become fluent in the tongue; he did not consider what a strain this was to her, and how she pined to speak her own language. Now that Asheton and she were rattling along about persons and things that did not particularly interest him, he left them together, that he might give orders on the farm, or look at his horses, or clean his gun. He saw that it gave Jacquetta pleasure, and he was glad at no effort to himself to give her pleasure.

When her husband and Asheton were out—or playing billiards—the poor little wife sat by the fire in a dream, or with the bellows puffing at the logs to make them burn, and puff away her own troublesome thoughts. French houses are not, or were not, built with much consideration for comfort in the winter. The rooms are large, the doors and windows fit badly, and the open hearths do not throw out much heat.   There was about Nantes little or no oak, and oak is the only really excellent fuel for dogs or a brick hearth.   Next to oak comes beech, and there was as little beech available.   Pinewood there was, but that burns badly unless very dry, and worst of all was that which was most abundant, poplar which will not burn at all unless constantly impelled to do so by the bellows.

The weather was very cold.   Jacquetta suffered greatly, the draughts, the wretched fires, the absence of the thousand and one little comforts that render a room cosy in winter, made her feel unhappy, and drew from her many a sigh. She sat with the bellows on her knee as close into the hearth as she could draw, and looked into the dull, red ashes; she thought of the fireside at home, of the circle there, of the tea-table—Oh, for an English tea-table again! Then she began to wonder whether she had not made a mistake in marrying out of her own country, out of her own class, anyhow, one who did not understand English ways and thoughts, and requirements.

The Ashetons had got grates in their fireplaces, and burnt coals.   They had furnished their rooms like those of an English house, with thick rugs, and a Chinese gilt leather screen which cut off draughts, and had plugged the windows with wadding, and had sandbags to the doors. She had been to their house at tea, and seen a kettle with a spirit lamp, and heard they had an urn, a copper urn, brought in at breakfast.   Oh, she would so like to hear the singing of an urn again! Also the parlour-table was covered with English cloth-backed books.   She was weary of the sight of the yellow paper-backed French volumes that fell to pieces and looked ragged whilst in process of being read.

Alphonse was a dear, good fellow, but he was very absurd in some things. He was exaggerated in his sentiments, and—she could not help admitting it—rather niggling in his mind. He lacked the breadth and solidity she had found in Englishmen. She would never quite understand him, never know exactly what he would be at.

She had made acquaintance with most of the French nobility around, and had been received with kindness and an eagerness of hospitality which touched her, but she had made no friends among them; acquaintances in plenty, but she felt that they were acquaintances who would never be dearer to her, because they would not understand her thoughts, nor she theirs. They belonged to different orders of mind. The education she had received had been at all points so opposite to that received by French girls that they lacked the community of ideas and sympathy which are necessary for the growth of friendship. So Jacquetta was lonely, utterly lonely, and likely to remain lonely. She sighed. Had she made a grievous mistake? Would she not have done much better to have married an Englishman —a plain merchant, instead of a French noble? She began blowing vigorously with the bellows.

All at once she started up. The two old ladies, who had been talking to each other in a low tone without noticing her, were surprised, and asked what was the matter.

'Nothing. I am going to the *presbytère*, to see Mdlle. Gracieuse.'

' But it rains.'

' In my own country we think nothing of rain.'

No further objection was raised. She put on her hat and cloak, and took her umbrella and trudged forth. The poor deformed woman was pleased always to see her, she was just then specially pleased, because she was suffering. Cold and wet always gave her rheumatic pains in her body. The room in which she sat was much more draughty and bare than that at the chateau. Gracieuse was not very warmly clad.

Jacquetta told her how grieved she was to find her so ill, and suggested various comforts.

'Oh, I am right as I am,' said the deformed woman. 'I was thinking as you came in how happy the children were at your Christmas tree, I was repicturing to myself their look of astonishment and delight. Ah! madame, that was a beautiful idea of yours!'

'But you are suffering, mademoiselle. See, I have this thick knitted jacket. Oh, be kind, and do let me take it off and put it on you.'

'No, no!' the poor creature raised both her hands. 'Not for the world.'

'What, not to give me a great happiness?'

Then Gracieuse tried to shuffle to her and kiss her hands, crying, '*Mon Dieu!* what have I done to deserve such goodness, to be shown such kindness. Oh, madame, God has been good to me! I have so many dear friends, I have everything I can desire, more, a thousand times, than I can deserve.' She considered, and said, half to herself and half to the young baroness, 'What a happy, happy life mine has been, what then is a little rheumatism when the rain comes!'

Jacquetta sat some time with the cripple. Her society

did her good. It calmed her troubled mind. Gracieuse
had received very little education. She had read few books.
Quintus Curtius even, the one volume of light reading on
her brother's shelves, was a sealed book to her. As for a
novel, she had never read one in her life. Her ideas were
very narrow. Her interests very few. She and Jacquetta
had little to link them to each other. She was the daughter
of a poor peasant, and Jacquetta was rich and the wife of a
baron. Yet there was one tie that united them, a tie
unacknowledged yet existing, the tie of sorrow. Poor
Gracieuse, however cheerful she might be, had lived a life
of pain, and Jacquetta's spirit was suffering. The curé
came in.

'Madame, you are not well.'

'M. le curé, I have nothing the matter with me.'

'You have tears in your eyes.'

'I am pitying your sister.'

'Ah, bah !' Just then, in came the baron and Asheton.
They had heard that the baroness had gone to the parsonage
in the rain, and were shocked and had come to fetch her.

'Hold, M. le baron !' said the curé. 'Will you do me
the honour to step into my little room. I have there a
Quintus Curtius, a most interesting book, giving the history
of Alexander the Great. What a pity that the first two
books are lost ! The style is so fine ! Will you come in
and see it ? I will lend it you. It will serve to make pass
the time of rain.'

When the baron was with him, ' *Mon ami*,' he said, ' it is
not my place to interfere, but—but I cannot help. Mdme.
your wife does not look well, or happy. She is growing

paler every day.   The life at the chateau does not suit
her.'

'She makes no complaint,' said the baron.

'No, certainly,' answered the curé. 'But for all that
I can see that she is not happy. She is like a fish on land.
Your mother and aunt do not behave properly to her.'

'But, my dear curé, what can I do?'

'Do, sir! devote yourself more to your wife than to
Guernsey cows and foreign sheep. She is more precious
than they. It would have been better had you not married
her. I said so, your mother said so. But you made your
choice and you have taken her, taken her away from her
own country and home and plunged her in uncongenial
surroundings. She is in a new and strange world here, and
she cannot accommodate herself to it. You must be more
with her. You must lay yourself out to interest her, and
brighten her life. She is good-hearted as an angel. That
is well for you, for mischief comes of it when a woman is
left alone too much by the companion God has given her.'

'I will think of what you have said.'

'Act on it. Act on it.' The curé held out his big hand
and shook that of the baron.

On their way back to the chateau the baron said, 'My
dear Jacquetta! What do you say, shall we make an
excursion in the spring, after Easter, to England, and see
your dear father and mother again?'

She flushed with pleasure, then turned pale; she put her
little hand to his and pressed it.

'You have not answered me,' he said.

'We will talk it over together when we get home. It is
a surprise. You are very kind, Alphonse.'

He felt her trembling at his side.

When they were together in their room, and he was helping to take off her wet things, 'Well, Jacquetta, what do you say? Shall we go over that same pleasant route again, and pass another honeymoon in the Channel Islands, and then on to Plymouth and spend some time with your dear parents? You are not looking well, little woman.'

'Oh, Alphonse!' she burst into tears and clasped his neck, 'it cannot be just when you offer—for—I expect I shall—sometime be a mother.'

CHAPTER XI

When the dowager baroness knew that her daughter-in-law was about to become a mother, she became excited, and was more gracious than she had been before. Jacquetta was required to take the greatest care of herself, to follow the old lady's prescriptions, to take exercise when and how she ordered, to eat this and refuse that, and to submit to an infinity of minute and unnecessary restrictions. Jacquetta yielded because she was thankful to find her mother-in-law unbend towards her, and show some interest in her, though she did not hide from herself that the old lady thought much more of the future heir to the title and estate than of the mother. The dowager had quite made up her mind that the child was to be a boy. Jacquetta hoped it would be so, or she would be completely out of favour. Her only chance of ingratiating herself with the mother and the aunt was to become the mother of a boy.

As Jacquetta wrote to her own dear mother, and confided to her her anticipations, Mrs Fairbrother wrote back a gushing letter, declaring her intention of coming to

Nantes to be with her daughter. She took it as a matter of course that she was to nurse her.

Jacquetta would dearly have liked to avail herself of this offer, but she hesitated and showed the letter to her husband.

'You must do as you like,' he said; 'but I doubt whether your mother and mine will get on together. My mother has planned everything, she has her ideas, she has her rights. Would Mdme. Fareboutier consent not to take the lead?'

Jacquetta's eyes filled. 'I should like to have my mother here. I—I don't like to be among strangers.'

'Strangers!'

'I beg your pardon, dear Alphonse, the word slipped out of my mouth unconsidered. I mean that the dowager is not, cannot be, and does not wish to be, in a position towards me such as my own mother occupies.'

'I know that,' said the baron sorrowfully; 'but wait— in time! You do not know what a pretty thing the curé said about the frost going.'

'Yes, dear husband, the frost may go, and the dear little primrose that will show his sweet face will banish it, may- be, but, in the meantime, it is not merely a white frost that reigns, it is a black frost, and I want some home warmth when I am in trouble.'

'You must decide. It would be painful if your mother and mine did not agree, and the sickroom were made a battlefield and the baby's body the bone of contention.'

'I will go and consult Aunt Betsy.'

'Do so. But I do not think it would conduce to your health and happiness to have bickerings about you.'

Jacquetta drove to Champclair. She was never allowed now to go out alone; one of the old ladies attended her.

Mdlle. de Pleurans accompanied her to Aunt Betsy's but refused to go in, she would not even look at the house lest she should see the face of the assassin. She allowed the baroness to descend, and then ordered the coachman to drive along the road for a little league and return. 'When you see the carriage,' said Mdlle. de Pleurans, 'I hope you will come out and not keep me and the horses waiting.'

'I will be as quick as I can,' answered Jacquetta with a smile. She was quite sensible of the effrontery of the old lady, but too sensible to take offence.

This was a sample of their treatment. Everything that was bought with the young baroness's money was accepted ungraciously as a contribution to the family, a paying of her footing to be acknowledged by it. It was an honour to her that mdme. the dowager used the carriage and horses sent out to Jacquetta from her father, the grocer. The fact of the baronial arms and coronet being painted on the panels made them the property of the family, and Jacquetta used them as she used the house, and bore the name and title, on sufferance. What was hers became theirs, but what was theirs was only grudgingly lent her.

'My dear,' said Aunt Betsy, 'I don't know what to say. I wouldn't, if I were you, offend the baroness in any way. If she would like to have your mother, send for her, if she would not, it will never do to go contrary to her wishes. She might make the house very unpleasant both for you and for your mother.'

'She is capable of doing it,' said Jacquetta. 'I will tell you what it is, Aunt Betsy. I do care a little for myself, and I would dearly love to have my darling mother with me. Oh, aunt, suppose anything were to happen to me and I were never to see mamma again, or papa! Oh, aunt, I cannot bear the thought. Do you think I can run home and be there?'

'Certainly not. That would give mortal offence.'

'Then, if I must remain here, it does seem hard that mamma should not come to me. But I am afraid for her sake. I would not for the world have her snubbed by my mother-in-law; and I would not have her think that I am unhappy. Perhaps if she were here and saw some of the ways of going on, she might fire up. Mamma has plenty of spirit, and a strong sense of justice, and she speaks out her mind—only the dowager cannot understand English, so mamma would be attacking Alphonse, and setting him, perhaps, thereby, against me. He does not like to be worried, he takes matters easily.'

'My dear, you must decide for yourself, but—be quick, there is the carriage. Mdlle. de Pleurans is in it with her head turned away, looking at the rope-walk. Do not keep her waiting. I do not suppose she is really interested in seeing the man spin ropes.'

So, both by her aunt and her husband, Jacquetta was thrown back on herself for a decision. She did not talk in the carriage, the old lady at her side told her she was under strict orders not to let her talk much, as too exhausting. But Jacquetta had no wish to talk. James Asheton passed and removed his hat. The young baroness leaned back in the carriage. Had she made a mistake? If she had been the wife of an Englishman, her mother would of course have been welcome to be with her in her troubles. She knew perfectly how unpleasant the dowager could make the house to her mother, she knew that the old baroness was resolved to have her own way in everything with the baby. It would be a Montcontour and not a Fairbrother, and therefore what had Mrs Fairbrother to do with it? Properly it was for her, the Dowager Baroness of Montcontour to take the charge of everything connected with the advent of the heir to the barony. Jacquetta was quite aware that her mother-in-law saw matters in this light and would act on her conviction. Then Mrs Fairbrother would refuse to give way. She would want everything in English fashion, and if the dowager was obstinate in one way, Mrs Fairbrother was obstinate in another. There would be storms, and her mother would return to England very unhappy, and make her old father unhappy as well—convinced that their daughter was miserable. No, it was better that Mrs Fairbrother should not come out. So poor Jacquetta wrote home a letter which cost her many tears and much thought to write, a letter which in spite of all her efforts to soften the refusal she knew must wound the dear mother, because it declined her services.

'Don't cry,' said Alphonse, 'you have decided wisely. It will never do to bring two strong heads in juxtaposition. Wait, and when the child is strong enough, we will go together with it on a visit to its grandparents.'

The prospect was far off, but after all it was something to look forward to. Jacquetta submitted with a sigh.

At last the eventful day arrived. The hopes, the ambition of all were gratified. The baby was a boy, a very fine boy. Jacquetta laughed and cried, and hugged the little thing. 'It is an English boy; see Alphonse, is it not?'

Now mdme. la douairière was in her glory.   She assumed absolute management of everything.   As for Mdlle. de Pleurans she bounced about the house like a bird in snowy weather which bobs its head against everything.   She was here, there, and everywhere, in wild excitement getting into every one's way, and doing nothing.   The dowager had provided a lusty peasantess as wet-nurse, but Jacquetta absolutely refused to give up her baby to the woman.   She would have it and nurse it herself.   At least her baby should be her own; the dowager and aunt might appropriate her carriage, and her green-house—anything else she had—but she would not surrender her baby.

On the eighth day it was to be christened.

'But, Alphonse, we have not decided on a name yet.'

'Oh, yes,' he replied, 'my angel, that is all settled by mamma and Aunt Celestine.'

'But—I have not been consulted.'

'You have been too unwell; besides, the names are admirable.'

'What are they?'

'Joseph Marie Celeste.'

'What! a boy called Marie!   Nonsense.   I won't have my boy given a girl's name.   And Celeste! it is ridiculous. I don't half like Joseph even.'

'But it is not uncommon for a man to be called Marie.'

'I cannot suffer it.   Why, how he will be teased at school, all the boys will call him Molly!   And Celeste—it is really too absurd.'

'My mother is Josephine, and my aunt Celestine.'

'Yes, but my boy is a boy, and must have a boy's name.'

'You must persuade my mother.'

'Look here, Alphonse. I will not have my boy grow up a milksop, and if he is called by girls' names he will very likely be that. I am determined he shall be manly, and go to Eton, play cricket, and football. He shall not wear baggy red trousers, and a peaked pink cap, and wear stays and have a wasp's waist. I put my foot down at once at the name. If he be called by these girls' names be will be brought up effeminately. It is the first step which costs.'

The baron looked distressed. He did not know what to do.

'Alphonse,' pursued his wife, 'you know that little shrimp, Anatole de Puygarreau—he is just ten years old and walks about in uniform like a soldier. Well, one day when your aunt and I were in the garden we had Anatole with us, as his mother was with the baroness. We were in the shrubbery, and as he lagged I said to him, turning round, "Come, follow us, Anatole." Whereupon, will you believe it, he removed his cap, bowed, and replied, "*Madame, je vous suivrai jusqu'aux enfers.*" And he—Ten years old. I should die of shame if my baby were to address me thus.'

'But why, Jacquetta? It was a pretty speech.'

'It was absurd—especially in a child of ten. No; my boy shall be brought up English fashion, and as a beginning he shall not be Marie, neither shall he be Celeste. I do not like Joseph, but—I will call him Joe.'

'I fail to see anything in Anatole's answer, but great readiness and spirit.'

'There we think differently. I will not have my boy brought up to be a *petit-maître* like Anatole. I will write home at once to mamma—give me a book and a pencil and paper. I will write in bed.'

'What for, Jacquetta?'

'A set of stumps, and a ball, and cricket bat. My boy shall be manly—he shall not be a girl.'

Of course Jacquetta was not present at the baptism. She was not sufficiently well. When the ceremony was over, she asked her husband eagerly, 'Well! what name was given him?'

'Joseph Victor.'

'Why Victor?'

'First, because your Queen is Victoria—'

'What a hankering you have after female names!'

'We thought it a delicate compliment to you; and also because his godfather, the Comte de Puygarreau is Victor.'

'That first and the compliment to me second. My boy shall be only plain Joe to me.'

Alphonse did not tell her, but she discovered it afterwards, that her wishes had been disregarded, her boy had been baptised by the names of Joseph Marie Celeste Victor. When Jacquetta did learn this she was very angry and scolded her husband.

'I could not help it,' he said. 'I conveyed to my mother your objections, but she overruled them. Besides, at the ceremony, when the curé asked the names, she, as sponsor, answered and gave them—it was not possible for me to interfere.'

'I shall never forgive it. But I do not care. He shall be Joe to me, and Joe only. I have written for the ricketing things.'

CHAPTER XI

It is difficult to describe the pride, the delight, of the two old ladies, they would have engrossed the baby altogether had it been possible. Jacquetta trembled to see Aunt Celestine holding it, she was unaccustomed to infants and seemed so nervous when carrying the heir that out of fear of letting him fall she very nearly dropped him. The dowager wanted to have the little Joseph Marie always on her knees. She crowed to him, she snapped her fingers, she jingled her keys, she made the most hideous grimaces, and outrageous noises, in order to attract his attention. She discovered that he was the image of the great-great-grandfather of her late husband, a general, whose portrait was in the *salon*, a grim old officer with a mouth like a rat-trap. She called Alphonse to admire, to adore the infant. She went into ecstasies, she chattered, she prayed, she laughed, she cried over it.

Unfortunately she concentrated her love on the babe to such an extent that she could spare none for the mother. She rather resented that Jacquetta should lay any claims to it. She would have preferred that the child should be nursed by a peasantess who would have been under her own control, and quite taken away from its mother and brought up in her own suite of apartments. She plagued the poor young wife with her exhortations, remonstrances, advice. If this was vexatious before the child was born, it was doubly vexatious now. But Jacquetta endured her mother-in-law's fidgets with patience; in some matters she held her own, would not yield, and then the old baroness gave way, not without a secret respect for Jacquetta for being able to show firmness. In trifles Jacquetta yielded, yielded graciously, smilingly. She was pleased to see the withered old hearts unfold and bloom like roses of Jericho. The baron resumed his country occupations, and but for her baby, the young wife would have been almost as solitary as before. Thoughts which she could not crush down worked in her head. Life at Plaissac was insupportable. The two old ladies took advantage of her amiability, and Alphonse was culpable in not sustaining her against them. She thought that they would try to set her baby against her, as he grew up. They would carry their ideas into effect with his education as they had overridden her wishes in the matter of his name. She drove out to visit Aunt Betsy. An idea had been fermenting in her mind which she was afraid to give utterance to, yet resolved to hint at. She could not put up with the life she was leading any longer. She wanted to go home to England, to her father and mother, and carry baby with her. She had no dislike to Alphonse, she loved him, but she loved her little fellow better. She had not had a really happy day since she had been in France. Would Aunt Betsy abet her in her plan of running away? She beat about the bush, she turned white and red, she had her eyes filled with tears, she hid her face, and at last, when Miss Pengelly failed to take hints, her whole scheme was revealed.

The dismay of Aunt Betsy was great. Jacquetta to desert her husband and chateau, to throw away, as naught, her position as baroness, to bring a slur on the name of Montcontour!

'My dear!' she exclaimed, 'it may be all innocent and true what you say, but no one will believe that you have run home—I mean to your father and mother—just for baby's sake. They will say horrible things of you. They will believe every kind of evil of you. Never—never! No one will admit that you have been badly used. Of course, you are a grocer's daughter, and an English girl, and you are married into a noble family that is French. You knew all this when you married, and as you have married, you have taken all the disadvantages as well as the advantages in one lump, and you cannot shake them off at pleasure.'

'But, Aunt—those old cats.'

'What old cats?'

'The dowager and Mdlle. de Pleurans. I did not marry them. I do not quarrel with Alphonse, but I do not think it fair I should be plagued with those old women—cats!'

'They are not cats, they belong to a very good family, and must not be spoken of in this way. My dear, the thing is monstrous, not to be thought of. Put it out of your mind at once. You make my blood curdle.'

'If I go, will you go with me?'

'No, certainly.'

No encouragement was to be got from Aunt Betsy, however Jacquetta put her case. She became sullen and angry. For several days she was changed in her manner towards her husband. She resented his conduct. He was bound to see that she was not flouted and imposed upon by his mother and aunt. He did not fulfil his duty, therefore she was relieved of responsibility to fulfil hers. She was more than ever resolved to take an opportunity of running away, and carrying off baby with her. She drove into Nantes and inquired about the vessels sailing for the English ports. If she went by road, she might be pursued and overtaken before she reached St. Malo: but by sea she would be safe, and once in England nothing would induce her to return.

One day the curé and his sister came to pay their respects to the baby and his mother, and congratulate as well the grandmother and great aunt.

'Oh, *mon Dieu!*' exclaimed the deformed woman, 'what splendour, what luxury! What superb furniture! I have never dreamed of anything like it. This *fauteuil*, my faith, one could dance on it. See! it is full of springs!' The poor little creature laughed shrilly. She was a child in mind as in stature, but not a child in spirit, in that old, experienced, trained by suffering.

The curé fixed his keen eye on the young mother.

'Well! How goes?—happy, thankful to the good God! Why, madame, with such a child, and such a husband, and such a home—' He had read her heart. He saw the cloud that hung over it. 'Ah, yes! there is something wanting, and that'—turning to the dowager—'you must supply.'

A rough man, who smote hard, but with a kind hand, a

man who had no scruple to blurt out his opinion in the face
of any one.

'I am very thankful, M. le Curé,' said Jacquetta, 'for
my dear, dear baby.'

He looked at her with his shrewd eye, and grunted.
Her colour was heightened and there was a sparkle in her
eye. She did not like his steady observation, and she
moved impatiently.

'Humph!' said the curé. 'Madame, may I ask you
kindly to show your greenhouses to my sister? She loves
flowers passionately.'

'Certainly,' answered Jacquetta, 'if mademoiselle will
follow me—but perhaps she is tired and would first rest.'

'Oh, no, madame, not at all; it is itself a rest for the
soul to contemplate beautiful flowers.'

Jacquetta rose stiffly; she was offended. The curé had
as much as told her he wanted her out of the room.
Another slight, offered her now by one from whom she
did not expect it. However, one more mattered little,
she thought. In a few days she would be beyond the
reach of these petty insolences.

She hardly had left the room before the sound of carriage
wheels on the gravel before the door drew Mdlle. de
Pleurans to the window. 'But who is coming? It is a
hired carriage. *Mon Dieu*, Josephine, what is to be done?
It is—it is——'

The door opened, and the servant announced, 'Mdlle.
Painaulait.'

The two old ladies of the house looked at the incomer
with speechless astonishment, and with a contempt that

transpired from every feature, and finger, and from the very rustle of their gowns.

'You have come, mademoiselle,' said the baroness haughtily, 'to see my daughter-in-law. She is in the garden. Jeanette, take mademoiselle into the garden to Mdme. la Baronne.'

'Pardon, madame,' said Aunt Betsy timorously, 'I have not come to see my niece, but to see you.'

Ah! Mademoiselle Painaulait! To be sure!' exclaimed the curé walking up to her with both his great hands extended. 'I have not seen you for long, not since the death of Madame de Hoelgoet, to whom you were so devoted, so good, so like a sister. My faith! how she suffered! And she was a saint. She bore her pains with such fortitude; and you, mademoiselle, have laid up a store of merit, you were ever with her, night and day, and hers was a trying illness, not to herself only, but to those who ministered to her. Well, well! You know the saying in the gospel about ministering to the suffering. Did I say you were like a sister? You were more than a sister.'

The baroness and Mdlle. de Pleurans looked at each other. The curé was a provoking man; he was deficient in tact. He made great blunders.

'I am sure, ladies,' said the curé, 'that I am only expressing your feelings when I tell Mdlle. Painaulait that the debt of gratitude owed her by the family is one that can never be repaid.'

'M. le Curé,' said the baroness sternly, 'we can speak for ourselves. What is it which Mdlle. Painaulait wants with us? I assure you, M. le Curé, that neither my sister nor I can conceive of any occasion for Mdlle. Painaulait having called on us.'

'M. le Curé,' said Aunt Celestine, 'I am equally surprised at this visit of Mdlle. Painaulait. I assure you, M. le Curé, that I also cannot imagine an occasion for the intrusion.'

'Oh, Madame la Baronne!' pleaded Aunt Betsy with great humility, 'I am perfectly aware that I have no right here, and that it is great presumption on my part, but I do want to speak in private with you, two words, if you will graciously consent, madame.'

'M. le Curé, I am sure that Mdlle. Painaulait can say anything she desires before you. Is it not so, monsieur?'

'That, madame, concerns her. She wants a word in private with you.'

'But, monsieur, I must request that whatever is said be said here. I am indisposed to accord a more private interview.'

'Madame!' pleaded Aunt Betsy, 'it concerns your family. It concerns Jacquetta—'

'She means Madame la Baronne de Montcontour.'

'It concerns the baron, and the baby baron too.'

Not a word. The old ladies sat stiffly on their seats, they had not asked her to take a chair.

'Oh, Madame!' burst forth Miss Pengelly, 'I have only just discovered it. She has made all preparations to go away—she has taken her place in a vessel that sails on Tuesday, and the coachman's wife is to go with her as nurse, and the baby will be carried away also—I mean the Baron Joseph Marie de Montcontour.'

'What is that? What?'

The ladies started to their feet in dismay.

'She has been so unhappy. She cannot bear to live in France any longer. She pines to be home in England with her dear papa and mamma. You have not understood her. She has been neglected, treated coldly. She is out of her place here. I have only just discovered her plan. Do not tell her I have betrayed her secret, but—it must not be permitted—the scandal.'

'*Effroyable!*' exclaimed both ladies at once.

'*Hein!* have I not said it?' shouted the curé thrusting his hands through his cincture, and striding up and down the room. '*Hein!* it is come to this? This is the result of your detestable pride and airs! I tell you, baroness, and you, mademoiselle, you call yourselves Catholics but you are heathens at heart. Why did not you go and nurse your sister, Mdme. de Hoelgoet? Why did you keep away from her? You were afraid lest the disorder should attack yourselves. Miss Painaulait had no such fears. She is a heretic, but she is a better Christian than either of you. Then, when you get a charming, angelic daughter into the chateau, with your wicked pride and uncharitableness you make the place unendurable to her, and drive her away! *Hein!* it makes me angry. I would like to take your two noble heads and knock them together—*que Diable.* Heaven forgive me, I was swearing,' and he crossed himself. 'Mdlle. Painaulait, we thank you; all will be well. Do not let the baroness see you; return at once. Let me be your chevalier and escort you to the carriage. Say nothing to your niece. All will be well. Hold!—what is the name of the vessel?'

'The *Petrel.*'

'Come, march !　Excuse me, mademoiselle, I am impatient to see you drive away before your niece is aware that you have been here.　I have an idea in my head.　All will be well, on my faith as a priest.　Believe me.'

As he handed Miss Pengelly into her carriage he said, ' Drive at once to the quay.　Secure two more berths, four in all, for　M. le Baron, and Mdme. la Baronne de Mont-contour.'

Then the good old man strode away into the garden in quest of Jacquetta and his sister.　They were not on the terrace, not in the conservatory.　He called 'Gracieuse.' Then he heard voices, and he went to a window that was open, and looked in.　The window was that of a day nursery on the ground floor.　On a chair sat the young mother with her babe on her knee, and before her kneeling, was the little hunchback, holding the child's feet to her lips and kissing the soles, and laughing with her shrill cracked voice, so as almost to frighten the baby.

'Haha ! madame,' said the curé, placing his arms on the window sill, ' making an idolater of my sister.　How the world has changed !　In pagan times infants were sacrificed. Now we sacrifice ourselves to the children.'

'Will you come in, monsieur ?'

'With the greatest of pleasure.'　He went round to a glass door and entered.

'Madame,' he said, ' you have done me a great favour in admitting me to this sanctuary of innocence and maternal love ; I feel myself a culprit before you.'

'How so, M. le Curé ?'

'Because I am keeping from you a secret that concerns you intimately.'

'Me!'

'You and the *petit policon là.*'

'What secret?'

'I have no right to tell it; but I consider that secrets
may be carried too far; and a pleasure spoils if it bursts
on one too suddenly.'

'What pleasure is in store for me?' asked Jacquetta
with bitterness.

'A visit to England, to your father and mother.'
Jacquetta started. 'Yes—so it is. The berths are all
engaged, you and the Baron, and the little baron (with a
small *b*), and your coachman's wife as nurse, and the coachman himself because he cannot be separated from his wife.
All are to sail on Tuesday. The berths are secured in the
Petrel, and you are to stay in England as long as you like.
There—gracious heavens! I am a traitor, I have betrayed
the baron's secret.'

CHAPTER XII

The curé rushed away in search of the baron. He knew that he was to be found somewhere on the farm. When, after some search and inquiry he came upon him, he read him a lecture, and told him exactly what he knew and what he had done.

'*Mon ami*, you have not treated your little wife rightly. Now you must act as I advise, and prevent a great catastrophe. On Tuesday you leave Nantes in the *Petrel* with your wife and child and two servants—the coachman and his wife.'

'But why the coachman? My mother will want the carriage.'

'Let her want it. It will do her good to feel what she loses by losing her daughter-in-law.'

'But how long is this visit to England to last?'

'Six months, nine months, a twelvemonth—I cannot tell, till your wife wants to return, and till madame your mother has learned how to treat her when she does return. Leave the dowager and your aunt to me. I know what medicine they require.'

'The farm! This is a busy time. I cannot leave it.'

'It must be left. Either the farm or your wife and child —which do you value most?'

So it was settled, and much to Jacquetta's surprise and humiliation she found that she was taking the journey home in company with her husband, which she had meditated taking without him. He did not allow her to suppose that he had any suspicion of her intended flight. The scheme was his own, a planned surprise, only to be disclosed to her at the last moment. Had he not offered to take her home to her parents at Easter? Had not the arrival of the '*petit bon homme*' interfered with this? Now what more right and reasonable than that the deferred visit should be made? True, Mr and Mrs Fairbrother had not been informed as yet, but there was time. They would get a letter before the *Petrel* arrived, and it would give them a great surprise and unbounded pleasure. Jacquetta was touched and humbled. She had doubted her husband's affection. She knew that this expedition cost him something. It drew him away from his favourite pursuits.

'My dear Alphonse, what about the farm?'

'Ah, bah! farm! What is a farm to wife and child.'

'But why do we go by sea from Nantes instead of by coach to St. Malo?'

'It will be better for baby, and your cheeks are pale, the sea air will restore your health.'

'I am afraid, Alphonse, you will miss your occupation on the estate and farm.'

'But I shall have to cultivate my wife's society, and that will be better.'

A day or two after the departure of her son and daughter-in-law and grandchild, the old baroness said to her sister sharply, ' *Mon Dieu,* Celestine, how silent you are.   Why do you not talk?   We might be in a city of the dead, one hears no sound in the house.'

'I do not know what to speak about now, Josephine.'

'You are becoming insupportable.   It is two days since they went away, and instead of enlivening me you make me more *triste.*'

'I cannot help myself, sister, the air of the chateau is becoming *triste.*'

'I wonder how the baby is?'

'I have been unable to sleep.   I have been in terror all night lest a storm should break.   My faith!   I wonder whether the baby will be sea-sick?'

'All babies are sea-sick, everywhere, on the solid land. I think nothing of that.'

'After all,' said Mdlle. de Pleurans, 'we are rid for a while of Jacquetta.'

'Yes—but—we have lost the baby.'

'I wish we had never seen Jacquetta.'

The baroness did not answer for a while; she was thinking.   Presently she said, argumentatively, 'That may be, but without her we should not have had Joseph Marie Celeste Victor.'

'But—my sister!   If Alphonse had taken someone else —it is conceivable—there might have still been a baby.'

'It is possible,' answered the baroness.   She considered for a while and then said, 'But not such a baby!'

'*Sainte Vierge!*   Why not?'

'Why not?—Celestine, I blush for you. This is an incomparable baby.'

'Yes, Josephine, I allow that. But why not an equally incomparable baby.

'Another! Then this would be non-existent! Celestine, in mind you assassinate this pearl, this angel, this—Celestine, I look upon you with horror.'

'But why, my sister?'

'Why?—another baby not only could not have surpassed this perfection, but—it is conceivable, might have been a girl.'

'I had not thought of that, Josephine.'

'Besides, the Montcontours are all of a delicate constitution, and they do not inherit robustness from our side. The little man had the constitution of a Jean Bull—though he has the soul of a Frenchman. Have you heard him roar? It is the roar of a lion. I never heard a little Montcontour, nor a de Pleurans, nor a Puygarreau, nor any babe of our ancient nobility roar like Joseph Marie. Veritably it shook the house; the foundations quaked. Those must be lungs which could roar like that! Lungs! they are forge bellows. We must give Jacquetta her due, she has given us a constitution in our baby, and she has considered my wishes in giving me a boy.'

'The time passes heavily without him.'

'Yes, Celestine. Now is the hour when he should be washed, and we are not there to assist!' The tears came into the old lady's eyes, and Mdlle. de Pleurans began to sniffle.

'I hope they will write as soon as they arrive,' said the

aunt. 'Perhaps they may send a letter back in mid-ocean by a passing vessel.'

'If Alphonse writes, I know his letter will be full of inquiries concerning the farm, and the cows, and the crops—he will say baby is well, but there will be no details, and it is the details which are so fascinating.'

'Yes,' said Aunt Celestine, 'it would be more interesting to us if Jacquetta wrote four pages crossed, and all about the baby, how he eats and sleeps and looks, and what the English nation think of him. When will he cut his first teeth?'

'I do not know; that depends. It is two days since they left. *Mon Dieu*, it is an age.'

'And we do not know when they return!'

'It is terrible! Celestine, we will have the carriage and drive to the Puygarreaus and talk there of the baby. You are so dull.'

Orders were given for the carriage, and the old ladies went to their rooms to dress.

When they descended and came to the door, they simultaneously uttered a cry of dismay. Jean, the factotum, was on the box of the old family yellow carriage, in his old faded livery, with his brown hands ungloved, his leather hat on his head, holding the reins awkwardly. The carriage looked vastly worse than it had ever looked before, the sides dull, the varnish not only dead but cracked, the leather without a sign of gloss, and full of roughnesses at every crease. The old horse that ploughed was in the wretched harness, ready to dance along the road as of old, throwing out his legs sideways, as though performing on a tightrope. Now he stood pensive with his nose towards the gravel.

The creamy white hair hung about his fetlocks unclipped, his hoofs were stained with stable manure, unwashed, the mane was very thick and tangled.

'Jean! What is the meaning of this? Tell the coach-man——'

'But, madame, the coachman is gone to England with M. le Baron.'

'Then, Jean, bring round the proper carriage and horses.'

'Madame, the shoes have been taken off the English horses, and they have been turned out to grass.'

'Very well, take this old carriage away, and bring the new one. Harness Coquillicot into it.'

'Certainly, madame, but we have only this single harness. The other, the splendid, the silver, is double harness.'

'Do not argue with me. Obey, Jean.'

Accordingly Jean drove into the backyard. The dowager was hot and fuming. 'How unreasonable of Alphonse! How could he be so thoughtless? He might know we would require the carriage.'

Presently they heard the sound of wheels, and went again to the door. Coquillicot was harnessed into the victoria, and Jean sat on the box. Coquillicot was in his old dingy harness, mended in many places. The contrast was too grotesque between the stylish English carriage and the shabby driver and harness, and horse from the plough.

'This will never do,' said the baroness. 'Every one will jeer as we pass through Nantes. I had no idea how mean Coquillicot was. He is unfit to be put in this victoria. I had no conception the harness was in such a condition. Drive back, Jean, and reharness Coquillicot into the old family coach. We will say, Celestine, that the new

carriage has gone to be re-painted and re-varnished, and
we are constrained to put up with this for a few weeks.'

For a third time Jean came round, this time as he had
driven to the door at first.

'Jean,' said the baroness in a sulky tone, 'where are
your white gloves?'

'In my pocket, Mme. la Baronne. I will put them on
as I drive through the town.'

'Put them on at once, and do not take them off till you
return.'

'As you will, Mme. la Baronne; but—the economies?'

'Never mind the economies. Do as you are bid.'

The ladies got into the carriage, and Coquillicot danced
along the road with them.

'The motion in this equipage,' said the dowager, 'strikes
me as—as bouncing. I never remarked it before. I do not
feel well. I think it will give me sea-sickness.'

'Oh, Josephine, think of baby on the ocean, tossed on
the waves. The feeling is alike in this conveyance and in
the boat. Be it so. I also am unwell. We are—are like
baby at this moment. It is very touching! It is poetical.'

'Jean! Drive round by the presbytery. We will summon
the curé to sup with us. We must have society. There is
a stillness as of death in the house, which makes black
thoughts and horrors come into the mind.'

Accordingly the curé was invited to supper. The baroness
said on her return, 'Go to the cook, Celestine, and tell
her to give us something good. If we cannot have the baby,
we must have to eat, and stifle our sorrow, and fill the void
as we may. *Fricandeau de veau aux truffles.* It is the
time of larks—*anges à cheval.*'

Presently Mdlle. de Pleurans came back in agitation. 'My sister—the cook has gone. The baron dismissed her with a month's wage, and old Germaine is back—and her cooking, as you remember, is detestable. What is to be done?'

'What was Alphonse thinking of? One must eat. One cannot devour leather. If he had a good *cuisine* whilst his wife was here, why not now that his mother is in the place?'

'Germaine tells me there is a letter addressed to you on Alphonse's table.'

'I have not been into his room since he left. I have only visited the spot where the cradle stood, and wept there. Run, Celestine, run and bring me the letter.'

Mdlle. de Pleurans returned turning the envelope about. It was addressed to the baroness. She tore it open and read—

'My dearest Mother,—You know that I adore you—only second to my wife, who occupies the first place in my heart. Always having your wishes and interests near my heart, mamma, I believe that I have acted as you would have desired. I know and deplore the fatal estrangement that exists between you and my beloved, angelic Jacquetta. But—it exists. You view her with an eye devoid of tenderness. Knowing this, and reading your inmost soul, I have taken provision that everything shall be carried on in the chateau during our absence, as if Jacquetta *had never been*. With your tender sense of honour you would shrink from using anything that was supported out of her means. I am therefore only saying what you say a thousand times to your own self—Perish all the comforts, the luxuries, rather than that I should be indebted to Jacquetta for them!   If you had spoken the words, mamma, I could not have understood you better.   I have therefore dismissed all the servants who were engaged on my marriage and received wages out of Jacquetta's purse, all but those we have taken with us.   You have Jean, who is a host in himself, who is butler, gardener and coachman, and bailiff to the estate.   You have Germaine, who has been with you more years than I have.   You will order everything with the greatest economy, as far as our means derived from the Montcontour estate will go, not one sou of Jacquetta's is available for the purpose.   I know that the money would burn your fingers—those fingers which I kiss passionately, and which I would spare the agony and the humiliation of touching money which they would regard as dishonouring to receive and to spend.   Our residence in England may be long.   Jacquetta is desirous of her son being trained as an English boy, and of his going to Eton, which is a famous school frequented by the sons of the nobility.'

The baroness uttered a cry, and fainted.

When she came round she gasped :   'I shall never see Joseph Marie Celeste Victor again !   I shall die of *ennui*.'

'What is the matter?' asked the curé coming in.

'Matter, monsieur !   Read this letter.'

The curé read the epistle, then waved his arms, and paced the room.   'It is just !   He has echoed your thoughts. Ah, madame, come !   Away with all this splendid furniture. Let us tear down the damask curtains, and put up the shabby old green rags instead.   Roll up the carpets.   Call in Jean and Germaine and all hands available.   We will remove everything—to the glass ball on the terrace. Down with these lustres, and mirrors, and paintings. Everything shall be transported to the attic, and stowed away till Mme. la Baronne returns to use them when the young baron is of age.'

'But,' M. le Curé,' protested Aunt Celestine, 'you do not mean this? Every room will look bare. The old furniture is worn out. The chairs are too high for comfort. There was not a *fauteuil* in the house that had not the springs out of order, and when you sat in one it was like sitting on a set of inverted pattens.'

'I know it,' said the priest. 'But honour is above all. You will not wear out the furniture of the woman you despise and insult. You will not eat off the pretty porcelain given her as her wedding present by English friends. You will banish to the attic everything that she brought into the house, everything that reminds you of her. Hold! I will come here to-morrow. I will take off my cassock, and help, and by evening we shall have gutted the house, and—how elate you will be, Mme. la Baronne, and you also Mdlle. de Pleurans.'

'Supper is served,' announced Jean.

'Bring the Médoc for M. le Curé, and the Burgundy for me and my sister. Burgundy is fortifying,' added the baroness.

'Madame,' answered Jean, 'I regret, but M. le Baron has taken away the keys of the cellar, and nothing is left but *vin ordinaire*, which was here before Mme. the young Baroness came.'

'*Mon Dieu !* I want fortifying.'

'Fortify yourself, madame,' said the curé, 'with the heroic thought that you are doing without your daughter-in-law.'

CHAPTER XIII

Jacquetta was received by her father and mother with rapture, they were very pleased to see the baron, but the grandchild was the great focus of attention and object of devotion. Old Fairbrother was almost as absurd about the child as was his wife. Mrs Fairbrother had been hurt because her daughter had declined her assistance, but this unexpected visit healed the wound.

How small the old house of her childhood now seemed to Jacquetta, accustomed to the large rooms of the chateau. The house was comfortable, but lacked elegance. The furniture was heavy, the papers tasteless, the ornaments ugly. She noticed how much duller was the sky of England, how much more changeable the climate, how little sun was seen, how depressing was the air.

'We will run to Cheltenham,' she said to her husband. 'I want to let the Misses Woodenhead see my darling.'

So they visited Jacquetta's old schoolmistresses, and presented the young baron to be worshipped by those old spinsters. Thence they were to go on into Sussex on a visit of a week to Jacquetta's school friend.

'Alphonse,' she said, 'have you written to your mother and Aunt Celestine? They will be longing to know how Joe is doing—dear little pet! sweet boy! was ever such a cherub seen? And oh! tell them there is a tiny, tiny peak coming through his angelic gum, and that he dribbles a great deal.'

'I have written to mamma.'

What did you tell her?'

'I said how happy you were, and how that I proposed on our return from Sussex to your father's, to go through studies in equitation, and that—'

'But what did you tell her about the baby?'

'Nothing.'

'How cruel of you. I know she will be wanting to hear. Now, Alphonse, I have news for you. My friend in Sussex whom we are going to visit tells me she is engaged to be married, just engaged to—whom do you suppose?'

"I cannot guess.'

'To Mr James Asheton.'

'That is unfortunate,' said the baron. 'I have just received tidings that the firm of Asheton has failed.'

'But my friend has money.'

'So much the better for Asheton. The poor blond, Miss Graham, will break her heart. She was much attached to him. He has acted unhandsomely by her.'

They paid their visit. On their return to the Fairbrothers, Jacquetta found a letter awaiting her, written in a beautiful foreign hand, like copper plate engraving.

'Why, actually, Alphonse, a letter from Aunt Celestine!'

The letter was formal as the writing, but gracious. The dowager and aunt were fairly well, and besieged heaven with prayers for the welfare of their dear baby. They had heard nothing about him since he left. Alphonse's letters were meagre, and scarce alluded to the one subject which most interested them. They thought night and day about their baby, and were anxious for full particulars concerning him. Madame the *belle mère* was especially alarmed lest exposure to the prevailing fogs which envelop Great Britain should endanger the health of the child.

'I must write,' said Jacquetta, 'for *them*, this is a great condescension.'

'Write very little,' answered the baron. 'Describe to them fully that charming bonnet you bought at Cheltenham, also the trousseau your friend will have, and say only of baby that he is as well as can be expected, and add—and underline it—that small-pox and scarlet-fever, measles whooping-cough are raging in the neighbourhood, and sweeping away thousands of children.'

'Why so, Alphonse?'

'My dear, I wish it. The curé advised it.'

'The curé! What has he to do with this?'

'The curé is a very shrewd man.'

'I cannot see why he should meddle in our affairs.'

'Then again, Jacquetta. Observe how Aunt Celestine and mamma always call Joseph "Our baby?" When you reply, say "My baby!"'

A week later came a very peremptory letter to Alphonse from his mother. She had heard in a roundabout way that there was much sickness in England, that an epidemic of the most dangerous kind had broken out there which was carrying off children by the millions, therefore she insisted on his immediate return to Plaissac.

The baron wrote a letter back full of filial affection and assurances of obedience. He would submit to his mother's wishes, and return, but he was undergoing a course of studies in equitation, which made it exceedingly inconvenient for him to leave at that time. Moreover, as his wife and child would remain, and he had himself undergone all childish maladies, he did not—if his mother would excuse his saying so—see the necessity of his running away from measles and whooping-cough.

Then came another letter from the baroness, rating him soundly for misunderstanding her. She did not desire *his* return. She was in alarm about the baby. Joseph Marie Celeste Victor must be placed beyond the reach of danger.

Alphonse replied, thanking his mother for the reprieve. It would have broken his heart to have interrupted his studies in equitation. He was able now to trot, rising in his stirrups with such elasticity and energy, and elevation, that it was possible to place a watch between his saddle and himself and withdraw it with the regularity of machinery, as he made the course round the riding-school, without his even starring the glass of the watch. He had found the greatest difficulty in turning in his toes, but by assiduous attention he hoped in time to surmount this difficulty also. He wore straps to his trousers now, but the professor of equitation had assured him that a master of the art of riding was able to go at a trot, or the canter, or the grand gallop, without his trousers working up his legs. Not a word about the baby !

Jacquetta, against her desire, was sensible of a difference between the manners of her dear parents and of the noblesse of the neighbourhood of Nantes; she knew it, and it troubled her.   She was herself a thorough lady in mind and manner, she had been given advantages not possessed by the old people.   At Nantes she had associated with the best French families, where traditional culture and refinement had produced an ideal delicacy and beauty of movement, mode of speech, manner, thought.   She had been received with great kindness, and had been shown the most delicate and graceful attentions.   Her perception of the charm of high culture had been sharpened.   Now she was in daily contact with these worthy old people who were by no means polished.   The Fairbrothers had acquaintances and friends who were called together to dine with their daughter the baroness and their son the baron.   With much difficulty and persuasion Jacquetta had induced her mother to cease from speaking of her husband and her as 'Lord' and 'Lady.' The old lady could not get hold of the name nearer than Monkeytower.   Now the title of baron and baroness was for ever in her mouth.   'Polly, where are the baron's boots?'   'Charity, bring the baroness her umbrella.'   To her friends there was no cessation of talk about the baron and baroness, and Jacquetta took a loathing to the title. Her mother's blunders were painfully obvious.   Her lack of taste forced itself on her daughter's notice, though she tried to blind her eyes.   She looked timidly at her husband when her mother committed herself egregiously, but the baron seemed unconscious of the mistakes.   The sense of humour is not present in the Frenchman, he does not mark the absurd, as does the Englishman.

The friends of the Fairbrothers were more open to criticism than the old parents. . Jacquetta saw how common, uncouth, and deficient they were.   She could not make the allowances for them which she had been wont to make before she had seen such sweetness of superior culture in France and had learnt to love it. She was getting tired of doing nothing. Time began to hang heavy on her hands. She could not be always knitting socks for baby.

'Alphonse,' said she one day, 'what shall I do? I have made baby a dozen sets of flannels and as many pairs of socks. I am at my wits' end how to employ myself.'

'Learn equitation,' he said. 'It is a fine study. I can already ride at the canter without my trousers working up to my knees; but I cannot at the trot. It will come in time. I labour very hard. I sigh for the time when I can do without straps.'

'I know what I will do,' she said, brightening, 'I will begin working for the Christmas-tree. We will have another when we get home.'

'Home?'

'Yes—to Plaissac. It gave such pleasure last year. As the winter was so cold the warm things we made were very acceptable. How thankful the poor were! Here our poor people are overwhelmed with charities, and accept all as a right. It was so pretty there, the way in which the mothers thanked me, and how one brought me eggs, and another sun-dried apricots, and another honey. Alphonse, how is dear Mdlle. Gracieuse? I should like to see her again, even to hear her cracked voice laughing. She took such delight working for the children. I will write to her and propose she should begin again. I will send her money to buy the materials. Alphonse, shall we have the tree this year at the chateau?'

'If you like, Jacquetta.'

'Oh, I wonder how my flowers are! We came away just before some Japanese lilies, quite new, came into flower. I gave a great deal for the bulbs. It is said that the lily is the finest ever seen—it is the queen of lilies—and the buds had not burst when we came away. I should like so much to hear what the lily was like. I wonder whether Jean will manage the azaleas right. They must not be kept too dry after they have flowered. I almost wish you had done what your mother said, Alphonse, and run back to Nantes and seen all there, and then you would have been able to tell me. Poor little Mdlle. Gracieuse, I believe she will miss me. What a happy spirit hers is! And Aunt Betsy, she has got to love me, and whenever I went to see her it was quite a festival.'

Jacquetta considered for a while, and then said, 'After all, how pretty it is at Plaissac. I shall never forget those pink chestnuts behind the chateau in spring, how the nightingales sang in them, and, oh, Alphonse, I never, never saw acacia in flower before, white and delicate pink, such masses—no, ostrich-plumes—of blossom, and the air fragrant with them. It really is very pretty at Plaissac.'

'I am glad you think that,' said the baron, smiling with satisfaction. 'I may be partial, but I think Plaissac is charming. All it has needed hitherto has been sufficient means to keep it up and develop its capabilities, and that was what you had begun upon. In time Plaissac would become a Paradise, far more lovely than Les Hirondelles, of which so much is talked. But then, I may over-estimate it—it is my home.'

'You are very fond of it?'

'It is bound up with my childish associations.   Besides, I have my pursuits there.'

'Yes—to be sure,' said Jacquetta, and became silent and grave.   'Where are you going now, Alphonse?'   He had taken his hat.

'I do not know.   To saunter about, and look in at shop windows, and smoke a cigar.   Perhaps to have a game of billiards.   I have no occupation when I am not at my studies of equitation.   May I kiss the baby before I go out?'

When she was alone, she sat in a brown study.   Really, Alphonse was very good.   He had cheerfully thrown up his employment, and cut himself loose from his amusements, from his associates, for her sake, to fulfil her wishes.   Was she right in exacting so much of him?   Was she not making too long a visit in England, absenting herself too long from her home?   Was it wise of her to keep him dangling about the streets of a large town doing nothing but trying to learn to trot without his trousers working up to his knees?   He had made a great sacrifice for her sake. He had proved to her the sincerity of his affection.   She was startled from her reverie by the voice of her father.

'Well, Jacket! looking as if in a dream.   What is it? Want to be back on the Loire again?   I see—torn between two attractions.   Now look here, my girl.   Your mother and I have no call to remain longer here.   I've begun to arrange about getting rid of the business.   If you know of a snug little box near you——'

'Oh, papa, papa!   The Ashetons have failed and have to leave Nantes.   They had a charming little property and *maison de campagne*——'

P

'If it is nice in your eyes, it will do for us.   I will talk to Alphonse about it.   Here is a letter come for you, foreign post-mark ; by the hand, I guess, from Aunt Betsy.'

An hour later the baron came in.   He had done his cigar, and there was nothing new in the shop windows, and no one to play with him at the billiard table.   He found Jacquetta almost dancing.   'Alphonse!   You must read. From Aunt Betsy.   And papa is going to buy the Asheton's place and come and settle near us.   But read, read—no, not the first page, the second.   Here—I will read to you. "Wonders will never cease.   Would you believe it, Madame la Douairière and Mdlle. de Pleurans came here this afternoon in the yellow coach, Jean driving.   They actually came to call on me—on me, the old assassin and robber of the dead, the Painaulait.   And what do you suppose brought them?   THE BOY!   It seems they could get no news of baby, and the old ladies were perfectly frantic with anxiety.   They had heard nothing about him from the baron, nor from you, but they had received the most alarming reports.   So after a great struggle, they humbled themselves to come to Champclair, and behaved most graciously.   They asked to see your letters to me, and I showed them, especially where you told me such a lot about the darling, and his tooth, and the dribbling.   They perfectly devoured it.   I saw them kiss the letter where you said that baby said mum-mum-mum!   And when you told how he cooed like a dove, and about that lovely little dimple in his cheek which is like a rose leaf, they fairly cried and threw themselves into each other's arms and wept like a pair of watering cans.   And they wanted to carry off the letters, but I did not think myself quite justified in allowing that. And I do believe they were more rejoiced to hear that the little pearly tooth was through than they would have been to hear of the return of the Comte de Chambord —I mean Henri Cinq. And they said, if I had another letter from you, I was to mind, instantly, and take a *voiture de rémise*, and drive to Plaissac with it, and show it them. And they spoke so beautifully and handsomely of you—"'

Then a gulp came in her throat, she could read no more; but she put her arms round her husband's neck, and drew his face beside hers, and whispered into his ear, 'Put on your hat, run to the steamer office, and find out when the *Sir Francis Drake* starts. I am full of impatience. We must go *home*.'

CHAPTER XIV

ONE beautiful evening on the Loire. At the entrance to the grounds of the Chateau de Plaissac a triumphal arch has been erected, covered with laurels, and green birch boughs, with paper flowers and streamers of coloured ribbons. Ranged outside are the children of the parish in their best dresses, with flowers in their hands and hats; their dark eyes twinkling and their little red tongues chattering. The curé is sometimes with them, then striding away to the house to see if all is well there. Yes— there all is well. The furniture has been brought down from the garret, the pictures, lustres, mirrors, curtains re-hung. The drive has been weeded, at last. The ladies are in the entrance-hall, burning with impatience.

'Has he grown much, I wonder?' asks the dowager.

'Will he know us again, Josephine?' asks mademoiselle.

'She must be good—very good, or she could not have given to the world such a boy. It says so in the gospel. The curé read me the passage—"Grapes do not come of thorns, nor figs of thistles."'

'It is very true.   And she *is* good.'

'I don't believe such a boy could have been had without her.'

'Hark!   I think I hear carriage wheels.'

'Silence, Celestine.   It is the step of Coquillicot.'

'Ah! what a pity the victoria could not meet the diligence.'

'What! that carriage, that pair, in that harness, driven by Jean! Impossible! The English coachman returns with them.'

Then as the yellow-bodied carriage became visible, approaching the triumphal arch, with the ambling Coquillicot going before, and Jean on the box without his gloves, leaning forward persuasively holding the reins in both hands, the curé waves his great shovel-hat, and shouts to the children—'*Allons! mes enfants.   Heep!*'

A faint response from the children. '*Heep!*' Their eyes are on the carriage, their attention also.

'*Allons! encore! plus fort! Heep!*'

A still gentler response.

Allons! mes enfants! Comme un coup de tonnerre Hourah!'

'Ah! Mme. la Baronne! *Bon jour* Mme. la Baronne!' from all the little boys. 'Ah! *le bébé! le bébé!*' from all the little girls, and a thrust of little brown hands into the carriage with posies picked from every garden in the village. The *Hourah!* was unuttered, though it had been diligently rehearsed.

The carriage drew up at the door, and there, on the steps, uttering exclamations of joy, and salutation, and love, and admiration, were Mme. la Baronne—the dowager,

Mdlle. de Pleurans, Miss Pengelly, and Mdlle. Gracieuse. No wonder they exclaimed. Jacquetta sat in the carriage holding up the *petit polison*, above her head.

'How he is grown!' 'He is like a rose! like la Douairière!' '*Mon Dieu!* he laughs!' Let us see his tooth!'

But before the tooth is looked at, the sparkling, proud, delighted mother is hugged to the hearts of three old women, the mother-in-law, Aunt Celestine, and Aunt Betsy, while the little hunchback is dragging at her gown to get hold of her hand and cover it with kisses.

What is this?

Outside the window on the terrace are ranged the children in a semicircle, the boys on one side and the girls on the other, and the curé stands in the middle with his hat raised. Down it goes, and at once a strain is sung, familiar to Jacquetta, yes—surely familiar, but united to very funny words or to very funny rendering of words—

> ' Coat shave de gracieusse Kveene,
> Longue leefe de glorieusse Kveene
> Goat shave de Kveene!'

Where was Alphonse? Actually forgotten in the excitement of welcome accorded to the young mother and the glorious boy. Now he made himself conspicuous by rushing forth on the steps and saying: 'M. le Curé, my children! Mme. la Baronne and I and the young Baron Joe—that is, Joseph Marie Celeste Victor—thank you with all our hearts for the honour you have accorded us, and we beg that you will wait and all partake of some cake and

wine which Jean will bring to you when he has unhar-
nessed Coquillicot.'

'You have heard that, my children!' exclaimed the curé,
'and now then, all attention, eyes in front, on my hat, all
ready? Once more, *Heep! Heep! Hourah!*'

This time the children responded, effectually, up-
roariously.

THE END

MOTH-MULLEIN

CHAPTER I

To the outward or homeward bound traveller on the Thames what a contrast betwixt the Kent and the Essex sides of the river : the Kent side, with its pleasant chalk hills, woods, and apple orchards; the Essex side flat, tree-less, receiver-general of the London sewage !

When Jutes and Saxons invaded Britain, and came to divide the land, then the Jutes said, 'We have had the flats in our ancestral Jutland, time out of mind; we will take the hills, and if you don't like the swamps you must fight us.' The Saxons growled and accommodated them-selves with the Essex side of the river, and the Jutes kept their feet dry, and rheumatism out of their bones, and ague out of their blood, on the Kent side.

Once on a time the Thames and Medway were all one— that was a grand mouth for the river, and then the hills looked down on the water from Greenwich to Gadshill; but now Kent has made a concession to Essex, and acquired a flat alluvial tract that divides the Thames from the Medway.

Above Greenhythe the chalk hills are much honeycombed with quarries, and huge kilns smoke perpetually, resolving the chalk into cement. Further inland the hills are covered with trees, and form that region so dear to naturalists— Darenth Wood. Now to one unfamiliar with the district, who first traverses Darenth wood, the trees are calculated to excite surprise, for every other is patched with a viscous, sweet, and dark substance, and he will stop and say, ' What is the matter with these trees? Have they got some sort of disease with which I am unfamiliar?'

He will be answered, 'Nothing of the sort. This is done by the moth-hunters. Darenth Wood is famous for the rare lepidoptera caught in it, and it is for the Noctuina group that the collectors hunt here. They spread treacle and beer, mixed, on the trunks of the trees, and catch the moths that are attracted by the mixture. There are as many as three hundred British species of Noctuina alone. Then there are the Bombycidæ, which are not caught by treacle. The collectors hatch out a female and place her on a tree, when numerous males of the species gather about her. This method is not peculiar to the Bombycidæ, though I know of no sort that assembles so vigorously as that species ; it may, however, be satisfactorily tried with many of the Liparidæ and Chelonidæ, as well as with the *Eudromis versicolora*, and *Saturnia Pavonia minor*.'

' Exactly. I merely asked about the smears, without wanting to plunge into lepidopterology. Of course this moth-catching takes place only in summer.'

' Not at all. The *Eriogaster lacustris* appears in

February, and the *Pœcilocampa populi* in November and December. Of course the majority of moths are found in warmer months.'

At the edge of Darenth Wood stood, and perhaps stands still, a little house; it was inhabited by a forester, a man who trimmed and attended to the trees, thinning, pruning, planting. His name was Mullins; his wife was dead, but he had a daughter of the age of twenty—a remarkably handsome girl, with clear complexion, blue eyes, and singularly fair hair, that in the sun looked almost white; it was not quite silver, but of a yellowish tinge, an amalgam of gold and silver. She was tall and straight, had been spoiled by her father, and knowing herself to be a beauty was vain and coquettish.

If she had had only her father's little wage to dress on, she could not have adorned herself with such good clothes as those she affected; but Jessie Mullins had a subsidiary source of income—she herself collected and sold moths and butterflies, and she provided tea and supper for naturalists coming to Darenth Wood for lepidoptera.

The little room in which naturalists regaled themselves whilst waiting for the proper time to smear the trees was surrounded with cases in which butterflies and moths were displayed with spread wings. A whole case, containing many varieties of species, might be purchased, or else some of Jessie's small glass boxes, which she made herself, about a square or oblong block of wood, in which a single specimen or a pair of specimens was fastened by a delicate pin to a cork glued to the glass bottom.

Jessie furnished dealers with such specimens of British moths and butterflies as were to be caught in Darenth

Wood, or on the downs, or in the chalk pits. Her skill in setting up specimens was great; her dainty fingers manipulated the delicate insects without bruising their wings or brushing off any of their plumage.

Perhaps it was her observation of the colouring of these beautiful insects that gave training to her eye, and cultivated her taste. Certain it is that Jessie Mullins dressed becomingly. She never wore colours that disagreed with her complexion and hair. Her favourite tints were silver gray and pearl, and she wore a ribbon of pink or blue, but never much positive colour. That caused all the naturalists who came to Darenth Wood to say, 'Jessie Mullins dresses like a lady. To look at her you would swear she was a lady.'

Now this century is especially the age in which natural history is prosecuted with ardour, not only by spectacled professors but by schoolboys and young men. My own son began collecting butterflies when he was six, and I have a baby that catches flies. Accordingly Jessie had a regular sale for her collections, and throughout a large part of the year had gatherings of naturalists, old, middle-aged and young, at her cottage, who desired to be provided with lanterns, treacle and ale, and a supper when they returned from their chase in the wood.

Jessie was very much admired by the naturalists, and flattered by them; she made herself agreeable to them. Who could say but she might some day catch a naturalist on his way to catch a moth?

But, though the Bombycidæ are caught, the Bombycidæ catchers would not be caught. They were ready to joke with Jessie Mullins, flutter about her, keep up a simmering flirtation, but that was all. Jessie was too haughty to consider the pretensions of those of her own class. Those who ventured to approach were thrust off. For some time two or three of a genus above her own did buzz about her and were not absolutely repelled—they were tolerated ; but they retired, all of their own accord. One there was, one man persistent, unabashed, whom no rebuff would banish, about whom more presently.

Tom Redway, the young plasterer, had been very much struck with Jessie. 'Plasterer,' sneered the girl, 'what is a plasterer?' She sent him up an oak tree to catch Purple Emperors—gorgeous butterflies that fly high, and hover about the tops of the king of the British sylva.

So high do these splendid creatures fly that to catch them a ring net must be affixed to a pole forty feet long. But who can manage a net with the dexterity needed—that is, at the end of so long a pole?

Tom climbed an oak and brandished a pole with a net in vain throughout a day and caught nothing. Then Jessie laughed at him for his pains. He must be a fool not to know that the Purple Emperor loved home-made goose-berry wine, and might be enticed from his aërial altitudes by a bowl of that liquor. After this Tom was so joked by his comrades about being 'sent up a tree' by Jessie Mullins that he kept away from Darenth Wood and the forester's daughter, and soon after—it was said out of spite—married a spinster ten years older than himself.

The next to hover round Jessie was Joseph Ruddle, the carpenter. She sent him in quest of the caterpillars of the rare Cinxia, that were to be found in webs about plantains halfway down the side of the chalk cliffs.

Joe had fallen in his efforts to carry up a web of the caterpillars and had broken his leg. After that Joseph Ruddle went no more up the lane to the cottage of the forester.

Sam Underwood was another admirer. He was a young farmer. She encouraged him after a fashion. A match with him would not be a bad one at all. But Jessie trifled with him; she was like a player on musical glasses, who touches one, sets it humming, then another, and keeps a score in vibration at once. Sam did not appreciate this. He thought she carried on a little too much with a young Oxford man, son of Parkinson the brewer, and, in dudgeon, he withdrew.

There was a fourth, an owner of large strawberry fields, from which he supplied the London market; a sleepy man who took long to make up his mind. She bewildered him with her learned talk about lepidoptera, and became silent when he ought to have spoken, and no touches at last brought any quiver in his heart, or sound out of him.

There was a fifth, Mr Parkinson, but Jessie was not sure that he was sincere; a vain and impudent young man.

And there was a sixth, who would not be shaken off, little Dicky Duck, an active, cheerful fellow with no fixed profession or trade, but always ready in any quarter to make himself useful. He was usually called in to assist the naturalists at night in the wood. He carried the lantern or painted the tree boles. He was not so tall as Jessie.

It was preposterous of him, a fellow stunted in his

growth, to look up to her with matrimonial prospects in his absurd little head. Jessie snubbed him without compunction. But he remained a faithful follower, and held on after Tom Redway, Joseph Ruddle, Sam Underwood, and Benjamin Polson, who owned the strawberry fields had fallen away.

Everyone liked Dicky Duck; he was always cheerful, obliging, and good-natured; a wonderfully active little fellow, who darted about like a squirrel, and, as already said, was ready to turn his hand to anything. But, though everyone liked Dicky, everyone laughed at him: partly because he was small; partly because he never resented being made fun of, and so was a safe person on whom to whet the wit; partly also because his fresh, cheery face was laughter-provoking, it had a natural comicality about it. He was not bad-looking, there was no deformity about him, but there was an indefinable something about his face which set those who observed it a-laughing. I had a pair of fire-screens once, on which were two heads with gaping mouths, and whoever took up one of these screens was set a-yawning; so everyone who took up and talked to Dicky Duck was set a-laughing. He was not brilliant, he never said a witty thing in his life, and yet he was a good companion, because he excited risibility in those he was with.

The tall, dignified, handsome Jessie Mullins was ill-pleased that this absurd little whipper-snapper should be her persistent admirer; it offended her self-esteem.

As yet nothing has been said of the nickname given to Jessie. It was a nickname that could not fail to attach to her, partly from her business, partly from her appearance and colour. She was called the Moth-Mullein, and it cannot be said that she disliked the nickname, for the Moth-Mullein is a stately plant, that stands up and shows itself off. She was not a modest retreating violet, not ordinary as a daisy, not fresh as a buttercup, not sweet as a rose; no, she was a Moth-Mullein, that stood by itself and held its head high.

CHAPTER II

Two huge chalk quarries, worked by separate companies, had been opened many years before in the hill near Moth-Mullein's cottage, and these quarries had eaten their way towards each other till only a neck of chalk divided them. A line had been drawn from the cottage in the direction of Stone church-tower, that stood high on the hill to the west, and a concession had been made to one company on the north and to another on the south of this line. The companies had been wide apart at one time, but as years advanced they approximated, and now only a curtain of rock divided them, and neither might break through into the rights of the other. The ridge was called the 'Back o' the Knife,' and extended about two hundred feet where it was narrowest, and there it was in places only about a foot wide at top. The soft rock was continually sliding away after thaws, and threatened in time to break the continuity of the Knife Back, and convert it into a saw. But that time had not yet come, and when the forester or his daughter wished to go to Dartford or Stone, the way taken was over the Knife Back, which saved a long round by the lane down to the high road, and thence by the road. In fact, it formed the hypothenuse of a triangle. The companies were trying to arrive at a compromise whereby they might get through this curtain, but each demanded too much of the other, and each thought by withdrawing it could make the other accede to its terms. So the Knife Back, though menaced, remained.

Over the Knife Back came Dicky Duck one day. Jessie saw him coming, and she said—

'You're not afraid of going along that way, it seems, but it is not a safe one.'

'I'm not afraid. My light heart carries me over.'

'I should have thought a heavy one would have steadied your feet best. What do you want here?'

'I have come to see your father.'

'Oh! not me?'

'Of course you, Moth, but your father also.'

'And what do you want with him?'

'I want him to speak a word for me to the Squire that I may be taken on as a woodsman. I know as much about trees as anyone. I've smeared their bark with treacle, and caught scores of moths off them. I ought to know trees.'

'And what will you do when you are taken on in the woods, supposing my father does put in a word for you?'

'I'll marry you next day, Moth,' said Dicky boldly.

'Will you? It takes two to do that. If that is to be the consequence, I will not ask my father to speak for you. You! Why you would have to stand on a chair to kiss me.'

'I can do that without the help of a chair,' said Dicky, and with a spring he was by her, had given a jump and caught her round the neck. In a moment he was sent spinning from her. She had given him a hearty box on his ears.

'Look what you have done, you ape!' she said.

She had been knitting a stocking; he had entangled his legs in the wool, pulled the stocking out of her hands, and unravelled a great part of her work.

'You come here full of impertinence,' said she angrily, 'and unravel what it has taken me an hour to knit. Go away at once over the Knife Back, and if you break your neck I'll not shed a tear.'

Little Dick Duck looked sadly at her, and in spite of her annoyance she laughed—not good-naturedly, but in a manner to wound him.

He went back over the ridge.

'There!' said she, 'he came hopping over with a light heart; I have sent him lagging back with a heavy one.'

It is a curious feature in the character of woman that she finds a positive pleasure in making man miserable. As the weakest emperors and the feeblest governors are the most tyrannical and cruel, so is it with woman; because she is weak she likes to convince herself of possessing strength; she does this by treading on worms and making them writhe. She says to herself, 'By nature it is true that I am feeble, but see how strong my beauty or my craft has made me! I can take that man and snap his heart as if it were a dry twig; I can bend and twist that other man about my finger as a piece of grass.' It is not that woman delights in cruelty—far from it. She is full of sympathy and tenderness; but then, when she has power, she likes to exert it, and she can only convince herself that she is a queen when she hears the screams of her victims.

Jessie Mullins looked after Richard Duck as he walked the Knife Back, with a proud curl on her lip. She knew that he was unhappy, disappointed, and wounded, and she asked herself, 'Could anyone else have clouded that gay countenance and brought a twitch of pain into the corners of that laughing mouth? That fellow's spirits are so high that there is no one—no one but me—who can sink him under water. I have put lead into that heart of cork, and he will keep down for a bit.'

As Dicky Duck disappeared, from the Greenhythe road by the lane came the Oxford scholar with a case for specimens.

At once Jessie rose with a smile, and put aside the unravelled stocking. She folded it up and put it in a drawer, and met the visitor with a smile.

'How do you do, Moth?' He held out both his hands.

'Come after moths?' she asked.

'Moth in the singular,' he answered. 'Who is he that says our British lepidoptera are deficient in beauty? Why here I have a Queen—the *Endromis versicolora*, the Kentish Glory—by the hand, by both, and am lost in admiration of her loveliness. Are you going to help me to catch moths in the wood this evening?'

'The Kentish Glory, sir, only flies by day.'

'Then where is that little rascal, Dick? I must have assistance.'

'I have just sent him over the Knife Back.'

'I will run after him.'

'Not for the world! You might fall and break your

neck, and then I——' she hesitated, looked down and coloured.

'Then you would—what?'

'Of course, Mr Parkinson, I should be miserable.'

'Thank you for your sympathy.' He put his hands one on each side of her face, with a sudden action drew it towards him, and kissed her.

'Halloo,! halloo! what is the meaning of this?' shouted old Mullins, coming up.

'Moth really provoked me to take a liberty,' laughed the young man. 'She was so troubled lest I should hurt myself if I went over the Knife Back, that in gratitude I could not restrain my emotion.'

'I'll trouble you to keep your emotions of gratitude within proper bounds,' said the woodman.

'Master Mullins,' said the young man, 'I want some one to come with me this evening after moths. Dick is away; will you carry the lantern?'

'Can't,' answered the father, 'and what is more, you had better keep out of the wood to-night. The poachers— desperate fellows—are coming in a gang. They've had the impudence to send word to the head keepers to look out for them; there is a large gang of them going to drive the wood. Can't say this night for certain, but some night in the week. They were in Swanscombe Wood yesterday, and no one durst stop them. There must have been ten or a dozen. We've been asked to help the keepers; we'll stop them if they come this way, and not give way as did them in Swanscombe. But they're desperate men, and there may be shots fired. So I say—keep out of the wood.'

'Not at all,' answered the Oxford man. 'I'll go with

you, and amuse myself looking out for moths whilst you
are looking out for poachers.'

'And I'll sit up,' said Moth-Mullein; 'I've got a beef-
steak pie, and I'll have potatoes ready, and hot water for
use when you both come back, that you may enjoy a good
supper.'

'Supper!' said her father, 'it will be breakfast rather;
we shall not be in till long over midnight.'

CHAPTER III

At the head-keeper's house were assembled all the under-keepers and those men who had been engaged to assist in watching the wood. A round of beef and ale had been provided for them. The party had regaled itself on the provisions, and waited to start for the wood.

'It's no use going too early,' said the head-gamekeeper; 'they won't come, if they come at all, for another hour.'

'I say, Finch, do you think Long Jaques will be there?'

'Sure.'

'Who is Long Jaques?' asked Mr Parkinson.

'Long Jaques! Why, Long Jaques,' answered one of the keepers; 'everyone knows Long Jaques; there ain't a more desperate blackguard in the county of Kent. I never will believe but it was he killed Tom Prentice.'

'Sure of it!' said the head-keeper, Finch.

'The fellow is so daring and crafty there is not a cover he has not been in and got a pheasant out of, and yet has never been caught.'

'I axed him t'other day,' said a man, 'whether he was working on the new line. "New line," said he, "at ninepence an hour! Thank you! when I can get ten rabbits a day, and sell them at ninepence, and have the sport thrown in.'"

'If he'd stick to rabbits I wouldn't mind,' said the head-keeper, Fred Finch.

'What brings you here?' asked Mr Parkinson of Richard Duck.

'No offence, but I might ax the same of you, sir, answered the little man. 'Lord, sir! I can run sharper than them that is bigger, and I see in the dark like a ferret.'

'What are you doing there, Mr Finch?' now asked the Oxford University man. He saw that the head-keeper was melting lead in an iron pan over the fire.

'Going to run a bullet or two,' answered the keeper; 'not, please God, that I shall use 'em, but with Long Jaques and two or three of them other ruffians about, I like to have a bullet to fall back on. I'll tell you a story of Long Jaques. I can't swear it is true, but I believe it is. The story is told of him, but it never could be brought home. You know his wife died, leaving him a little child of a year, or perhaps a month under. Sometimes when he went out after his snares, he took the baby with him. He went out one Sunday when his housekeeper was not at home, and he had to mind the child; he went into the nearest wood, of course, to see after a pheasant. He had just got sight of one sitting in a tree, gone to roost, for it was evening——'

'But why did he not leave the child at home?'

'Because the child would not go to sleep, so he took it out on his arm, and his gun in pieces in his pocket, on the chance of getting a shot. Sunday evening, he thought, no one would be about. He could not leave the babe alone in the cottage, and he could not keep at home when there was a chance of a pheasant. Now you understand?'

'Yes—go on.'

'Well. He saw a big cock roosting in a tree. So he put down the babe on the grass at his feet, screwed his gun softly together, loaded it—not too heavy, and pop—down came the cock pheasant. He picked the bird up, and was just clapping it into his pocket, when he heard voices. Two keepers were coming that way. They had heard the report. Long Jaques went into the bushes, picked up the child, and whispered, " Poll, not a sound. Hush, and be still." Then he stood back where the leaves were thickest and listened. He heard the tread of the men hard by, and heard what they said. One was sure that the crack of the gun had come from thereabouts. The other thought he smelt the powder. Then they saw where the grass was trampled, and one picked up some feathers of the bird. Long Jaques was mortal afraid the babe would squeal out, and let the keepers discover him. In his mind he darned his housekeeper for going to chapel that evening and leaving him with the child. He put his face down and whispered, and then drew his coat round the little creature. Then he heard her make a little noise and begin to struggle to get the arms out ; but he drew his coat the tighter, and ever tighter, as the keepers kept prowling near. Curiously enough they did not see him, but it was some while before Jaques could loosen his coat, and let the child out from under cover—not till their voices had died away in the distance. Then he saw the babe had gone to sleep—but it was to a sleep past waking—he'd suffocated her! So he took home a shot cock pheasant and a stifled hen babe—that came o' poaching on a Sunday.'

'It was 'crowned, I suppose?' asked one man.

'To be sure, it was 'crowned and sat on, but the true story never came out at the inquest. That got wind afterwards. Long Jaques told it of himself, when he was drunk, and many a curse did he send after those two who had disturbed him that Sunday, and led to his smothering his child.'

'And who were these two?'

'Mullins, there, and me. Now you know why I think it well to-night to have a bullet by me. Jaques is not particular and like to deal tenderly by either of us, if he recognises us.'

'I say, keeper,' interposed Mr Parkinson, 'as you are not using all that molten lead, let us have some of it.'

'What for?'

'It is All-Hallow E'en,' answered the young man. 'In Scotland, whence I come, we make a great deal of to-night, and run lead into water, and find out what our fortunes will be for the ensuing year by the shapes the lead takes in water.'

'That's all gammon,' said Finch.

'Of course it is gammon, but as we have an hour to spend here before the moon rises, we can have some fun out of it. Let Dicky Duck try his fortune first.'

The proposal created interest. A bowl of water was procured and set in the middle of the table, and an iron ladle or spoon heated, and dipped in the molten lead. The men, laughing, talking, chaffing each other, crowded round the table.

'Who shall try first?   Dicky Duck?'

'No,' said Mullins, 'give it me.'

He took the ladle, and poured the lead into the water. It fell fizzing, and sent up a puff of steam.

Then there ensued shouts of laughter, and guesses and queries.   The lead was too hot to be extracted immediately.

'What is it?   A tree?   A house?   A wife?   A bag of money?   A son-in-law?   Eh, Mullins?'

James Mullins put his hand in and drew forth the lead. It had formed a compact, oblong mass.

'It looks to me ·uncommon like a coffin,' said he. 'Thank heaven, I lay no store by such things, or I'd not go out to-night and face Long Jaques.'

'Now it is your turn, Dick.'

The lead was again melted, and little Dick got on a chair, stood above the table, and let the fluid metal pour down from a height into the bowl.   Again a burst of queries, guesses, and jokes.

The lead was extracted from the water; he had poured it in two masses, and two separate formations were in the water.

'What is this?' he asked, holding up the largest mass, which was shapeless.

'It looks to me like a dragon,' laughed the head-keeper, Finch.

'And the other?'   That was passed from hand to hand, and one conjecture after another was made concerning it.

'It is—a pair of hearts, a pair o' linked hearts,' shouted one of the keepers.

'To be sure it is, but look,' said Parkinson—'both broken!'

CHAPTER IV

THAT night there was an affray with the poachers, an affray
that was much talked of, and one about which the newspapers gave leaders.

Towards nightfall the keepers had been through Darenth
Wood, and had driven the pheasants towards the path, or
road, that traversed the wood from Greenhythe to the
village of Darenth on the further side of the hill. Their
object in doing this was to get the pheasants to roost on
trees beside the open road, where, in the event of the
poachers coming after them, they could be most easily surrounded and caught. In the depths of the wood it might
be hard to seize them, and it would be less easy to identify
them ; but if the fellows came along the road and popped
at the birds in the trees on each side, they would be perfectly visible to those in conccalment watching for them,
and it would be easy to cut off their retreat along the road
by throwing a body of men across it. A good deal was
made by some papers of this action of the keepers. It was
represented that they had laid a trap and baited it for
inoffensive men ; the keepers provoked them to commit an

illegal act, and then precipitated themselves upon them. On this text much indignation was expressed at the game laws ; and the wealthy were held up to reprobation for reserving wild birds and beasts for their own table, and allowing the poor and deserving to starve whilst abundance was within their reach.

As it happened, the poachers belonged to a set—a set which lived on poaching, which moved about the country from place to place, and which supplied, or helped to supply, the London market with game. The men had no other business—they lived by poaching. They slept or loafed about by day. Where navvies were engaged on a line they followed them, and brought these hardworking and generally honest men into disrepute. It was said that the navvies were desperate poachers. This was not so. The gang followed the navvies, and its components were men who never willingly did a bit of honest work—scorned the hard toil to which the navvy bowed his back. They lived by night sport, and let the navvies bear the blame of their misdeeds. Sometimes—so bold did these gangs become— they sent warning beforehand to the head-gamekeeper of my Lord or of Squire Acres, to say that they were going to visit his covers. Then the keepers had to consider whether they would muster a large force and go out against them, or keep close and let them do their worst. By no means infrequently the latter course was pursued. An affray with these rascals led to serious results. Shots were exchanged, blows dealt, and lives were lost. When the head-gamekeeper came to my Lord or to Squire Acres and said, 'I have had notice that the gang is coming. There are daring devils among them—Long Jaques for one, who smothered his child rather than be took,' then my Lord or Squire Acres said, 'Well, well, don't let there be a row and bloodshed. Go to bed, go to bed. They can't exterminate the game.'

But in this instance the head-keeper was not willing to go to bed, and the Squire was inclined to have the poaching stopped. He had reared the pheasants, and he calculated that they had cost him a guinea a-piece. 'I don't see,' said he, 'why I should let a man pick my pocket without trying to stop him,' and he was right. If the landowners had combined, and altogether had said 'The gang must be put down,' it would have been put down; but so many were timorous that the gang gathered courage, strength, and audacity.

This night—this All-Hallow E'en—there was an affray that created a sensation. It created a sensation both because one man was shot dead in it, and also because the man who killed the other was caught and carried to gaol, and that man was Long Jaques. He who was killed was Mullins the woodman, and he who revenged his death by catching the murderer was little Dicky Duck.

If the man shot had been a poacher, what an outcry would have been made!—what commiseration, what political capital would have been made out of his murder! But as the man shot was only a fellow acting for the nonce as a keeper, there was not much fuss made about him. All the Radicals said, 'Serve him right!'

This is how it came about.

The poachers had come along the road and had fired at three of the pheasants, when the gamekeepers and their party appeared and surrounded them. There were thirteen poachers, and all strong, desperate men. They turned to break their way through. The moon was shining. Long Jaques was face to face with Mullins, and the moon was on Mullins' face.

Jaques uttered a curse. 'It's you, you dog, who made me smother my kid!' he said; put his gun to his mouth and shot him dead. Then he made a leap to pass the man as he fell, and in another moment would have got into the coppice and have escaped, had not Dicky Duck been too alert for him. In an instant he was after him, gave a leap, was on the poacher's back, clung, and would not be shaken off. Jaques could not easily get at the adversary who was on his back, and who kicked him in the sides and fastened his grip with all his strength about the throat of the poacher, compressing the windpipe that he could not gasp. Jaques became bewildered, ran against the trees to beat off his little assailant, tried to wrench his hands away, but was unable. Duck clung like a ferret to a rat, and screamed for help, till Jaques, stumbling over a root, fell prostrate in the wood. Then the poacher would easily have mastered Dicky, had not some of the keepers come to his assistance, rescued the plucky little man, and bound the poacher.

Moth-Mullein had the kettle on the fire puffing steam, and the potatoes on the boil. The table was spread, the cold beef-steak pie was on it, and her father's pewter tankard, brightly polished, reflected the firelight. Moth knew how to make a table look well. She had had experience. In the middle was a glass full of crisp, nutty celery; there was a piece of American cheese ready, and, balancing it, a plate of tartlets of her own making.

A little after midnight her father was brought home,

dead. Finch came first to break the news to her. Mr
Parkinson followed with the body. Moth bore the shock
better than might have been expected: she was deadly
pale; but she was a girl of nerve and self-control, and she
did not go into hysterics.

'I am very, very grieved,' said Mr Parkinson, looking
out of the corners of his eyes at the beef-steak pie. 'This
is most dreadful. You have my deepest sympathy. Dicky
Duck behaved like a man,' then he left. The young man
was quite out of his element in a house of sorrow and
bereavment; he really was grieved, but he was at a loss to
know what to say, and how to console the girl. 'I must
come after the funeral and see her,' he said to himself;
'what a bore that matters should have turned out like
this! I must take care not to compromise myself. She is
awfully pretty, but I'm not a fool.'

Dicky Duck remained. He was of the greatest assistance
to Jessie. He ran messages for her. He found an old
woman to lay out the corpse, and to keep her company.
He contrived about the inquest, he saw the undertaker
about the coffin, he arranged for the funeral. He would
have ordered the mourning for Jessie had she suffered him.
What would Jessie have done without the help of Dicky?
She did not consider that it would have been inconvenient
for her, had he not been at her beck and call. She did not
consider that he gave up his work and wage to attend her.
She was grateful to him in a cold, ungracious manner only
for having arrested her father's murderer. And the reason
why her gratitude was ungracious was because Dicky had
caught Long Jaques in such a grotesque manner, so that
when anyone spoke of the capture a flicker of a smile

passed over his face. At the inquest, when the evidence was taken, and it came to the account of the taking of the poacher, there was a general laugh, and the coroner and jury laughed with the public. It was not possible to avoid laughing,—the idea of little Dick clinging to the poacher's back, kicking him in the wind with his heels, and grabbing his throat with his hands was vastly ludicrous, especially when the little man was present with his comical face drawn in an effort to look sad.

Jessie was angry with Dick because he had not stopped her father's murderer in a more heroic and dignified, or romantic, manner. The sense of his absurdity irritated her, and his very officiousness, though she accepted his services, helped to annoy her. She could not well do without his help, and she wished some one else—Mr Parkinson for instance—had been there instead to minister to her wants.

Mr Parkinson did not reappear till after the funeral. Then he called in a black coat with a hat, not his usual 'billicock.'

He seemed shy. In fact he did not know what to say. He was unaccustomed to paying visits of condolence.

'What are you going to do, if I may ask, Moth?'

'I shall have to leave this house,' she answered, and sobbed. 'It will go to the new woodman.'

'Where are you likely to go to? Have you any nice relations?'

'I have no relations at all—that is, none whom I could stay with.'

'But you have friends?'

'Friends'—hesitatingly—'yes, but I cannot go to them unless they ask me.'

'I hope you are not left badly off?'

'Of course I must work for my living. I should like to live near this wood and go on collecting moths and butter-flies, but that would not be enough to support me, I fear.'

'And you have no one who can put in the claim of a near and dear tie?' Mr Parkinson turned red. He was really sorry for the girl, and also much afraid of compro-mising himself. 'I mean—I thought that Dicky Duck—'

'Sir—Mr Parkinson!'

'I meant no offence. I have a suggestion to make. It occurred to me. It may have occurred to you. Why not go as one of the girls in a refreshment room at a railway station? It seems to me you are just the right sort of person for that, very good-looking, and like to chaff with young chaps, and don't mind a little cheek. You are cut out for it.'

'Mr Parkinson! is this all you have to say to me?'

'Yes, Moth. No offence meant. 'Pon my word I have been thinking a lot about you, and I do believe you were made for a refreshment room—and now the new line is being finished——'

Jessie rose, white with anger, and left the room.

Somewhat abashed, Mr Parkinson came outside the house. Dicky was there.

'I say, Dick,' said he, 'the lead told true—a coffin for old father Mullins.'

'Yes, but not so for me. I got a dragon, and St. George

killed the last of them.   And two hearts, but I've got only one on the right and none at all on the left.'

'And both broken.   No, Dicky, your heart is in the right place, and like mine, sound.'

'I take it, that matter of the lead is all rubbish.'

'Who can say?   Wait till next Hallow E'en.'

CHAPTER V

THE road from the Forester's Cottage to Greenhythe Church happened, curiously enough, to lie between the grounds occupied by certain of Moth-Mullein's admirers. The farm of the Underwoods was at the corner where the lane joined the main road. The house was a substantial modern one, square, with a stack of chimneys in the middle, and the slated roof drawn together from all sides to the stack, without showing a gable anywhere. It was one of those houses in which people of no taste delight, because so compact, but which are eyesores to such as have a sense of beauty, houses which, even when ugliness-hating Nature reduces them to ruins, will never make even picturesque ruins. With the advance of civilisation and cultured taste, and with increased facilities for the employment of dynamite, all these abominations will disappear ; the men of culture and light will go about the country and blow them up for the common good.

It was, however ugly, a snug house, and the farm was a good farm. As Jessie Mullins followed the hearse in which her father was conveyed to the churchyard, seated in a

mourning cab, she looked over her white pocket-hand-
kerchief at the Underwoods' farm, and saw that Sam was
standing in the gate with his hat off, watching the mourn-
ful procession. Perhaps he would forgive her for having
sent him away because she flirted with Mr Parkinson—that
is, if Mr Parkinson did not offer her consolation. Further
along the road was Joseph Ruddle's shop. Joseph was a
carpenter, with a good business, a handy man, steady—
never drunk. He had been thrown back by breaking his
leg in going after the Cinxia caterpillars for her. Perhaps
he would be on the look-out—yes, he was. Jessie over her
handkerchief saw him with his paper cap on his head,
flattening his nose against the window of his workshop.
Who could tell? Other things more unlikely might happen
than that young Ruddle should offer her to share his home,
and love her all the more dearly because she had broken
his leg. He was a good-looking fellow ; Jessie rather liked
him. True he belonged to a lower stage on the social ladder
than Sam Underwood, and Sam Underwood was a rung
lower than Mr Parkinson, who was a brewer's son. By
the side of the main road, on the side opposite the carpenter's shop, were the strawberry-fields of Ben Polson.
He was a heavy, stout fellow with a flat face, who walked
about with his hands in his pockets ; he, however, looked
after his interests well, and in the time of strawberries was
active, and drew his hands out. Well—if Mr Parkinson
did not propose to make her Mrs Parkinson, she would
have Sam Underwood, and if Sam Underwood still sulked,
she would waive the difference in social standing between
the other two, and for the sake of his handsome face and
general steadiness take Joe Ruddle. If, however, his

broken leg made the carpenter halt in his love-making, she could always fall back on Ben Polson. Sure enough, there by the side of his hedge, with his hands in his pockets, was Ben, looking on at the funeral train, and—dolt that he was !—had forgotten to take off his hat, or thought, because he was on the other side of the hedge, that it was not necessary. That, in the time of her bereavement, she would not be overwhelmed with offers from these chivalrous young men did not occur to her. They had all admired her ; it was true they had turned sulky, but then lovers' quarrels are proverbially short, and are, as the Eton Latin grammar says, ' the reintegration of love.'

Jessie cried a great deal for her father. She had really loved him, and was genuinely grieved at his sad end. But to all bitters, by a merciful provision of nature, there comes some sweet, and every cloud is given a silver lining ; so Jessie thought that perhaps—nay, certainly—her great sorrow must lead to her advantage in the end. Some one or other of her lovers would—she did not put it in words, but she thought it—' come to the scratch.'

As already shown in last chapter, Mr Parkinson did not at all come to the scratch, or only came within a near risk of getting his face scratched because he proposed that Jessie should become waitress at a refreshment-stall, instead of becoming Mrs Parkinson. Nor did Sam Underwood rise to the occasion. He still harboured his grudge. Nor did Joseph Ruddle ; the lane was wet and rough, and he would not risk his leg on it. Nor did Ben Polson ; he took time to think about it, and his hand was not available ; it was in his pocket. So weeks passed, and Jessie was without a prospect of a fixed home. Little Dicky Duck had applied for the situation of woodman, vacated by old Mullins, and had got it.

'At Lady-day,' said Dick, 'I shall have this house. I don't want to turn you out, Moth; why should you not put your hand in mine, say the word—be my Duck and stay on?'

'Because I'm not come down so low as that woman who

> '"Had a little husband
> No taller than her thumb
> She set him in a pint-pot
> And bid him drum."'

'No offence meant, Moth; but as you have been accustomed to this house all your life—'

'I suppose I am tired of it, and wish for a change.'

'Why, Moth? I get now the wages your father had, fourteen shillings a week; the cottage I shall have—and then—'

'O, if you are calculating on the cottage, I will turn out at Christmas. You need not wait till Lady-day. I'll have a sale, and the house shall be clear for you then.'

'I wouldn't hasten you for the world, Moth. I don't want you to leave the house, nor lose your sticks of furniture, but take me—'

'I wonder that you can have the face to make such a proposal, so soon after my father's death.'

Moth-Mullein's temper did not improve that winter. She was subjected to slights, and was the victim of disappointment. She was constrained to leave her house, and she had not means of earning a livelihood. Partly because she would not be indebted to Dick, but also because she could not afford to be idle, she was led to the resolve to

have a sale at Christmas, and to vacate the cottage.
Though she made light to Dick of leaving, she was sore at
heart. When she knew that go she must, the cottage all
at once became dear to her, and the retrospect over her
past life presented to her singular charms. She had been
very happy on the edge of the wood, and very interested
in her work collecting moths and butterflies.

She was vexed with herself, but would not admit to herself that she had acted foolishly. She had trifled with her
chances and had lost them. Neither Sam Underwood, nor
Joseph Ruddle, no, nor Benjamin Polson showed tokens of
relieving her from her difficulties by offering her the shelter
of his name and roof.

Christmas Eve arrived; she had been down into Greenhythe to see the auctioneer. The sale was to take place
two days after Christmas. It might not be on Christmas
Day, and the day following was a Bank-holiday. Moth
had also been about inquiring for lodgings, and had been
unsuccessful. Greenhythe is a place which in certain
seasons is very full of yachting men and their families.
These guests are ready to pay a good price for lodgings,
and those who have lodgings to let are indisposed to let
them for a permanency at a low rent; they prefer a short
and rich harvest in yachting time. Moth did not wish to
leave the neighbourhood, because she desired still to collect
lepidoptera for her usual customers. The pay was not
great, but it was something, and something certain. Besides, it was an occupation she liked.

The days close in fast at Christmas, and, as it happened,
that Christmas Eve was murky. The weather was rough,
with a south-west wind, and heavy clouds discharging every

now and then rain, and the darkness settled in earlier than Moth had anticipated.

The wind had shifted a little, a few points more to the north, whilst she was out, and after she left Greenhythe on her way home—to a dismantled and solitary home—the darkness fell like ink about her, and a storm of rain came on, so driving and so cold that Jessie took refuge from it in an old kiln that stood beside the road. The kiln-mouth was large, vaulted, and the shelter it afforded perfect. She retreated to the back part of it and seated herself on an overturned broken barrow, to wait till the storm had swept away and the sky was lighter.

As she sat there her utter disconsolateness made itself felt. She must vacate the cottage in three days, sell all her furniture, and be homeless. She had not settled whither to go. No friends had come forward to help her. Her pride had offended the young women who might have been her friends, and her want of consideration had alienated the men who might have offered her their homes. But it must not be supposed that Jessie blamed herself. She was bitter at heart against all the world. The fault was in her neighbours, her suitors, her acquaintance, not in herself.

Then, as she sat brooding, angry in soul, and with knit brows, she heard voices of men talking, and, a moment later, three persons entered the old kiln-mouth. As they talked she recognised them.

'I say, Underwood,' said the voice of Ben Polson, 'we shall do in here. What a slashing shower! It can't last long. I've just mulched my beds, and, darn it, this flood will wash all the goodness away into the runnels, and carry it to the Thames. What I like is a soft drizzle—*that* carries the goodness into the ground and nourishes the roots.'

'I'm glad to be out of the storm,' said the third, and the voice was that of the carpenter. 'Since I've broke my leg I get twinges of rheumatic in it.'

'I guess it is just as well you broke your leg instead of your heart about Miss Moth-Mullein,' said Underwood.

'Rather so,' was the reply. 'If I'd married her, she'd have broken my life, she's that giddy and cruel and self-willed. But, Sam Underwood, I thought you were after her?'

'So I was, but there were too many after her, and she kept our Oxford scholar skipping about her, and I didn't like that.'

'And I was after her, too,' said Polson slowly. 'I say, mates, what larks! she's been trying to splice broken ties. She sent to say she'd be glad to earn a few shillings by weaving strawberry pottles; but I wasn't to be taken in by that. I answered that I bought 'em wholesale, by the thousand.'

There ensued a laugh.

'And she's been down every day to my farm for a ha'porth of milk, thinking that she might find me in the way some evening, and the ha'porth of milk would bring the cow and the stable and the house and the farm and Sam Underwood. I keep out of the way. I see through her little games.'

'And she has ordered of me a couple of boxes for her clothes and them odds and ends as don't go into the sale,' said Joseph Ruddle. 'She thinks we're moths to be caught, she's such a dab hand at hunting; but we're wary coves—eh, Sam? eh, Ben? In vain is the net spread in sight of the bird.'

'The rain is ceasing, I'm off,' said Underwood.

'So be we,' said the others.

When the three men were gone, Moth put her head down on her knees and burst into tears, tears of shame and wrath. She had been unjustly treated. She had not hunted these three men; she had really needed milk, really needed boxes, really needed work. In her inner mind she had hoped that one or other of the three would come and throw himself at her feet, but she had not asked for milk, boxes, and pottle-plaiting in order to bring them there. She was very angry with all three; so angry, that had any one of them come back and offered himself to her she would have rejected him disdainfully.

She had been sobbing for some time, when again she heard steps, and again someone entered the kiln-mouth.

'Brrh!' said a voice, 'I must shake myself like a dog. The wind is so high I cannot light a pipe out there, and I must dry my fingers before I can get at the lucifers.'

The voice was that of Dicky Duck.

The girl shrank further back. She put one hand over her mouth, the other she pressed against her bosom, to check the sobs. She would not for the world be found there by Dicky Duck.

Then, whilst his fingers were drying, he began to whistle. Dick had a sweet pipe, and he whistled with taste and in tune. He whistled now 'Home, sweet home!'

All at once a compressed, struggled-against sob broke from the heart of Jessie.

Dick stopped his whistling.

Another sob. Now the convulsive emotion had got beyond her control.

'There's someone there, someone crying!' exclaimed Dicky. 'Who is it?'

No answer.

'Anyone unwell?'

No answer.

'Tell me who you are? I will not hurt you.'

No answer.

Then Dicky stepped in as far as he could go in the dark, and fumbled for his match-box, and struck a lucifer.

The match flared up and filled the white vault with light. Dick stood with it in his fingers, motionless, looking with open, astonished eyes at the girl.

'Why,' said he slowly, 'it is Moth! Moth crying!'

He held the lucifer till the flame reached and burnt his finger, then he threw it away.

'Moth,' said he, when they were again in darkness.

She did not answer him.

'Moth,' said he again, with pity and tenderness in his voice. 'I won't say nothing to you till you've got over them there hickups.'

Presently she felt something on her face. He had removed the silk kerchief from about his throat, and with it was gently wiping the tears from her cheeks.

'Lord,' said he, 'it have been raining, and has wetted you, awful.'

Still she said nothing.   Her sobs ceased at last.

'Now them hickups is over, said he, 'suppose you stand up, Moth, and give me your arm, and——Lord! Moth, never another word, there'll be no sale, you ain't going to leave the cottage.   You unpack whatever you have put away, and we'll be married.   Why, I put it to you.   If you was to leave this part of the country, the moths and the caterpillars and the butterflies and the grubs of every description would multiply to that enormous extent, that the plagues of Egypt would be child's play to the state of Greenhythe.   For the good of your native country and for the keeping down of warmint you must remain and become Mrs Dicky Duck.'

'Very well,' said Jessie after a pause, 'on one condition.'

'And what is that?'

'That we have a grand wedding.'

'We'll have the wedding as soon as the three banns have been called.'

'Banns!' exclaimed Jessie.   'You don't mean that we are to be married by banns?   We must have a licence.'

'That will cost a lot of money,' said Dick, 'and won't make us faster together than banns.'

'It is grander,' said the girl.

'There's one advantage in our being married and that so soon after your father's death, that it must be quiet.'

'Did you not hear?   I made it a condition we should be married in style.'

'But why so, Moth, when we're humble folk, and after what has happened hardly proper?'

'Because, Richard, I want to show Sam Underwood, and Ben Polson, and Joseph Ruddle, aye, and Tom Redway, too, and Mr Parkinson, who is here because it is his vacation, that we can do handsomely without them. That we can have a carriage——'

'A carriage, Moth!'

'To be sure, a carriage and white favours, and everything of the best.'

'It will cost a lot of money. We needn't have a carriage. Think, Moth. It won't cost less than a pound.'

'A carriage and pair,' said Jessie. 'I'll be taken to church in a carriage, and from church in a carriage, and in a carriage with a pair we will go on our honeymoon.'

'I don't think we can go anywhere,' said Dicky; 'it will come expensive.'

'We must go and do all in style, so as to let those fellows see that we have money to spend as well as they.'

'But I have not the money, Moth.'

'Then you must borrow it. A carriage and pair, and white favours, and a honeymoon I will have'—she stamped impatiently. 'Do you think I want *you*? I want a stylish wedding, and I take you for the sake of the wedding, and to make these men open their eyes.'

Moth Mullein carried her point. She was poor, she had nothing but her father's furniture, and Dicky was poor, except in prospect of a good wage for tending to the woods. He had no money laid by, but Jessie would listen to no excuses. To satisfy her Dick had to borrow money, to borrow the carriage and horses of the host of the 'Blue Boar,' with promise to pay when he could. When the wedding took place Jessie drove to church, and drove slowly

in state past the farm of Sam Underwood, the shop of
Joseph Ruddle, the strawberry field of Ben Polson, and the
plasterer's yard of Tom Redway; yes, and past Mr Parkinson too, who stood on the kerb of his door and threw rice
after her.

'Now,' said Jessie, with flashing eye, 'now do you understand, Dick, why I insisted on a grand wedding?'

'No, I do not, Moth.'

'Because I wouldn't have them say I took up with you
because I could get no other: because, also, if we didn't do
it in style they might have laughed at such a handsome,
tall girl as I am taking such a cock-sparrow as you. But
they can't laugh when they see us drive away as gentle-
folks in a carriage and pair.'

'It'll cost a lot of money,' sighed Dick.

'There is one thing more,' said Jessie as she laid aside
her bonnet and fumbled in her pocket. 'Do you remember
unravelling a stocking I was knitting one day?'

'I cannot say I do remember.'

'But *I* do. Here it is!' She held it under his eyes—in
his face. Now I'll take care that you are paid out for unravelling that stocking.'

CHAPTER VII

A year had passed since the woodman had been shot.
Dicky Duck was in the cottage ; Jessie had not made his
life more cheerful. The mouth that was formerly puckered
with smiles was now drawn and compressed. It really
looked as though Dicky were on the edge of a cry rather
than on the brim of a laugh.

There is a child's toy that represents a number of feathery
birds on a platform on wheels. When the little thing is
thrust or drawn along, a quill is set in motion that strikes
fine wires and catgut. The little birds are on the quiver,
and then ensues a twittering and chirping as though
they were all singing. Dicky's heart had been like this
hitherto ; anyone could set it in motion, and produce a
twittering and chirping that provoked laughter. But the
strings and wires must have been broken or relaxed,
or the quill tongue out of order, for now, either no
merry sound at all issued from him, or only a plaintive
little tweet ! tweet ! such as a shivering finch gives forth
when hail and frost have stripped the trees and made the
face of the land desolate. The spring had gone out of the

little man's walk, the straightness from his back, the sparkle from his eye, the whistle from his lips.

Poor little Dicky Duck! What had altered him? Not the getting of regular employ with the weight of responsibility for the young trees. There was nothing else to account for it but his marriage. Jessie made no attempt to curb her tongue. She cast jibes at him, scorned him for his smallness of stature, turned contrary when he was merry, distorted his funny little sayings and gave them an ill-natured turn, as though they were thrusts aimed at her, when nothing was further from his thoughts than to break a lance with his wife. His light-heartedness was made a cause of reproof; his amiability was treated as callousness. Every day some scornful allusion was made to the ridiculous manner in which he had caught Long Jaques, and Dicky heartily wished he had let Long Jaques escape.

Moth was a disappointed woman, and her disappointment had soured her. Did she love Dicky? Who can say? Love expresses itself in various ways. Love in some is tender, considerate, pitiful. In others it is exacting and cruel. Yes, there is a fashion of love that is ashamed to own itself, but wraps itself up in hardness and defiance. There is a story of a princess who was clothed in gold, but over the gold brocade she drew a vesture of horsehair and hog's skin. Everyone thought she was a wild woman, and those who came near her were scratched; but one day, through a rift in the coarse outer covering, the gleam of the gold shot, and then it was seen that she was a princess in disguise. Was there an under-vesture of cloth of gold, the fine gold of true love, in Jessie? If so she covered it up and hid it, chief of all from her husband, lest he should surmise its existence.

'It is a year to-night since your father died,' said Dick, 'and just about eight months since we were married.'

'Ah! I have cause to know that; afflictions never come singly. First I lost my father, then I got you.'

'I've a mind to stay at home to-night, and not leave you to your sorrowful thoughts, Moth.'

'I do not want you. Go again if you like to the "Blue Boar." You seem to be most at home there.'

'Well,' said Dicky, 'I can't say that, exactly, but, you see, I meet them old friends, and they ain't sharp on me, but uncommon kind. And then, Moth, I haven't yet paid for the carriage and pair, and I must keep the landlord in good humour, lest he press for payment. That carriage and pair do weigh on me like lead.'

But he hesitated whether to go or not. He waited for a word from her to make him stay.

'Moth,' said he, 'I shall go round by Greenhythe. I must fetch a bundle of tarred cord for the trees.'

He would have given a year of his life—a leap-year, even, which has a day extra—for a good word from her, but none came. Then he went away, with a heavy tread. She heard his steps; how they dragged!—there was no elasticity in them now.

After he was gone, it suddenly occurred to her that since the rain of the preceding night a portion of the Knife Back had given way. It would be dangerous to cross it in the dark. Would Dicky venture on this when he returned from the 'Blue Boar'? In her sullen mood she muttered, 'If he does it will serve him right for going away from me

—on such a night as this.'   But she did not mean what she said, not in the depth of her heart; and because she did not mean it, without staying to cover her head she ran out of the cottage after him, down the lane, to give the caution. She had delayed too long before starting in pursuit, for he was not in the lane.   She came out on the road, and almost ran among some men who stood there in a cluster.   Their heads were turned in an opposite direction, and they did not observe her; but she recognised them, and to escape being seen slipped into the mouth of the old kiln.   She did not wish to be caught running after her husband, and running after him with nothing over her head.

The men were Mr Parkinson, Sam Underwood, Joseph Ruddle, and Ben Polson.   Dusk had fallen, and in the kilnmouth all was dark.   Jessie heard the voices approach it, and as once before, so now she drew back into the depths.

'I say,' said Mr Parkinson, 'it is warmer here out of the east wind.   Are any of you going to the "Blue Boar" to-night?   There's Dicky Duck trotting off there, not knowing what is in store for him.'

'What is in store for him?' asked the carpenter.

'Don't you know, Ruddle?   Well, I dare say you do not.   It has been kept quiet that the surprise may be complete. ' Some of us who were with him this day last year, when he took that scoundrel Jaques, also the Squire and some others, have clubbed together to make him a testimonial—a beautiful clock, with a silver plate let in on the stand, engraved with a few lines, to show it is a mark of esteem for his pluck and readiness.   He has been told to come to the "Blue Boar" to-night, but has no notion that the Squire will be there to present him with the testimonial, and that he'll be the lion of the evening. I am going.'

'I fancy something ought to accompany the clock,' said Underwood. 'The poor little chap is under water with the extravagance of that fool of a wife of his, who would have a grand wedding, with a carriage and pair. I've heard the host of the "Boar" say that was never paid for, and he believes the reason why Dick is so down-hearted now is because he is in debt.'

'I think we're all of one mind,' said Ben Polson, 'that we owe him something—we who've not been asked to subscribe to a testimonial of which nobody told us anything. First, because we all respect the little man ; though small in body he is big in heart. Second, because he tackled what was worse than Long Jaques—the Dragon of Darenth.'

'The Dragon of Darenth has been too much for him,' said the carpenter. 'It is my opinion that it is because of *her* he is so altered in looks and spirits, not because he is in debt. Lord! we had a lucky escape, all of us.'

'I say, mates,' spoke Sam Underwood, 'shall we send the cap round here in the kiln to raise a little sum among us to pay for the coach and pair and the white favours ? Mr Parkinson has already subscribed to the testimonial.'

'But my thankfulness at my escape from the Dragon is not exhausted. I insist on adding my mite. Take my hat and pass it round.'

Jessie heard the clink of coin. Her face was on fire. She nearly choked with anger. Her heart beat so furiously that it was a wonder it did not reveal her presence.

'I must tell you a joke,' said Mr Parkinson. 'On this night, a twelvemonth ago, Dick and I, old James Mullins, and the keepers, were in Mr Finch's waiting to go after the poachers, and some took to running lead to find out their fortunes.   What do you think Mullins ran?'

'I've heard,' said Underwood, 'a coffin.'

'And that is what he got.   Dick ran the lead next, and he ran—a Dragon!'

There followed a burst of laughter, and a general exclamation of 'And that he has got.'

'There was something more he ran in lead,' continued the Oxford man.   'He ran two broken hearts in lead—linked together.'

'One broken heart is accounted for already,' said Underwood.   'His wife has pretty nigh broke his—but the other!'

'The other can't be hers,' said the carpenter.   'For why? He is that gentle and considerate he would not say a word or do a thing to hurt her.'

'For why?' put in Ben of the strawberries.   'Her heart is too hard ever to be broke.'

This elicited another burst of merriment.

Then the men went forth.

Jessie, angered, ashamed, with burning head and bounding heart, rushed out and ran up the lane to her cottage, and threw herself on her bed, with her hands over her eyes, tossing, muttering, then at length with the tears of mortification streaming between her fingers.   She was no longer the Moth-Mullein, but the Dragon of Darenth.   Her husband was in high esteem, and she—she was despised and disliked.   What had her grand wedding, with carriage and pair, brought her?   Ridicule; and the cost of the luxury was defrayed by her slighted suitors.

CHAPTER VIII

NEVER—no, never, was a man more taken aback, more utterly amazed, than was Dicky Duck when he found himself an honoured guest at the 'Blue Boar,' where a supper was spread, and the Squire himself was present to hand over to him, in behalf of some of those who valued his excellent character and esteemed his courage, a Testimonial of Respect and Regard.

What for?

For his daring conduct on the night of the murder of old Jim Mullins.

Dicky looked from side to side, opened his mouth, but never a word came from it. He turned white with astonishment and emotion. *He* given a testimonial for *that?* Why that was an act thrown daily in his teeth at home, a subject of daily humiliation. Heartily ashamed of himself had Dicky Duck become, because he had jumped on the poacher's back, kicked him in the wind, and behaved altogether ridiculously. Whenever he had heard an allusion to that affair, in the tavern, or among his acquaintances, he had winced. He supposed that others viewed his conduct in the same light as did Moth, his wife. If it had not been for her—that he was tied to her, and bound to look after her, to support her, and make her happy—he would have run away to America where he might be out of hearing any more of the capture of Long Jaques in Darenth Wood.

Dicky looked at the Squire, then at Mr Parkinson, who sat at the Squire's right hand, then at Finch, the head-keeper, who sat on the Squire's left; then at a fly that sat on the ceiling immediately over the Squire's head; and then with an expression of distress at the host of the inn, who stood behind the Squire, and was making a trumpet of his hands, and sounding a hoarse stage-whisper through it, of 'Say something.'

Dicky knew he must say something, but every object spun round with him, and the Adam's apple in his throat went up and down like the knob of a piston in a steamer and choked him. But at length he became sufficiently composed to gasp 'Thank-y,' gentlemen '—he touched his forelock—'I can't underconstumble it noways, a little chap like me—no higher than her thumb, as was ordained to be put in a pint-pot and forced to drum; as made himself a laughing stock and mockery, and made a fool of himself—but I fancy, gentlemen, you're now poking fun at me ? '

'No, no, no ! Go on, Dicky; bravo ! '

'It can't be for me.'—again he touched his forelock—'more of a monkey than a man—who can't do anything but he must do it absurdly; who——'

There welled up in his memory the many harsh, cutting,

cruel things that his wife had said, and which he had accepted from her lips as his due.

'Gentlemen,' said he, 'I'm that amazed, I ax you of your great kindness to let me run home and take this here clock with the beautiful silver plate and inscription, and show it to my missus. And——'he saw the host thrusting a paper into his hand; he looked at it. The host was not perfect in his orthography, but Dicky understood what was written :—

'For a Carridge and Pear, etceterer,
'Sottled.'

'Gentlemen,' he looked at the paper, 'I'm that upset I shall be unwell unless I run home, and show 'em to Moth-Mullein—show her the beautiful clock and the silver plate, and last, not least, "For a Carridge and Pear, Sottled."'

His voice was quivering, his eyes filling.

'Yes, let him go,' said the Squire. 'He is right. He must go to his wife. He will break down if we detain him, and that may hurt his pride.'

'Then, Dicky,' called Mr Parkinson, 'not by the Knife Back.'

'Lord, sir! It saves over a mile, and I could cross it the darkest night at a run.'

He went forth—went with the clock hugged to his breast, and holding the receipt in his right hand. He had but one idea then—his mind could hold but one. He must tell his triumph to her who had despised him. His heart made a great leap—towards her. Now, now at last, she would come to see he was not the despicable little monkey she supposed, and now, now at last, as she would respect him, would come to love him.

Jessie had lain long tossing and weeping on her bed. She had beaten her head with her clenched fists, and then struck her head against the wall and the posts of the bed. She would have liked to kill those insolent, mocking men! How dare they make game of her as she had made game of Dick? She lay for a while staring up at the ceiling out of hot eyes, biting her fingers, and then again threw herself over on her face in a fresh paroxysm of tears.

Why was Dick away now? Now—when she was insulted, wounded, in pain? Dick! he was amusing himself at the 'Blue Boar,' laughing, telling his silly stories, cracking his inane jokes, making everyone laugh at him and pity her for having for her husband such a jackanapes. But, no! She gave a gulp. No, Richard was there respected. The Squire had gone there on purpose to meet and honour him with a testimonial. No, Dick was not the laughing-stock she had supposed. Her eyes had been blind to his merits, to his courage, his gentleness, his patience, his tenacity of purpose. But she could not forgive him for being absent now, when she was so unhappy—now, on the anniversary of her father's death.

As these thoughts dark and wild chased through her head, as clouds across a stormy night sky, still crying she dozed off into troubled slumber.

How long she slept she did not know, whether for seconds or for hours. She awoke with a start. There came to her suddenly, in the midst of her sleep, a thought that seemed to strike her sensibly, not as a stunning, but as a rousing blow; and the thought was—the Knife Back has been broken through, and Dick does not know it. He may return that way. Dick! Was it a cry she heard? With a shiver, and her hair standing electrified, and audibly rustling about her head, she stood on her feet. Had she heard a cry, or had she dreamt it? With trembling hands she struck a match and lighted a lantern, ran out before her house, and listened. She trembled so that her teeth chattered in her jaws. Had she heard a cry, or had she dreamt it? Should she run to the ' Blue Boar ' and caution Dick? or should she stand on the broken edge of the Knife Back and call? She would do the latter first.

She stole to the brink of the old quarry and along the ridge as far as it went. Then came a gap; the rain and frost had undermined this portion of the path, and it had given way the preceding night.

' Dick !' she called, ' Dick ! Dick, dear ! '

Then from far below she heard a faint 'Ting! ting! ting! ting!' a clock that struck—what hour she could not tell, she did not count; but immediately after a Dartford clock struck far away, and nearer, but still distant, the Greenhythe clock tolled ten.

What was that she had heard? No echo; it came before the town clocks had struck.

There was, a little way off, a steep path—almost a slide —down the cliff of chalk. She went to the place, and descended cautiously. Her heart was sick with fear.

She reached the bottom, and there she stole along with her lantern near the ground before her, fearing greatly what she might see irradiated by the yellow light.

Her heart stood still, and every drop of blood was arrested in her arteries. Within the circle of light was a foot in boot with brass eyelet holes for the laces. She knew the boot; it belonged to Dick. She uttered a cry and raised the lantern, and it threw its halo over the little man, lying huddled among the chalk lumps, hugging something.

She stooped, she touched, she called, she kissed him. He took no notice. His eyes were closed, but his lips slightly moved, and one hand that clutched a piece of paper was lifted, and the paper thrust in her face, much as once she had thrust the unravelled stocking in his. But she did not look at the paper.

What should she do? She was a woman of nerve and strength in emergency. Should she leave him there, and run for assistance? She could not; no, she would not do that. He was a little man, and she a strong, tall girl. She bent to him, put her arms under his body, and lifted and carried him away.

She carried him through the old quarry. She paused at intervals and panted. Then she went on again. She came out into the road. She must go some way round to reach her cottage, must pass Ben Polson's strawberry field, and Joseph Ruddle's shop, and Sim Underwood's farmhouse. Should she halt at any of these and ask for help? She set her teeth; she toiled on. She had left the lantern in the quarry; she could not carry that as well as her husband. No, she would seek no help. No! along that road she had driven in the carriage and pair which had so troubled Dick because he could not pay for it—the carriage and pair for which the hat had been sent round. No, no, no! She would carry him all the way. He could not be better than in her arms; she would traverse, bearing him, every step of that road over which she had driven scorning him in her heart.

The night was dark. No one was in the road, no one in the lane when she reached that. She halted at the kiln, and as she was exhausted, carried her burden within, and sat on the ground with him lying across her knees.

She had matches with her. She struck one, and it flared up. His eyes were open now. She saw that he was looking at her, and again he thrust the paper that he clutched towards her, and a smile broke on his face.

'Dick! O dear, dear Dick! Speak to me! Forgive me! O Dick, speak, speak!'

Then he said, 'Moth!—A carridge and pear, etceterer—sottled,' closed his eyes, and the lucifer went out.

He had held tightly to him all this while the presentation clock; it was a clock that would go in any position, and it had gone in spite of the fall. As Jessie carried the little man, she had felt or heard the tick, tick, tick against her own heart, and had thought at first it was the counter-beat of his. Now, in the darkness, as the lucifer expired, the clock stopped, stopped as the light went out, stopped as he said 'Sottled.'

In the stillness, in the vault of the kiln-mouth, she listened for his breath, but could not hear it. She stooped to his heart, laid her ear against it, and heard nothing. That piece of mechanism was stopped also. She unloosed, in the dark, his red neckerchief, the kerchief with which he had dried her tears in that same kiln-mouth, when in his kindly considerate way he had called her sobs 'hickups.' She sobbed now, and none tried to stay her sobs. She wept now, and no hand was extended to wipe away her tears.

CHAPTER IX

A⊤ the refreshment stall of the junction to the new line, some time after what has been related, might be seen a young woman in black with wonderfully light hair, so light as to be nearly if not quite silver, a young woman with a beautifully delicate, pure complexion ; one with an expression of sadness on her face, but with that sadness tinged with a certain sweetness, the sweetness of humility and modesty. The guards, and the young men who came to the bar, never ventured on any familiarity with her, but always treated her with deference, and addressed her as 'Mrs Duck.' A year passed, and then, one day between trains, when the girls were away, and only Moth was there, Sam Underwood came into the refreshment room. He looked round, saw that no one was within earshot, leaned across the counter, and said, ' Moth !—I mean Mrs Duck —what do you say? Will you take me now? I'm well off; and we'll have a splendid wedding and a carriage and pair.'

She shook her head.

' My first carriage and pair is not yet paid for.'

' Indeed—I know it is.'

' Yes, the host of the "Blue Boar" is satisfied. But I still owe it to Dick.'

No, she would not have Sam Underwood. No, nor Joseph Ruddle, when he asked. No, nor Ben Polson, when he came for the same purpose. And when Mr Parkinson hung about the bar and asked for a glass of bitter, or a nip of cherry brandy, and looked tender things, did she encourage him to make any further advance? No, not by a sign.

On All-Hallow E'en the old head-keeper, Finch, came to look in on her at her lodging.

'Mrs Duck,' he said, 'now I understand it. That lead-running was not all gammon. The second heart after all was broke—that is, all its pride and hardness gave way. The shell was broke.'

She liked to talk to Finch as to a father; he had known her from a child. She told him how troubled poor Dick had been because he had incurred debts—especially about the wedding conveyance—through her pride; and how she thought about the wrong she had done him, and grieved over it.

'Mrs Duck—Moth,' said he; 'Dick was the gentlest and most forgiving creetur there ever was; what was that paper he thrust on you as he died?

'" A Carridge and Pear, etceterer,
                        Sottled?"

What is "Etceterer"? Everything between you scored off—sottled. He bore no grudges—not Dick!—sottled!'

THE END

UNIVERSITY EXTENSION SERIES.

Under the above title MESSRS. METHUEN will shortly commence the publication of a series of books on historical, literary, and economic subjects, suitable for extension students and home-reading circles. The volumes are intended to assist the lecturer and not to usurp his place. Each volume will be complete in itself, and the subjects will be treated by competent writers in a broad and philosophic spirit. A full list of the series will be issued shortly. The first volume, to be published in August, will be :—

THE INDUSTRIAL HISTORY OF ENGLAND. With Maps and Plans. By H. DE B. GIBBINS, M.A.

EDUCATIONAL WORKS.

BRADFORD SCIENCE SERIES.

Under the above title MESSRS. METHUEN propose to issue a Series of Science Manuals suitable for use in schools. They will be edited by Mr. R. Elliot Steel, M.A., F.C.S., Senior Natural Science Master in Bradford Grammar School, and will be published at a moderate price. The following are in preparation :—

The Elements of Natural Science	... ...	... Sept., 1890.
Elementary Light and Sound		... Oct., 1890.
,, Electricity and Magnetism		... Oct., 1890.
,, Heat		... Jan., 1891.
,, Inorganic Chemistry (theoretical).		
,, Practical Physics.		
Advanced Inorganic Chemistry (theoretical).		
,, ,, ,, (practical).		

Other Volumes will be announced in due course.

By A. W. VERRALL, M.A.

SELECTIONS FROM HORACE. With Introduction, Notes, and Vocabulary. By A. W. VERRALL, M.A., Fellow and Tutor of Trinity Coll., Cambridge. Fcap. 8vo.   *[In the Press.*

By R. E. STEEL, M.A.

PRACTICAL INORGANIC CHEMISTRY. For the Elementary Stage of the South Kensington Examinations in Science and Art. By R. E. STEEL, M.A., Senior Natural Science Master at Bradford Grammar School. Crown 8vo, cloth, 1s.   *[Now ready.*

By R. J. MORICH, M.A.

A GERMAN PRIMER. With Exercises. By R. J. MORICH, M.A., Chief Modern
Language Master at Manchester Grammar School.   [*In the Press.*

By H. DE B. GIBBINS, M.A.

GERMAN ACCIDENCE. By H. DE B. GIBBINS, M.A., Assistant Master at Nottingham High School.

WORKS by A. M. M. STEDMAN, M.A.,

WADHAM COLLEGE, OXON.

FIRST LATIN LESSONS. Fcap. 8vo, 1s.

FIRST LATIN READER. With Notes adapted to the Shorter Latin
Primer and Vocabulary.   [*In the Press.*

EASY LATIN PASSAGES FOR UNSEEN TRANSLATION. Fcap.
8vo, 1s. 6d.

EASY LATIN EXERCISES ON THE SYNTAX OF THE SHORTER
AND REVISED LATIN PRIMERS. With Vocabulary. *Second
Edition.* Crown 8vo, 2s. 6d. Issued with the consent of Dr. Kennedy.

NOTANDA QUAEDAM : MISCELLANEOUS LATIN EXERCISES
ON COMMON RULES AND IDIOMS. Fcap. 8vo, 1s. 6d.

LATIN VOCABULARIES FOR REPETITION : arranged according to
Subjects. *Third Edition.* Fcap. 8vo, 1s. 6d.

FIRST GREEK LESSONS.   [*In preparation.*

EASY GREEK PASSAGES FOR UNSEEN TRANSLATION.
            [*In preparation.*

EASY GREEK EXERCISES ON ELEMENTARY SYNTAX.
            [*In preparation.*

GREEK VOCABULARIES FOR REPETITION : arranged according to
Subjects. Fcap. 8vo, 1s. 6d.

GREEK TESTAMENT SELECTIONS. For the use of Schools. *New
Edition.* With Introduction, Notes, and Vocabulary. Fcap. 8vo, 2s. 6d.

FIRST FRENCH LESSONS.   [*In the Press.*

EASY FRENCH PASSAGES FOR UNSEEN TRANSLATION.
            Fcap. 8vo, 1s. 6d.

EASY FRENCH EXERCISES ON ELEMENTARY SYNTAX.
            [*In the Press.*

FRENCH VOCABULARIES FOR REPETITION : arranged according
to Subjects. Fcap. 8vo, 1s.

SCHOOL EXAMINATION SERIES.

EDITED BY A. M. M. STEDMAN, M.A.

Cr. 8vo.   2s. 6d. each.

In use at Eton, Harrow, Winchester, Repton, Cheltenham, Sherborne, Haileybury, Merchant Taylors, Manchester, &c.

FRENCH EXAMINATION PAPERS IN MISCELLANEOUS GRAMMAR AND IDIOMS. By A. M. M. STEDMAN, M.A. *Fourth Edition.*

> A KEY, issued to Tutors and Private Students only, to be had on application to the Publishers. Cr. 8vo. 5s.

LATIN EXAMINATION PAPERS IN MISCELLANEOUS GRAMMAR AND IDIOMS. By A. M. M. STEDMAN, M.A. *Second Edition.* KEY (issued as above), 6s.

GREEK EXAMINATION PAPERS IN MISCELLANEOUS GRAMMAR AND IDIOMS. By A. M. M. STEDMAN, M.A. *Second Edition.*
[KEY. *In the Press.*

GERMAN EXAMINATION PAPERS IN MISCELLANEOUS GRAMMAR AND IDIOMS. By R. J. MORICH, Manchester Grammar School. *Second Edition.* KEY (issued as above), 5s.

HISTORY AND GEOGRAPHY EXAMINATION PAPERS. By C. H. SPENCE, M.A., Clifton College.

SCIENCE EXAMINATION PAPERS. By R. E. STEEL, M.A., F.C.S., Chief Natural Science Master, Bradford Grammar School. In three volumes.

> Part I.   Chemistry.
> Part II.   Physics (Sound, Light, Heat, Magnetism, Electricity).
> Part III. Biology and Geology. *In preparation.*

GENERAL KNOWLEDGE EXAMINATION PAPERS. By A. M. M. STEDMAN, M.A. [KEY. *In the Press.*

EXAMINATION PAPERS IN BOOK-KEEPING, with Preliminary Exercises. Compiled and arranged by J. T. MEDHURST, F. S. Accts. and Auditors, and Lecturer at City of London College. 3s.

ENGLISH LITERATURE, Questions for Examination in. Chiefly collected from College Papers set at Cambridge. With an Introduction on the Study of English. By the Rev. W. W. SKEAT, Litt.D., LL.D., Professor of Anglo-Saxon at Cambridge University. *Third Edition, Revised.*

ARITHMETIC, Examination Papers. By C. PENDLEBURY, M.A., Senior Mathematical Master, St. Paul's School. KEY, 5s.

English Leaders of Religion.

UNDER the above title MESSRS. METHUEN propose to commence in the Autumn the publication of a series of short biographies, free from party bias, of the most prominent leaders of religious life and thought in this and the last century.

Each volume will contain a succinct account and estimate of the career, the influence, and the literary position of the subject of the memoir.

MR. A. M. M. STEDMAN will edit the series, and the following are already arranged—

CARDINAL NEWMAN.	*R. H. Hutton.*	*[October.*
JOHN KEBLE.	*W. Lock.*	
CHARLES SIMÉON.	*H. C. G. Moule.*	
BISHOP WILBERFORCE.	*G. W. Daniell.*	
JOHN WESLEY.	*J. H. Overton.*	
F. D. MAURICE.	*Colonel F. Maurice.*	
THOMAS CHALMERS.	*Mrs. Oliphant.*	

Other volumes will be announced in due course.